W9-CCK-780

Angel's Verdict

"Exciting . . . An entertaining mystery."
—*Genre Go Round Reviews*

"The latest Beaufort & Company mystery is sure to please series fans and newcomers alike. Stanton has penned a tale that will keep the reader's interest to the very end . . . Larger-than-life characters—human and temporal—infuse the story with humor and empathy." —*Romantic Times* (4 stars)

Avenging Angels

"Stanton's third Beaufort & Company mystery is a gem. It's an original and thought-provoking concept, and Stanton's imagination knows no bounds. Her characters—both dead and alive—are ones you want to spend time with and get to know better." —*Romantic Times* (4 ½ stars)

"An engaging tale due to a strong cast starting with the lead attorney. The storyline is fast-paced on earth and in court . . . Fans will enjoy this still unique quirky angelic spin on the afterlife." —*Genre Go Round Reviews*

"A witty and engaging mystery of life after death . . . An entertaining and fun read."
—*The Romance Readers Connection*

"Quick paced with an unusual twist . . . [A] devilishly good read." —*The Mystery Reader*

"Stanton has taken an unusual premise and given it wings."
—*Fresh Fiction*

continued . . .

ANGEL
Condemned

Mary Stanton

BERKLEY PRIME CRIME, NEW YORK

THE BERKLEY PUBLISHING GROUP
Published by the Penguin Group
Penguin Group (USA) Inc.
375 Hudson Street, New York, New York 10014, USA
Penguin Group (Canada), 90 Eglinton Avenue East, Suite 700, Toronto, Ontario M4P 2Y3, Canada
(a division of Pearson Penguin Canada Inc.)
Penguin Books Ltd., 80 Strand, London WC2R 0RL, England
Penguin Group Ireland, 25 St. Stephen's Green, Dublin 2, Ireland (a division of Penguin Books Ltd.)
Penguin Group (Australia), 250 Camberwell Road, Camberwell, Victoria 3124, Australia
(a division of Pearson Australia Group Pty. Ltd.)
Penguin Books India Pvt. Ltd., 11 Community Centre, Panchsheel Park, New Delhi—110 017, India
Penguin Group (NZ), 67 Apollo Drive, Rosedale, Auckland 0632, New Zealand
(a division of Pearson New Zealand Ltd.)
Penguin Books (South Africa) (Pty.) Ltd., 24 Sturdee Avenue, Rosebank, Johannesburg 2196,
South Africa

Penguin Books Ltd., Registered Offices: 80 Strand, London WC2R 0RL, England

This is a work of fiction. Names, characters, places, and incidents either are the product of the author's imagination or are used fictitiously, and any resemblance to actual persons, living or dead, business establishments, events, or locales is entirely coincidental. The publisher does not have any control over and does not assume any responsibility for author or third-party websites or their content.

ANGEL CONDEMNED

A Berkley Prime Crime Book / published by arrangement with the author

PRINTING HISTORY
Berkley Prime Crime mass-market edition / November 2011

ISBN: 978-0-425-24462-3

BERKLEY® PRIME CRIME
Berkley Prime Crime Books are published by The Berkley Publishing Group,
a division of Penguin Group (USA) Inc.,
375 Hudson Street, New York, New York 10014.
BERKLEY® PRIME CRIME and the PRIME CRIME logo are trademarks of Penguin Group (USA) Inc.

PRINTED IN THE UNITED STATES OF AMERICA

10 9 8 7 6 5 4 3 2 1

Cast of Characters

The Winston-Beauforts

Brianna "Bree" Winston-Beaufort . . . attorney-at-law

Antonia Winston-Beaufort . . . Bree's younger sister, an actress/stage manager

Francesca "Chessie" Carmichael Winston-Beaufort . . . Antonia's mother, Bree's adoptive mother

Royal Winston-Beaufort . . . Antonia's father, Bree's adoptive father

Franklin Winston-Beaufort (deceased) . . . Royal's uncle, Bree's birth father

Leah Villiers Winston-Beaufort (deceased) . . . Franklin's young wife, Bree's birth mother

Celia "Aunt Cissy" Carmichael . . . a wealthy divorcée, Francesca's younger sister

Beaufort & Company

Ronald Parchese . . . angel and secretary at the Angelus Street office

Petru Lechta . . . angel and paralegal at the Angelus Street office

Lavinia Mather . . . angel and owner of the 66 Angelus Street building

Armand Cianquino . . . retired law school professor, director of Beaufort & Company

Gabriel . . . angel and investigator
Sasha . . . a dog and angel
Emerald "EB" Billingsley . . . secretary at the Bay Street office

In the Chatham County Judicial System

Sam Hunter . . . police lieutenant, Chatham County
Cordelia "Cordy" Blackburn . . . assistant district attorney, Chatham County
Gavin . . . Cordy's assistant
Karen Rasmussen . . . an assistant district attorney
John Stubblefield . . . a lawyer
Payton McAllister III . . . a lawyer
And various public defenders, justices, and members of the police force

In (and around) the Celestial Court System

Goldstein . . . angel and court recorder
Zebulon "Zeb" Beazley . . . a lawyer
George Caldecott . . . a lawyer
Mr. Barlow . . . an advocate
Lloyd Dumphey . . . paralegal, Beazley, Barlow & Caldecott

Some Residents of Savannah

Prosper Peter White . . . director, Frazier Museum, and a specialist in Roman antiquities
Alicia Kennedy . . . assistant to Prosper White
Allard Chambers . . . archeologist and co-owner of Chambers Antiques and Reclaimables
Jillian Knoles Chambers . . . archeologist and co-owner of Chambers Antiques and Reclaimables

Charles "Bullet" Martin . . . a wealthy buyer of antiquities

Lewis McCallen . . . a famous defense attorney

James "Jim" Santo . . . a famous defense attorney

Schofield "Scooey" Martin (deceased) . . . graduate student in archeology

One

"Would you believe the *nerve* of this wormy little bozo Allard Chambers? Bringing a lawsuit against Prosper, of all people?" Celia Carmichael patted Prosper White's knee with a protective air. She didn't wait for a response from the other people sitting in Brianna Winston-Beaufort's law office but ran on like a train with no brakes. "And that *scruffy* little creep who forced Prosper to take the papers, Bree. He was a toad. Not only that—what'd you call him, darlin'?" She turned to the elegantly dressed man seated at her side and batted her eyelashes appealingly.

Celia Carmichael was Bree's aunt—her mother Francesca's youngest sister. The family called her Cissy—and until her recent engagement to museum curator Prosper White, she'd been a woman of cheerful insouciance and a certain artless flamboyance. She'd burst into Bree's office some minutes ago, her face red with indignation, Prosper White trailing arrogantly in her wake.

"He was a process server, Celia." White smoothed his fingers over his knee, dislodging Cissy's hand with barely suppressed irritation. "I do wish you'd moderate your voice."

Cissy's fiancé was tall and lean. His hair was prematurely white, his eyes blue, and his face had a permanent tan. When Cissy had first introduced White to the family a month ago, Bree had guessed him to be in his late forties, although he looked younger. Cissy herself admitted to forty-five and looked like what she was: a well-cared-for Southern gentlewoman holding off the ravages of fifty-nine with charm and judicious applications of Botox.

"Whatever. This *server*," she veered off into irrelevancy, "although I can't think of a restaurant within a hundred miles of Savannah that would take him on as a waiter. The man had tattoos on his tattoos and a gold ring in his nose. Anyway, this person walks right into the gallery and shoves the papers into Prosper's pocket. Then he grins like a hog on ice and scoots on out. I wanted to slap the smirk right off his mouth."

Bree murmured sympathetically.

"So I brought Prosper over here sooner than quick. Well, we had one quick stop in between, but I have to tell you, I hustled. What we need, I told him, is the best lawyer in the state of Georgia, who I just happened to be related to by marriage, thank God. And since *he's* going to be related to us by marriage in less than a week, I knew you'd be even more anxious to help us, Niece. You will, won't you?" Cissy settled back into Bree's only visitor chair with a snort, and then added, apropos of nothing in particular, "When *are* you going to get some decent furniture here, Bree?"

Bree couldn't decide which question to answer first. She

wasn't anxious to take on a case for her aunt's suspect fiancé, so she decided not to answer that one at all. And she didn't have a dime to spend on fancy office furniture, so she wouldn't answer that one, either. She'd bought the essentials when she'd reopened the office a few months ago: two desks, three chairs, and a steel-gray five-drawer filing cabinet from Second Hand Rows, the used furniture store on Whitaker Street. The place looked just fine, as far as she was concerned.

She looked at Prosper White and wondered at the instinctive dislike he'd raised in almost all of the Winston-Beauforts except the infatuated Cissy. The thumbs-down included Bree's younger sister, Antonia, who normally exhibited no common sense about men at all. Maybe it was the determined air of supercilious contempt. Or his too-fancy shoes. Or the faint drift of cologne that followed him. Bree sighed. Whatever it was, the man couldn't put a foot right with any of the family. She supposed she ought to feel sorry for him. But he wasn't a man who invited sympathy.

At the moment, White seemed to have an attitude about her furniture. He slouched in Bree's saggy leather office chair as if the touch of the worn-out leather was repugnant. Bree's secretary, EB Billingsley, had dragged the chair out from behind the small screen that partitioned Bree's desk from the rest of the office space. White also seemed to have an attitude about EB, whom he'd ignored when Cissy had made the introductions. EB was clearly one of "the little people" who didn't count in the twin worlds of art and commerce.

EB herself commanded her space behind her battered pine desk with her customary air of majestic aplomb. The desk faced the mahogany office door eight feet away. The upper half of the door was made of the opaque glass popu-

lar when the Bay Street building went up in 1822. Black
lettering read LAW OFFICES B. WINSTON-BEAUFORT, only
backwards, if you were standing inside looking out, the
way Bree was. Gray wall-to-wall carpeting covered pine
floors too gouged and splintered from a former fire to be
successfully refinished. The office had one window,
double-hung, that looked out over Bay Street. You could
glimpse the Savannah River between the rehabbed warehouses that lined the other side of the street, but the sight
was so familiar Bree rarely bothered.

"We're keepin' an eye out for some nice new office furniture, Ms. Carmichael," EB said blandly. "But I'll tell you
true, we've got so much business comin' in that Bree hasn't
had time to spit." This was a fib but a generous-hearted
one; EB kept the accounts for this, the Bay Street office,
and Bree's Angelus Street office, too. She knew the dismal
state of their finances better than anyone.

"This summons is such a small matter; I doubt it will
take up much of your time," Prosper White said. "I can
certainly send it along to my counsel in New York." He
smiled with a glimpse of artificially whitened teeth. "But
it's such a trivial matter I hate to bother them. And Cissy
insisted. When Cissy gets her mind made up, I just follow
along. If you'd rather I passed the case along to someone
else, I'm happy to do so."

Bree, arms folded, one hip cocked against EB's desk,
paused a moment before answering him. She looked at her
aunt, instead.

Like all the Carmichael girls, Cissy was small, with
good bones, and an upright, graceful way of moving. But
where Bree's mother, Francesca, was rounded, Cissy was
spare, with the wiry body of a woman who spent too much
time at the gym. Francesca's own red-gold hair (refreshed

every six weeks at a quiet beauty salon near the Winston-Beauforts' North Carolina home) was one of the reasons Bree's father had fallen in love with her. Cissy's was bright, sun-streaked blonde, the sort of color that demanded her aunt's frequent trips to plastic surgeons to maintain a youthful image. Or so she claimed. Both sisters had clear blue eyes and soft, musical voices.

Cissy's first husband had run off with his executive assistant some fifteen years ago. Bree's memory of Cissy's ex-husband was spotty. Ash—what was his last name? Smallwood, that was it—had been a heavy-set guy with reddened cheeks, a fondness for bourbon sours, and political views to the right of Attila the Hun. The family hadn't liked him much. Cissy hadn't, either, and nobody was too surprised when he lit off for California after he'd made a very generous settlement on her aunt. Since then, Cissy had happily dated every eligible bachelor in Georgia over the age of thirty-five. She hadn't bothered much about a second husband.

Until now.

Prosper White was Ash's antithesis: tall, skinny, and with buzz-cut prematurely white hair. Bree had never seen him wear anything but slim black suits; crisp, open-collared white shirts; and those sleek Italian shoes. He drank martinis (sparingly) and seemed to have no political views at all. He looked just like what he claimed to be: a museum curator from New York City. He certainly acted the part.

He was as different from Ash Smallwood as chalk from cheese, although the Winston-Beauforts didn't like him any better. Bree felt very sorry for her aunt. She might even be persuaded to feel sorry for Prosper White, and she hoped he wasn't as arrogant and uncivil as he seemed. But she really didn't want to handle his lawsuit. She was short-tempered these days. Keeping civil would be an effort.

Bree gave her aunt an affectionate smile and turned to White. "The thing is, criminal law isn't really my strong suit. You might do better referring the case to your people up north. Or I'd be happy to refer you to somebody here."

"Not your strong suit?" Cissy said. "That's a hoot! You got that Chandler child off! You solved four murder cases bam-bam-bam! And you've only had Uncle Franklin's practice open for a few months!"

White scowled. "This is a criminal case? You're telling me there's a jail sentence attached to a possible conviction? This flap is over my acquisition of a magazine cover, for God's sake. And he wants damages!"

"Did I say criminal?" Bree said, hastily. "I'm very sorry. I misspoke." Her biased opinion of White's character was another reason to steer clear of his case. Her job was to be an advocate, not a judge. "I'm a specialist in tax law. I should have said that I'm not an expert in torts. Most lawyers in Georgia are more experienced in tort law than I am. Is this a criminal case? No, of course not."

"Nonsense. Uncle Franklin believed you could handle anything, from torts to tarts," Cissy said confidently. "That's why he left you his practice."

"Absolutely," EB said loyally.

"Uncle Franklin was an optimist," Bree said, "but thank, you Aunt Cissy."

Nobody in the room knew just how much of an optimist. She'd taken over Franklin's civil practice, as he'd requested in his will. It was why she'd come to Savannah last October in the first place. What she hadn't known then, she knew now. Franklin's other practice, the criminal one, was carried out from the office on 66 Angelus Street, where

Bree handled appeals cases for souls who had been condemned to Hell.

Celestial jurisprudence turned out to be a lot less process-laden than the human/temporal one, but the beings she had to deal with—from the Opposition's prosecutors to the Divine Justices themselves—were an intimidating crew even to Bree, who was no pushover. In the last four months, Bree had handled four such clients with the help of her Angelus Street staff, five angels appointed by the Celestial Courts.

The last case had taken a lot out of her, and she was tired to death. She wasn't sleeping well. She'd lost another dress size. A car had tried to run her over, and she'd broken her leg. Despite her doubts about Prosper White, he did deserve the best advocate she could find for him, and she was pretty sure she wasn't up to it. Not without a couple of weeks off somewhere sunny.

"Let me see if I can get Marv Welch to give you a hand, Aunt Cissy. He's the best civil litigator I know. And he's not suit-happy, either. If this can be settled with a few phone calls, he's the man to do it."

"Fine," Cissy snapped. She pressed her lips tightly together. She cleared her throat. Then she said, "You want to shove this off on some stranger? No problem. No problem at all." She adjusted the cuffs on her blue-striped cotton shirt, tugged her short beige skirt over her knees, and slung the strap of her tote over her shoulder. Her legs were as tanned as White's face. She got to her feet and said stiffly, "Sorry to bust in on y'all like this."

EB cut her eyes at Bree with a disapproving frown and said soothingly, "Now just hang on a minute, Ms. Carmichael. You sit right back down. Of course Bree wants to help her auntie."

EB had a large, rambunctious family. She held decided
views on family loyalty. A middle-aged African-American
woman who'd left school in the eighth grade to have the
first of her five children, EB had come to work for Bree
very recently, just after her last child graduated technical
school. She wasn't, she told Bree at her job interview, having any more part-time jobs waitressing, housecleaning,
and cooking. She'd signed up for an online secretarial
course, and she was going to make something of herself or
die trying. She'd taken to Bree's temporal practice in a
New York minute. It'd taken her less time than that to make
Bree part of her extended family. EB lowered her chin and
peered at Bree over her wire-rimmed spectacles. "Isn't that
right, Bree?"

Bree gave it up. EB would never let her hear the end of
it if she sent Cissy somewhere else. Come to think of it,
Cissy wouldn't, either. "Certainly. If you're sure you want
me, Cissy."

Her aunt sat down with a sigh of relief. "Of course I do.
Thing is, I'd purely hate to have strangers poking around in
our personal business."

Bree hoped her distaste for both Prosper White and his
lousy case didn't show. "I may need to get an expert in tort
law to give me a hand. You okay with that?"

"You sure you can't keep this just between us?"

Bree began to be very curious about what skeletons
White might have in his closet. How complicated could a
lawsuit over a magazine cover get? "Sure," she promised.
"I'll do my best."

"Thank you, darlin'. I know you will."

"I'll let you know if I get in over my head and have to
call someone else in to help out." Bree leaned back against
the desk. She met Prosper White's chilly eyes with an in-

terrogative lift of her eyebrows. "You said a former ac-
quaintance is claiming damages for a work of art you took
from him? May I see the Summons and Complaint again?"

He pulled the long buff envelope from inside his suit
jacket and handed it back to her.

"As I was sayin'," Cissy said. "This what's-his-name
and his wife . . ."

"Allard and Jillian Chambers," Bree read aloud from
the summons.

"Allard Chambers," Cissy repeated scornfully. "He's
a—what did you call him, Prosper?"

"A failed academic. Also a fraud." White flicked his fingers dismissively. "I believe the dreadful Jillian is, as well."

Bree looked up. "The address here says they're the owners of Chambers Antiques and Reclaimables. First, the
plaintiffs are alleging fraudulent representation on the part
of said defendants, Prosper Peter White and his agent, Alicia Kennedy. Who is Alicia Kennedy?"

"Alicia Kennedy is my assistant curator at the Frazier.
She's not my agent. My agent's out of New York."

"'Agent' in this context means someone paid to act on
your behalf." Bree referred to the summons again. "This
basically says that Alicia Kennedy stole the magazine for
you. That the '1952 edition of *Photoplay* magazine, issue
number 3, edition 5, with cover featuring rock-and-roll star
Elvis Presley, currently on display in the Frazier Museum
exhibit *A Century of Magazine Americana* was, in fact, removed from the premises of plaintiff's site of business at
35 Whitaker Street, Savannah, Georgia, by fraudulent
means, pursuant to Georgia State statute' . . . Blah, blah
blah. I'll spare you the citation." She read on. "Second, it's
a demand for rescission."

Everybody looked blank. Bree clarified, "Chambers is

suing for the return of the magazine." She folded the summons into neat thirds. "Are you in possession of the magazine, Mr. White?"

"Of course I am. It's an integral part of the Frazier exhibit."

"Did the magazine come from Mr. Chambers's shop?"

White tapped his fingers impatiently on his knee. "The charges are ridiculous."

Bree waited for an answer.

"Yes, the magazine came from Allard's shop, and no, I didn't steal it or obtain it by fraudulent means. As I said, it's a critical part of the show at the Frazier. I sent my assistant down to buy the cover from him. Legally. We have a receipt."

"How much did you pay for it?"

A funny look passed over White's features. Sly—that was it. After a moment he said, "Twenty dollars."

"This brouhaha is over a twenty-dollar item? Surely you can find another magazine from the era to replace it."

"This isn't about a twenty-dollar item," White said. "It's about much, much more. It's Chambers's pitiful attempt at revenge. He's a nothing, a nobody, and a fool. I refuse to play games with the man or his dreadful wife."

Bree sighed. Arrogance could cost this guy a lot of money in legal fees. "Your assistant is the agent named as codefendant in the suit? Alicia Kennedy?"

"That's correct."

"A slippery little miss, that Miss Kennedy," Sissy muttered.

Bree glanced at her aunt and mentally filed the comment away for future reference. She turned her attention back to White. "There's something a little unusual about this. Mr. Chambers is represented by Marbury, Stubble-field. It's one of the largest firms in Savannah."

White cocked his head. "Meaning?"

Bree had a lot to say about Marbury, Stubblefield, but lawyers didn't throw dirt on each other in front of the laity. Unless they were all in court, with a judge to referee. "Meaning that John Stubblefield generally won't take on a case that doesn't represent a lot of potential fees. He's got such a high overhead that he can't afford to." She gestured at the floor. "One of the satellite offices is beneath us. They have the entire fourth floor. And if what you've told me so far is true, this is a violation of the Uniform Commercial Code."

"This doesn't have a thing to do with the military," Cissy said with an air of reassurance.

"The UCC is a set of federal regulations regarding business transactions," Bree said. "You're right. It doesn't have a thing to do with the military. It also doesn't carry much in the way of penalties for something like this—and it wouldn't seem to carry much weight with the likes of John Stubblefield. But it could cost a fair amount in legal fees if both parties are . . ." She searched for a phrase less inflammatory than "pig-headed." "Convinced of their positions."

"Chambers doesn't have two nickels to rub together," White said with malicious satisfaction. He smiled at Cissy. "If money is what it takes, I'm sure we can out-lawyer him."

Bree let the implied slur on her and her profession pass. "So what's this case really about?"

"It's bullpuckey that's what it is," Cissy said indignantly. "This Chambers is jealous, jealous, jealous. He always has been, and he chose this minute to make a stink because everybody in Savannah's beatin' down the doors to see what Prosper created. The *Magazine Americana* exhibit is the most successful thing the Frazier's ever done! And it's all due to Prosper! Before Prosper came on the scene to rescue the Frazier, it was the dowdiest museum in the whole damn South. A lot of molderin' old Confederate uniforms and a bunch of rooster feathers from Robert E. Lee's second-best hat! And now look at it! There was a line for tickets all the way down to St. Bonaventure's on opening day, and business hasn't slacked off since!" Cissy's face was pink with indignation.

"My, *my*," EB said. "Let me get you a glass of water, Ms. Carmichael."

Bree shifted against the hard edge of EB's desk. Her back hurt. The place where she'd broken her leg some weeks ago ached a little. Maybe Cissy was right. It might be time to get a few comfortable chairs in here or at least enough so that more than three people could sit down at the same time. "You said Mr. Chambers and Mr. White have known each other for a while, Aunt Cissy?"

"It's not 'Mister' Chambers; it's 'Professor.' Or 'Doctor.' Whatever. And I wish to goodness you'd quit callin' Prosper 'Mr. White.' He's going to be your new uncle, Bree, so at least you can start callin' him by his Christian name." Cissy fanned herself vigorously with one hand. "My goodness it's hot in here."

"Let me get you some of that water," EB said. "Or even better, some nice cold 'Co-Cola."

"No, thank you, EB. I'm just all of a doo-dah over this, and that's a fact." She took a deep breath and grinned a little sheepishly at Bree. "You can tell I'm upset, can't you? I'm going all over Southern."

"It's an unsettlin' situation," EB said. "What with Elvis on the cover of that magazine and all."

"Isn't that a fact."

The two women looked wisely at one another. Bree pinched her nose so she wouldn't laugh, then reached over and took a yellow pad from the stack on EB's desk. She uncapped her pen. "Let's try and get a handle on some facts. If you could give me some background, Mr. White? Does Professor Chambers have a grudge against you?"

"It's because *Prosper's* a genius with artifacts," Cissy said, with a meaning-laden look at her niece. "It's all on account of the Cross."

"Hardly genius, Celia," White murmured with an expression so self-satisfied Bree wanted to smack him, "but yes, Chambers has got a grudge. You may know that I have something of a reputation in the detection of fraudulent Roman antiquities. Chambers is—or rather was—an archeologist specializing in that period at one of our larger universities. He was on a dig near Constantinople—that's Istanbul to you—and claimed to have discovered the Cross of Justinian. Or rather, *a* cross of Justinian. A pectoral piece—"

"It's a necklace," Cissy cut in.

"Not a necklace, Celia," Prosper said contemptuously. "I do wish you wouldn't show yourself quite the fool. It's a piece designed to be displayed on the chest."

"And Constantinople is really Istanbul, to me," Bree said with an air of deceptive cordiality. "Thank you so much." She caught EB's look of alarm and managed to hang on to her temper. Her heart ached for Cissy. "Do go on."

"A pectoral piece seventeen centimeters by five centimeters, of hand-hammered silver over cedar. It's inlaid with jasper, coral, and lapis lazuli." White tugged at his ear. "Quite beautiful, in its way. Also quite fraudulent." He yawned and ran his hand over his short white hair. "Chambers tried to pass it off as a genuine antiquity. I knew it was a fake the moment I saw it." His jaw set. His face was flushed. "Why he thought he could pull the wool over *my* eyes I'll never know. Doctorates make some people arrogant."

Bree wondered at the venom in his voice.

"Of course, I let the insurance company and the university know right away. In the ensuing fracas, Chambers lost his cushy academic job. And she had to resign." He smiled in satisfaction.

"When did this happen?" Bree asked.

"Probably six months ago, just before I accepted the position here at the Frazier. Anyhow, I lost track of him"—he shrugged—"and it looks like he ended up here, running a junk shop."

"But the junk shop has some items of value, surely," Bree said. She refused to call a man who used the word "fracas" in normal conversation by his first name. Maybe she could get by without calling him anything at all. "It was where you found this copy of *Photoplay* for your current exhibit, isn't it?"

"Well, that's just it. I did find it, in a pile of unsorted scrap in the back of the shop. I knew Chambers would refuse to sell it to me. So I sent Alicia over to pick it up. She paid for it. In cash. She obtained a receipt. All perfectly legal."

"Did Professor Chambers put any verbal or written restrictions on the sale of the magazine when he sold it to Alicia?"

White shrugged dismissively. "There may have been

something written on the receipt. That it shouldn't go to Prosper White or the Frazier. Something along those lines. But hardly enforceable. Once Alicia sold it to me . . ."

"Didn't you say she was acting as your agent?"

"I *said*," he mimicked her, "that I sent her over to pick it up. It's Chambers who claims she's my agent."

"A good point, but it's moot." Cissy looked bewildered, so Bree added, "Not germane to the principle issue, which is the sale of the magazine to you, Mr. White. So you have a sales document with a condition of sale specifically forbidding the use of the magazine in the exhibit. It might save you a lot of grief if you just gave him the magazine back."

Cissy gasped. White's thin lips clamped shut. "Absolutely not. The cover is a critical part of the chronology of the *oeuvre*."

Oeuvre. Fracas. Phooey. Bree bit her lip.

"We have original magazine covers from 1810 on. If we took out the *Photoplay* cover it would leave an irreparable hole in the *oeuvre*."

Bree doubted that. There had to be hundreds of copies of *Photoplay* covers around. The magazine had been a huge success in the fifties.

"That magazine's worth a ton of money now," Cissy said, "but only as long as the exhibit is intact. You know we have some investors coming over just to bid on the whole thing? Alicia's set it up. It'd absolutely ruin the entire deal if we let that little worm wreck it. We offered to give that demented man some money to go away, and you know what he wanted?! Fifty thousand dollars! That's what he wanted! Then we get sued!"

White put his hand on Cissy's shoulder and tightened it. "Remember what we said about making that investor inter-

est public, Celia." He released her shoulder and straightened up. "Let's leave it at this, Miss Winston-Beaufort.
You do whatever you have to do to make this annoyance go
away. I'll pay any fee that's required. If you need help
going up against this John Stubblefield character, buy it.
I'll pay for that, too. It's a matter of principle to me. You
understand?"

"Sure," Bree said.

He gave her a thin, condescending smile. "I'm glad we
understand each other. Now. We've trespassed on your
time far too long. Get up, Celia. It's time we were getting
back to the Frazier. I've got people from New York in to
talk about moving the exhibit to MoMA next month."

"I'll drive you over, honey," Cissy said. "But I can't stay.
I have to see the caterer about the nibbles for the wedding
reception. And you remember that I'm meeting Bree for
dinner at seven? So I won't see you tonight at all." She
jumped lightly to her feet, and Bree caught a whiff of Prada
perfume. "Antonia's joining us, too, right, Bree?"

"She's looking forward to it."

"Antonia's an actress, Prosper. Bree's little sister. I told
you about her. She's with the Savannah Repertory Theater.
Doesn't that sound grand?"

He shrugged. "Regional theater's not quite my thing,
after New York."

If Cissy registered his contempt, it didn't show. "The
theater's dark on Mondays. That's what they call it when
there's no show on. She's even prettier than Bree. And
aren't I a lucky auntie, to have two such beautiful, darling
nieces." She kissed Bree's cheek, leaving a sticky mark
from her lip gloss. "Thank you, darlin'. Thank you! You go
talk to that man and slap him right up the side of the head."

Smiling, Bree kissed her back. "I'll have to go through

Stubblefield's office first. I promise to keep you in the loop."

"Y'all keep Prosper in the loop, too!" Cissy looked over her shoulder as she followed White out the door and mouthed, "Be sure and send the bill to me."

Bree and EB looked at each other in dismay.

Two

EB waited until the click of Cissy's heels on the terrazzo floor outside faded into the distance. Then she shook her head. "I don't know about this."

"You're not enchanted, enthralled, and enraptured by the elegantly dressed Mr. White?"

"Got up your nose, too?"

Bree exhaled with a huff. "Big time."

"Your aunt Cissy's got herself a fair amount of money, that right?"

"That's right."

EB shook her head again. "Mm-hm. Your auntie going to pay the bill for this lawsuit?"

"We're not going to charge her, EB. I can't charge my own aunt."

"She going to sit still for that? And you said something about hiring another lawyer if you need help. That lawyer going to work for free, too?"

Bree tucked a loose strand of hair behind her ear. It was silver-blonde and fell to her waist. Francesca said it was Bree's one vanity. She kept it tucked up in a coronet of braids during the working day, but it had an annoying tendency to work loose if she rushed the ritual of putting it up in the morning, or if she was tired and aggravated, the way she was now. "No," she admitted. "Supporting counsel won't work for free."

"Uh-huh." EB rocked back and forth in her chair, so that it creaked. "Your daddy hear anything about Mr. White from those folks he called in New York? I mean, what kind of trouble is your auntie in, here?"

Royal Winston-Beaufort had made a few discreet inquiries when Cissy announced her marriage plans. "White's very visible in the art world," Bree said cautiously. "He seems to live on grants, stipends, and donations, which is how folks in the art world tend to live, I suppose. There's no shame in that. But my father's not settled about this, EB. Not by a long shot. Neither am I. Anyhow, Daddy didn't get further than a couple of phone calls made when guess what?"

"Your aunt called your daddy up and asked him why he was poking around the affairs of her fiancé. Cryin', too, I'll bet."

"You're a smart woman, EB."

"It's why you hired me, isn't it?"

"It surely is."

"So what's your daddy going to do?"

"He apologized to Cissy for interfering. She demanded that we leave White alone. He apologized again. She told him to let it be. I don't know if he agreed to or not. But I didn't agree to let it be, and this case gives me the perfect excuse to find out a little more about Mr. Prosper White."

"So what are we goin to do now?"

"At the moment, we're going to try and make this case go away. It's a loser, no matter how I look at it."

"Good. Where do we start?" EB was dead set on becoming a paralegal after she got her GED through her night school courses, and she was adamant about understanding procedure.

"You mean if this weren't a beloved relative with too much money and no sense when it comes to predatory men? We'd file a motion to dismiss and perhaps a counterclaim for damages pursuant to the frivolous nature of the charges. But as you've so shrewdly reminded me, we don't have a clue about White's antecedents. And it's better to scope out the swamp before you wade in. I think I'll go on down to Stubblefield's office and see if Payton's in. I need a sense of what this is really about."

"Payton the Rat?" said EB. A grin spread over her face. "Last I saw of that boy was his backside when you kicked him out of the office a couple of weeks ago."

"Yep. Payton McAllister the Third himself. He's the attorney of record, according to this thing." She tucked the summons into her jacket pocket and glanced at her watch. "It's after two. He should be back from lunch."

"And you missed lunch. Now, me, I can afford to." EB patted one substantial hip. "You? I'm not so sure. Why'n't you go out and get yourself something real high calorie so those size two pants don't hang off of you like they do, before you whack Mr. McAllister over the head. I'm going wrap up those lease agreements for the Dwyer account and then get myself on home. I won't be here when you get back."

"You'll be in tomorrow?" When she'd opened the Bay

Street office, Bree had only been able to afford EB part-time. In the past few months—perhaps because of the no-toriety surrounding Bree's involvement in four high-profile murders—her temporal business had begun to pick up a bit. If she could afford the time to spend with her temporal clients, she might be able to start drawing a salary herself. She had a small stipend from a trust fund set up by her mother's family, but it was just enough to keep her head above water.

"Yes, ma'am," EB said in satisfaction. "Got myself two-thirds of a day's work at least. I might be hitting you up for a raise pretty soon if business keeps coming in."

"Why don't I pick up the tuition for your night school courses?"

EB shook her head. "We can't afford that right now, 'specially if you won't get a nickel from your auntie and most 'specially if you keep that Angelus Street office open." EB's curiosity about the Angelus office was intense, but so far Bree had managed to keep her curiosity in check without offending her. EB had never been there. It was not a place temporals other than Bree could find. "Besides, I got a grant to go to school. You'd do better to spend that money getting yourself some lunch."

"I'll pick up something after I go downstairs and talk to Payton," Bree promised. "Maybe I'll have a nice cold mar-tini, too. I always need a stiff drink after a talk with Pay-ton. I've got my cell on, if you need me."

She slung her tote and her black wool winter coat over one arm, and let herself out.

Marbury, Stubblefield was only two floors down, but she decided to take the elevator. Something about the gra-cious old Bay Street building demanded a certain amount of decorum. She preferred to arrive at the lavish offices below without announcing herself by clattering downstairs.

She spent the short ride thinking about Prosper White and what, if anything, he might have to hide. His casual erudition was pretentious, and there wasn't a law against that. His airy dismissal of Alicia Kennedy's possible complicity in defrauding Allard and Jillian Chambers bordered on the unethical, but it certainly wasn't a hanging offense. On the other hand, his rudeness to Cissy was unforgivable. If the guy was really going to be a member of the family, Bree foresaw a lifetime of biting her lip. She made a face at the mahogany wainscoting that lined the elevator car. Francesca would never interfere. Neither would Royal. They'd all just have to live with it.

The elevators doors hissed opened directly in front of the Marbury offices, and Bree stepped out.

John Stubblefield was sole head of one of the largest law firms in Savannah. If there had been an actual Marbury, other than the nineteenth-century advocate who had lent his name to the landmark legal case Marbury v. Madison, he was long dead or otherwise out of the picture. Stubblefield was notorious for late-night infomercials touting the services of the firm to victims of bad air, bad hip replacements, polluted wells, and fatty hamburgers from fast-food joints. Bree wasn't against class-action suits in principle—the successful litigation against the tobacco companies was a classic example of American jurisprudence in the right kind of action—but Stubblefield's notion of justice began and ended with what benefited him and his obscenely engorged bank accounts.

She pulled open the heavy glass door to the firm and stepped inside.

Stubblefield had remodeled the entire fourth floor at great expense. The thick wall-to-wall carpeting was crystal pink. The huge reception desk gleamed with brass fixtures inlaid in polished teak. The couches set out for clients were white leather. Silk flower arrangements overflowed every available surface.

The receptionist behind the desk looked up with a welcoming smile as the faint chime announcing a visitor bounced gently in the hushed air. Her smile died almost immediately. "Hullo, Miss Winston-Beaufort."

"How are you, Tiffany?" Bree was pretty sure Tiffany had been homecoming queen at her high school. She knew for a fact Tiffany had been Miss Peach Blossom the year after that. Beauty-queen credentials seemed to be a résumé requirement for Marbury, Stubblefield receptionists. That—and a demand to dye their hair to match the carpeting.

"Okay, I guess," she said warily. Bree's infrequent visits to the firm usually ended in disruptions of one sort or another. Tiffany twiddled the pen in her hand and then sucked cautiously at the tip. "You here to see anyone in particular? Mr. Stubblefield isn't in."

"Is Payton in?"

Tiffany's cherry-glossed lips twitched. "You aren't armed or anything, are you?"

"Just with my righteous sense of justice."

Tiffany nodded. "Okeydokey. I'll get him. I'd better not say who it is, though. He'll hide all day if he knows it's you." She lifted the phone receiver to her ear and hit the intercom button. "Mr. McAllister? Your two-thirty's here. I know, sir, it's a little early." She hung the phone up softly. "He'll be right out."

Bree sank down on one of the soft couches. "Does he actually have a two-thirty?"

"Nope. But he never remembers appointments anyhow. He says that's my job. You'll cover for me, right?"

"Goes without saying."

"Haven't seen you on TV lately," Tiffany said a bit wistfully.

"No, thank goodness. Things have been quiet."

"It's February. Things always slow down in the winter. It'll pick up right enough."

"I like quiet," Bree said. "And naps. I could go for a nap right now."

"You're lookin' a little wrung out," Tiffany agreed. "You ought to try going for a facial. Perks me up every time."

The thick wood door to the back offices swept open, and Payton strode into the room with an anticipatory grin. The sleeves of his pink Brooks Brothers shirt were rolled up to his elbows. He wore red suspenders, a silver tie, and beautifully cut gray trousers. He was also gorgeous. As a young, wet-behind-the-ears novice lawyer, Bree had fallen madly in love with his looks and his brains and just as madly out again when she discovered how slick he was. Not one of her smarter decisions in life, the affair with Payton.

Payton's shiny white teeth ground shut as she rose to meet him and he realized who it was. He shot a furious glare at Tiffany.

"Sorry," Bree said. "I told Tiffany I was early for my two-thirty and she bought it—hook, line, and sinker."

"You want to see me about a case, Bree, make an appointment."

"You can bill your time to your client without an appointment." Bree grabbed his elbow and steered him to the back door. "Let's talk in your office. Won't take more than a minute."

"It'll take less than that." He stopped dead and removed her hand from his shirtsleeve. "You're here about the Prosper White case, right?"

"Right. And talk about frivolous . . ."

"Who said anything about frivolous?"

Aware of Tiffany behind her, Bree amped it up a little and flung her hands in the air dramatically. "Payton, the cause of action *reeks* of frivolous. Baseless, causeless, and dumb. The case has zero merit. None. Nada. I'm filing a motion to dismiss, followed by a claim for frivolous damages based on the utter idiocy of arguing a mere violation of the UCC in court, followed by—"

"Just shut up a minute, will you?" He took a deep breath. Bree dropped the pyrotechnics, in a state of mild surprise. If she didn't know better, she'd say Payton was scared. "We've declined representation."

"Oh." Not looking surprised at anything was an essential defense mechanism in court, and frequently necessary elsewhere. Bree was pretty good at keeping a poker face. But she took a moment to digest this, and then she said, "Why?"

"Why? What do you mean 'why'? I don't have to tell you why."

Bree poked her forefinger in his chest. Payton backed up. "No, you don't. But you do have to tell me who has the case now."

"I don't know."

"Payton, Payton, Payton." She tapped her finger against his chest for emphasis. "I don't have to tell you how seriously the system takes ditching a client." Prosper White's disdainful voice echoed in her head—*Chambers doesn't have two nickels to rub together*—so she added, "Especially a needy, impoverished client. You'd be up before the

Bar Ethics Committee in ten seconds flat. Once the case is
in motion, you're legally bound to make a referral if you
drop a client."

Payton leaned back against the grass-cloth-covered
wall. "All right, all right. Will you get your damn finger off
of my chest? Look. I really don't know where the case
went, for sure. John handled the referral for me."

"John Stubblefield?"

"Yes. To some new firm. It all came down this morning.
Just too late to call off the process server."

"Anyone I know?"

"Doubt it. The firm's been around a month or so. I met
with them, and I . . ." Payton rubbed his hand across his lip.
"Didn't think too much of them, to tell you the truth. I even
recommended against it. John insisted. I honestly don't
know why. But I don't have to give a rat's ass about it because it's not my case anymore. So get off my back, will
you? Tiffany's got their business card, if you really want it.
But I'm out of it, okay? So just beat it." He was sweating
slightly, and flushed.

"I've got the name right here, if you want it, Miss
Winston-Beaufort." Tiffany waved the small card in the air.

Bree went back to the reception desk and took it from
her. It smelled slightly of rotten eggs. She read the names
embossed on the flame-colored background with a slight
sense of shock.

BEAZLEY, BARLOW & CALDECOTT
ATTORNEYS-AT-LAW
300 BAY STREET
SUITE 0
SAVANNAH, GA

"You heard of them?" Payton said.

"Maybe." She took a deep breath.

She knew them, all right. And when had they moved to her own office building?

Beazley & Caldecott were celestial counsel for the Opposition. She'd run up against them four times in her cases in the Celestial Courts. They were half demons from the darkest regions of the Celestial Sphere, and there was no way in hell Bree was going to involve her aunt with the two of them.

And who in the world was Barlow?

Three

"Beazley and Caldecott have a temporal practice?" Ronald Parchese said. The angel held the business card by one edge without looking at it. "And Suite 0? Who has a Suite 0?"

"Beazley, Barlow, and Caldecott," Bree said.

"Who's Barlow?" Ron demanded.

"Haven't a clue at the moment. But I plan to find out."

Bree had left the Bay Street building and walked to the Angelus Street office in a grim state of mind. Ron Parchese, her secretary, was in. Petru Lechta, her Russian paralegal, was in, too. Both angels were playing gin rummy at the old pine table in the kitchen. Their last case had wrapped up two weeks ago, and no new cases had come in. She supposed it was as good a way for angels to spend their time as any other.

Her offices occupied the ground floor of a small white clapboard house that sat smack in the middle of Georgia's only All-Murderers Cemetery. Her landlady, Lavinia Mather, lived on the second floor. From the various thumps overhead, Lavinia was probably up there, but with angels, you never knew.

Bree took the card back. "Suite 0 is in the basement. It's listed on the directory in the Bay Street lobby. The listing wasn't there this morning. I asked the security guard, and she said that a guy with bad fingernails came in and slotted the letters in about eleven thirty—just about the time the summons was being served on Cissy and Prosper White."

"Bad fingernails? That'd be Beazley," Ron shuddered. "Ugh."

Bree suppressed a shudder herself. Beazley's long, talon-like fingernails were usually caked with an unspeakable substance that smelled liked rotting corpses. She'd never gotten the wind up enough to ask—probably because she was afraid of the answer. "I went down in the elevator, and the offices were locked up tight."

"Maybe it's a blind."

"I doubt it, Ron. We knew they had a temporal practice. They represented the insurance company in the accident that broke my leg. I don't recall the address they listed then, but it sure as heck wasn't Bay Street. I would have remembered that."

"Bay Street is an excellent address," Petru said. "Perhaps they moved in the hope to attract a better clientele." He scratched under his thick black beard and peered at the cards in his hand. "I am knocking with three points in my hand, Ronald."

Ron picked up his hand and looked at it. He was tall, fair-haired, with bright blue eyes and an impeccable sense of style. Today he was in pressed blue jeans, a crisp white long-sleeved shirt, and a slouchy leather jacket. In sharp

contrast, Petru was short, thickset, and favored baggy
black suits that smelled faintly of mothballs. Sometimes,
depending on the light, it was possible to see the faint gold
glow that surrounded both of them.

Ron set his cards downs with a flourish, placed three of
his discards against Petru's meld, and sat back with a grin.
"Insult," he said. "That's fifty points for the good guys."

Petru muttered something into his beard and then re-
shuffled the cards. Bree snatched them out of his hand and
demanded, "Well?"

Ron leaped to his feet. "Is there something you want us
to do?"

"Perhaps we could discuss this in further depth?" Bree
suggested pointedly. "As long as it's not interrupting your
card game?"

"It is not a trouble to quit the card game," Petru said. "I
am glad to begin work again. I have been losing to Ronald
all week. But this case of yours is a temporal case. Nobody
is dead? This is a matter for Bay Street and Mrs. Billingsley. Not us, I think."

"This is a matter of my aunt. My mother's sister. I am
very fond of my mother's sister. I do not want her anywhere
near Beazley and Caldecott."

"Then of course we will be happy to consult." Petru got
to his feet with an effort and unhooked his cane from the
back of the kitchen chair.

"Good to hear that. Seeing as how both of you are on
the payroll." She paused. "For the moment." She let the silence that greeted this sally stretch out and then gestured
toward the doorway leading out of the kitchen. "Let's try
the conference room."

Bree had responded to the ad for the Angelus address
because it was amazingly cheap, close to her town house

on the Savannah River, and fairly spacious. This was before she knew it was an address that only she and those attached to the Celestial Spheres could actually find. The house dated from the 1820s and sat squarely amid the remains of the cemetery. She rented the entire first floor, which totaled about six hundred square feet, with just enough room for her office staff.

There was a small kitchen with a humpback refrigerator, a dinged-up porcelain sink, and a linoleum floor that peeled in inconvenient places. Petru's laptop computer occupied the square kitchen table, and his files and books were crowded into a battered china dresser near the back door.

The kitchen was off an equally small living room with polished pine floors. Ron's desk took up one end of the room. A battered leather couch with an old oak trunk that served as a coffee table offered space for clients at the other. At least, that had been the plan when Bree had rented the space initially. The house was hidden from temporals, and so far, only one damned soul had found its way there, and it hadn't needed to sit down, much less put a cup of coffee on the top of the trunk.

A brick fireplace was built against the long wall facing the cemetery. Above the fireplace was a painting of *The Rise of the Cormorant,* a horrific scene of a sailing ship in a fiery storm, with passengers drowning in the roiling waves. Bree hated the picture. Like her condemned clients, it was part of the legacy of celestial practice of her birth father, the man she'd always known as Great-Uncle Franklin. She couldn't burn it, bury it, or smash it with an ax. She had considered all three.

The remaining space on the ground floor was given over to a dining room used as a conference area and a small bedroom that she'd converted for her own use with Franklin's own desk and chair. The front door opened into a tiny foyer, with a stairwell that featured a parade of brightly painted Renaissance angels marching up the wall to Lavinia's rooms on the second floor.

Bree led the way into the conference room. She sat at the head of the table in a chair that faced away from the room's back window, since the view outside was depressing. A dying Spanish oak with an open grave beneath it dominated the backyard. The grave had once contained the corpse of Josiah Pendergast. Bree didn't know what had happened to the body and was afraid she was going to find out every time she had to work late and leave the office after dark. The other graves had decaying headstones that identified murderers long sent to their own particular circle of Hell.

Despite Lavinia's frequent efforts at gardening, the entire cemetery was filled with decaying leaves and the reek of foul decay, even in high summer.

"Coffee?" Ron asked brightly. "I've got some doughnuts left over from this morning."

"Not right now. Sit down, please, both of you. I want to know if we have a case or not." She handed the Summons and Complaint to Ron, who skimmed it and passed it along to Petru. Petru read it carefully, folded it up, and shook his hand. "I do not believe so. Nobody is dead."

"I don't think so, either," Ron said promptly. "Beazley and his beastly friend have the right to a temporal practice, if that's what you're asking. Just as you do with the Bay Street office. We all have to pay the bills somehow. And a temporal practice means temporal clients with real-time cash. As for this Allard Chambers and his wife, Jillian? Temporal, as far as I can see. They've got a real address on

Whitaker. I've gone by the store myself. Doesn't look too prosperous. Which would explain why he's reduced to the likes of Beazley and Caldecott. I mean, so far they're batting zero with us in the Celestial Courts. I can't imagine that they do any better in the Chatham County Courthouse."

Bree frowned. "Why haven't they shown up in a temporal practice before this?"

"Perhaps Goldstein has interceded," Petru said. "You and Ronald petitioned the Celestial Courts for better communication with your clients, did you not? Perhaps the establishment of this office for the defense is a step in that direction."

"Maybe." Bree leaned back in her chair. She'd been operating on an adrenaline surge since her run-in with Payton. Back here in the Angelus office, the only place she felt truly safe, she was suddenly aware of how tired she was. She wanted go to bed and sleep for a week. "Cissy's going to marry this guy Prosper White. All of a sudden, we've got two demons . . ." She thought about Barlow. "Maybe three?"

"Not demons, precisely," Petru said.

"Whatever they are, they aren't fully human, and they aren't nice, and they're involved with the plaintiff. I don't want any member of my family to come anywhere near what we do here."

"This is highly understandable," Petru said. "Perhaps you should go and see this Chambers to determine if there is a level of threat."

Bree tried to think of a bigger violation of the canon of ethics than contacting a plaintiff without the plaintiff's lawyer present. Embezzlement, maybe. Or hand-delivering your own client's written confession to the DA. Petru was studying for the Georgia Bar Exam. This didn't augur well for his success.

Petru caught her scowl. "Not in your capacity as an attorney, of course. He has a shop specializing in antiquities? Go and look to purchase one thing or another. Watch him out of the corner of your eye. You may be able to sense if he is a threat from the darker side of the Sphere. Take Sasha with you. That is what your dog is for. Today is Monday, I believe, so Sasha is at home with Antonia? He should accompany you to the shop."

"As a demon sniffer?" Bree smiled a little at that. Sasha was a cross between a Russian mastiff and a golden retriever and the gentlest soul in Bree's universe.

"T'cha! Sasha is an adept, if you will," Petru said. "He will sense danger, if there is any. This visit, it is not, I agree, a strictly proper thing to do. But if this were my sister Rose? I would not let such deter me. I could not."

"Love and duty," Ron said suddenly. "You shouldn't have to face that kind of choice, Bree. Call up Beazley and ask him if it's okay to take a gander at Chambers before you take on the case officially. You might want to hand off Prosper White to someone else, just like McAllister handed off Chambers to Beazley and Caldecott. Then you can keep an eye on your aunt Cissy without running into any potential conflicts."

Bree nodded. "That makes sense."

"There's a phone number on the card, isn't there?" Ron got to his feet. "I'll give the Weasel-Beasel a call myself."

"If he agrees, ask him either to e-mail or fax the permission to me," Bree said. "I don't trust his word. Petru? I'm not sure that you'll find anything, but if you could get some background material on the law firm of Beazley, Barlow, and Caldecott, I'd be grateful. If I'm going up against them in a court in the state of Georgia, I want to know what we're dealing with." She thought a moment and then added, "Ask him about this Barlow, too. I'm almost certain we haven't run into him before."

The two angels left the room. Bree closed her eyes and thought about lunch. She'd had a cup of yogurt at the town house for breakfast and nothing since. At least she was meeting Cissy and Antonia at B. Mitchell's for dinner at seven. The food was great there. Then she thought about Cissy in the talons of something like Caldecott, with his goat-pupil eyes and his sharpened teeth, and her appetite disappeared.

Her cell phone beeped. She flipped it open and read the text message:

OK Winston-Beaufort 2 see Chambers any time/no talk case/Z. Beazley/C U in court

"Charming." Bree tapped Save and snapped her cell phone shut. Fine. She had counsel's permission on record. She'd go see Allard Chambers for herself.

February in Savannah was chilly, but Whitaker Street was close enough that Bree decided to walk.

She strode along in the chilly air, an ache in her still-knitting bones. The break had healed exceptionally quickly, but an occasional pain lanced underneath her knee like a red-hot spike, and she felt as if her leg could give way without warning. She picked up her pace, as if trying to outrun it.

Winter had settled over the city like a silver shroud, veiling the trees and shrubs in the city squares and hushing the noise of the traffic. The sidewalks were damp and un-crowded. The skies were overcast, with a promise of rain to come. Bree crossed Oglethorpe Square, turned left onto

Mulberry, right again on Whitaker, and found Antiques
and Reclaimables halfway down the street.

It was located in a two-story, tin-roofed building that
had probably been a warehouse in the mid-nineteenth century. The aged stucco walls were streaked with rusty water
stains. The white-painted, peeling wooden frames of the
doors and windows were spotted with mold. The bottom
story was given over to storefronts. Reclaimables was
tucked between a hopeful coffee shop and something
called the City of Light Thrift Store and Grocery. The second story was faced with a long wrought iron balcony in
need of attention from a stiff wire brush. The balcony was
divided into three sections, each serving an apartment. The
balcony just above Reclaimables held two green plastic
lawn chairs, a rusty Weber grill, and a pot of vivid-red ge-
raniums. These items sat in front of a large window backed
by a pair of soiled drapes. Someone inside twitched the
drapes aside. The hand that held them wasn't young.

"You'd think the place would be full of posters for
Gauloises cigarettes and resin copies of the Eiffel Tower."

Bree jumped. She'd been concentrating so hard on the
upper story that she'd overlooked the small man standing
in front of the antique shop.

"The City of Light?" he said with a nod in the direction
of the thrift store. "Paris?"

"Paris. Of course."

"It isn't, though. It's a Christian sect, dedicated to charitable works. Although one could possibly trace its roots
back to Zoroastrianism, which was not a charitable reli-
gion at all. Quite the contrary, in fact. Pre-Christian, and
characterized by human sacrifice. Which isn't to say its in-
fluence has died out, of course."

This flood of interesting, but irrelevant, information

made think Bree of Petru, who'd turned didactics into high art. She smiled. "You'd enjoy a conversation with an associate of mine. He's Russian and very interested in antiquities."

"I might, indeed." He ran one hand nervously through his thinning hair. He was shorter by several inches than Bree, who stood five foot nine in her bare feet. His shoulders and arms were thick. He was dressed for the cold weather, in rumpled chinos, a worn denim shirt, and battered Frye work boots. He looked like every archeologist Bree had ever seen on the Nature channel, down to the wire-rimmed spectacles, L. L. Bean fishing vest, and weathered skin. All he lacked was a bush hat. She pegged his age at somewhere in the midsixties.

He didn't look possessed, evil, damned, or otherwise part of the darker areas of Bree's life as a celestial advocate. He looked like an archeologist shopkeeper on the verge of going down for the count.

"You are Professor Allard Chambers?"

His pupils widened, momentarily changing his eyes from washed-out blue to black. "The last person who asked me that, in that tone of voice, with that sort of specificity, was a process server." His voice remained cordial. If it hadn't been for his eyes, Bree wouldn't have known he was angry. "But you don't look like a process server. You look . . ." He shoved his glasses up his nose with one forefinger and peered at her. "You look like one of those statues of Athena the old Romans erected in imitation of the Greeks. Perfectly proportioned. Straight nose, broad brow, level gaze. You're too slender for your height, though. The Greeks wouldn't have approved. But the hair! More Norse than Greek, that white blonde. Hm. At a guess, I would say you're a lawyer? Here on behalf of that load of codswallop Prosper White?"

Bree raised her eyebrows. Chambers smirked. "I see my guess was an accurate one. Come in, please, to the shop. We can talk there more comfortably."

A bell over the door lintel rang loudly as she followed him inside.

The shop was a mess. That was the first thing to strike her. The second was the smell: a papery, moldy, very pleasant odor that was somehow familiar. Bree placed it, suddenly. Her family home smelled like that. Plessey had belonged to the Winston-Beauforts for more than two hundred years. It was the scent of age and history.

Reclaimables was long and narrow, perhaps sixty by twenty, with sixteen-foot ceilings. Cheap pine bookshelves stuffed with books, stacks of moldering magazines, narrow boxes, and a jumble of pots and other small objects lined the side walls. The uneven floor was covered in stained indoor-outdoor carpeting. It might have been hunter green, once. But maybe not. Three oak-framed, waist-high display cases ran down the center of the aisle. The glass fronts were smeared with thumbprints. Careless stacks of clay artifacts spilled from the interior shelving. Bree caught an occasional glimpse of bronze and silver metals among the piles.

"There's a couple of chairs in the back where we can sit, Athena."

"It's Brianna Winston-Beaufort." Bree dug into her tote for a business card as she followed Chambers to the back of the shop. He stopped at his desk—which was bare except for a laptop and a landline—and shoved a stack of catalogues off the desk chair onto the floor. "Have a seat, Athena."

Bree had only been practicing law for four years, but the first three and a half had been in her adoptive father's office in Raleigh, and he'd taught her well: the guy who stood had a psychological advantage over the guy who sat. She settled one hip on the edge of Chambers's desk and laid her business card on the cover of the laptop. Chambers looked bemused for a second, and then he sat in his office chair.

"I have your attorney's permission to come by," Bree said. "But I have to ask you if you're sure you're comfortable talking to me without him. And we can't discuss the particulars of your case with Prosper White."

"Zeb gave me a call. Said it'd be fine."

"Zeb?"

"Zebulon Beazley. Interesting name, isn't it? I'm wondering if his background includes one of those fundamentalist sects that adhere to a strict interpretation of the Christian Bible."

"I don't know," Bree said. "I wouldn't be surprised, though."

"Dirty fighter," Chambers said with cheerful spite. "Kind of lawyer who'll stand a lot of heat. Just who you want in the rough-and-tumble of a court case. I'm a lot more comfortable with him and Caldecott than that sniveling piece of work at Marbury, Stubblefield. Payton? Payton McAllister? Reminded me of a grad student I once had that plagiarized part of his thesis. Anyhow, Marbury's the biggest firm in town, so I thought they might be cheaper. I was wrong about that, too. Bastards have already e-mailed me an outsize bill, and they only turned me over to Beazley this morning." He patted his vest pocket and pulled out a well-used briar pipe. "Bad habit, I know. D'ya mind?" He didn't wait for her polite demurral but fished in another pocket for his tobacco.

"And you're at ease with them? Caldecott, I mean?"

"Don't like 'em much, if that's what you're asking. But who says you have to like your lawyer? Long as they hang White out to dry, I don't care about their character."

Bree regretted not bringing Sasha. Chambers seemed untainted by Dark Sphere forces, but who really knew? "You taught at a university before you bought this shop?"

He tamped the tobacco carefully into the bowl, struck a kitchen match against the sole of his boot, and lit his pipe. He puffed away for a second or two and then regarded her through the clouds of smoke. "How old are you? Twenty-eight? Twenty-nine?"

"Twenty-nine this year."

"Hm. Your expression's older than that, Athena. Bet you've seen a lot in those twenty-nine years. Which means you ought to figure the fools from the get-go. Do I look like a fool to you?"

"How can I possibly tell at this point?"

His bark of a laugh wasn't amused. "Take it from me, I'm not. Was, maybe, at one time. I learned my lesson about the kind of lawyer to hire a little too late. So if I look like a former fool to you, then you'd be right on the money. Yes, I taught at a university, and yes, your client Prosper White was instrumental in my teaching there no more. The bastard." His teeth clenched around the pipe stem so hard, she heard the wood crack. "You know he's called a press conference tomorrow? To tout his bloody magazine exhibit? With *my* cover? The man's a poseur and a fraud. We'll see just how far the bastard gets with the press."

Bree nudged Chambers back to the task at hand. "When did this all happen? The business over the provenance of the Cross of Justinian?"

"Started about eight months ago. I've been searching for the Cross for thirty years. And finally, finally . . ." He looked at Bree, without really seeing her. He was looking, she decided, at a memory. "My wife and I found it. In the back of a cave along the Dalmatian coast."

"Outside authentication was required by the university?"

"Yes," he said abruptly. "For the insurance. Insurance companies know damn-all about antiquities, much less the so-called experts they hire as consultants. It was my bad luck that they believed in White's bullshit credentials."

Bree made a mental note to check out White's background if this thing went to court—White's credibility might very well be on the line.

"He thought the Cross was, umm, not from the period."

"Said it was a fake. A twenty-first-century fraud." He rapped his pipe on his boot, spilling ash on the floor. "What's your interest in this case? You really represent Prosper White?"

"Yes," Bree said cautiously.

"Hope you got your retainer up front."

"That's not an issue. He's engaged to marry my aunt."

"You have to trust me on this, Athena. He's not a man you want in the family circle."

"I can understand your desire for vindication," Bree said. She would have to step carefully here. She couldn't discuss the actual case. "But why choose this way to do it? Surely there's a better opportunity to get Mr. White's attention than to quarrel over something like a magazine cover."

"Oh, it's more than that." Chambers smiled rather charmingly. "I didn't have any idea the bastard would show up here in Savannah two months after I bought this shop. You could have knocked me over with a feather when he came waltzing in here looking for old magazines. And"—he pointed the stem of his pipe at her dramatically—"true to form, the bastard tries to chisel me. The opportunity presented itself. How could I pass it up?"

Bree bit her lip so she wouldn't laugh. "It might be

worth reflecting on whether you want to confuse the two issues, sir. While I sympathize with your career difficulties over the relic—"

"The relic," he said. "A good man lost his life in pursuit of what you call 'the relic.' My wife lost any hope of a comfortable old age because of what Prosper White did to us over 'the relic.'" His face flushed dark red. He clenched one hand into a fist. "I'm going to take White down. I'll take you and your aunt down with him, if I have to."

Bree didn't like threats. She pulled herself up, concentrating on the man before her, pulling on the strength of will that made her what she was. A breeze came up from nowhere and stirred the catalogues piled at their feet. Her voice was icily level when she finally spoke. "If my aunt's determined to marry him, what I want or don't want doesn't matter. You should know—you need to let your lawyers know—that I'll defend him against anything they might try. Is that clear, sir?"

Chambers drew back and paled. "Who are you, anyway?" Then, as if ashamed of his momentary fear, he blustered, "What is this, some kind of threat? You can't bully me!"

Bree felt her lips part in a smile. She'd caught a glimpse of her face once, when she was angry like this. She hadn't liked herself much. "No threat. Just a statement of fact."

Chambers shoved his office chair as far away from her as he could get without standing up and running away. He hunched his shoulders and crossed his arms across his chest as if he were cold. "My wife says . . ."

Bree waited.

"My wife says the thing's cursed."

"The Cross?"

He nodded, mute.

"You're a scientist, Professor. I didn't think scientists believed in curses."

"Haven't had a day's luck since I found it again."

"Again?"

"Long story." He rubbed his hand over his face. "Bad story. Want to see the artifact that caused it all?"

"The Cross of Justinian?"

"Prosper would say the *purported* Cross of Justinian." He bent sideways and pulled open the lower desk drawer. He scrabbled around in its depths and then emerged with a small wooden box. He tossed it to her. Bree caught the box in midair. "Go ahead. Open it up. I . . ." The door chime rang, and he leaped to his feet, clearly glad for a chance to get away from her. "A customer, by gum! Here's a rare chance! Take a look at the piece of crap that started it all. I'll be right back."

The box didn't weigh very much. Bree hefted it in her hand. It was made of pine, with a cheap brass latch. She flipped the lid open with her thumb and took out the small jeweled cross and held it up.

White had described it perfectly, although the cedar base was so heavily inlaid that her first impression was that it was solid silver. The work wasn't refined, at least not to twenty-first-century eyes, but it was very beautiful. Semi-precious stones were inset with great care into the metal. The green must be jasper, and there were tiny bits of coral and lapis lazuli. Bree held it up . . .

And a wisp of dark shadow rose from its center.

Bree closed her fist. The Cross was warm, almost hot, in the palm of her hand. Her clients came to her through objects that had been near them when they died. She didn't want another client. Not now. Not this case, with her mother's cherished sister at the heart of it.

The dark light seeped through her fingers and coiled around her wrist with a touch that was almost loving. Bree closed her eyes. She didn't have to take every case that came along, did she?

"It's not a customer; it's a damn dog!" Allard Chambers shouted from the front of the store. "Ha!"

The shadow was an absence of light. A shape of nothingness. It crawled up her forearm and then rose in a slender pillar, taking shape in front of her eyes.

"Whoops! Heads up!" Chambers shouted. "It's headed your way."

Bree put the Cross back into the box, slid the cover shut and put it back on the desk. A familiar nose nudged her hip. Bree smoothed her hand over the golden head. "Hey, Sasha," she said. "Sniff out any demons, lately?"

Sasha looked up at her, his feathered tail waving a gentle welcome.

Take it.

"I can't just take it," she said. "It's not mine. Besides, I don't want to."

You must.

"Sorry about that." Chambers said. He was slightly out of breath. "Slipped right past me. The lock on the front door doesn't catch unless we slam it shut. All kinds of street people wander in when it's cold, but this is the first time I've had a dog take advantage. The street people drive Jillian crazy. The dog would really put her over the edge."

"Mrs. Chambers? She's joining you in the suit against my client?"

"Yeah." He looked at her hand on Sasha's head. "Dogs send her right around the bend. I see that dogs don't bother you, though."

"Not as a rule," Bree said. "Besides, I know this one."

"Yours, is he? Handsome animal."

"He is, isn't he?"

Sasha stood thirty inches at the shoulder. His chest was all mastiff: broad and heavily muscled. His thick, glossy coat was a color between amber and gold coins.

"Where'd he come from? He know how to open car doors, too?"

"I have a town house on Factor's Walk. I think he just decided to take a stroll and find me." She ran her fingers over his silky ears and stood up. "I'd better take him on home." She extended her hand and said politely, "I'm glad to have met you, Professor Chambers. I'll be in touch with your lawyers. I hope we can resolve this dispute amicably."

"I don't know about that. I'm not in a real amiable frame of mind." He sat down in his desk chair and squinted at her. "Did you take a look at the Cross?"

"I did."

"Doesn't seem like much to wreck a career over, does it?"

She hesitated. "How did you come to be mistaken about it?"

"I'm not," he said flatly. "Or at least I wasn't about the original."

"This isn't the original artifact?"

"Hell, no. This is a fake." He grabbed the box from his desk and threw it at her. Without thinking, Bree caught it. "Take it!"

"But you had the original?"

He glared at her, suddenly venomous. "I'm not saying another word to you, Miss Winston-Beaufort. You want the original? So do I. I want my job back. I want my life back. That isn't going to happen. So I want your client to roast in Hell. You want to know where the original is? You ask your goddamn client." He leaned across the desk, his face close to hers. His breath smelled of bread. "I know things about that bastard that your rich aunt isn't going to like to hear. You want to keep her out of a scandal? You tell her to pay up. Or else." He was so close that his breath was hot against her cheek. So close she could see the tears in his eyes. "I don't know how in hell I got into this mess. But somebody, somebody *owes* me something."

Four

"You have to tell Aunt Cissy that Prosper stole the real antique," Antonia said. "I mean, my God. The guy's a crook!"

"Shh!" Bree said.

Bree's little sister took after the Carmichael side of the family. She was small—an asset for a stage actress, since so many leading men were short—and had thick, dark red-gold hair that set off her blue eyes and camellia-like complexion to stunning effect. She'd insisted on acting lessons the day she turned thirteen, and the years of training gave her voice a resonance that could be heard in every corner of the restaurant. At seven on a Monday night in February, B. Mitchell's wasn't all that full, but several couples were openly listening. Antonia was a hard person to ignore when she was silent, much less when she was in full cry.

"Shh, yourself," Antonia said. "If you don't tell her, I will."

"Well, you can't," Bree said firmly. "All of this is unsubstantiated. The two men hate each other, that's clear. But I don't know a thing about Chambers, and neither do you. He could be delusional. He could be lying through his teeth. He could be setting White up."

"But you don't think so."

Bree sat back and looked at the menu. She didn't really need to look at the menu. She had the same thing every time she came here, and she'd have it again. Fish tacos.

"Bree?"

"Keep your voice down, Antonia. And no. I don't think so."

"So?"

"I think he's a pitiful little guy who's scared out of his mind."

"Scared? Of what?"

Bree shook her head in self-disgust. "Of me, probably. I leaned on him a little. He's in over his head, that's for sure. But he's stubborn. He really believes he's been cheated. But it's a guess, Antonia. Guesses aren't facts. Guesses don't settle lawsuits."

"You've always had an excellent baloney detector, Sis. Best in the family, except for Daddy. I say we tell Cissy that White's a thief. Then she'll ditch him, and we can all stop worrying about it, and this Chambers character can ride off into the sunset without Cissy's money."

"It doesn't seem to be that simple."

It wasn't—and she hadn't figured out why. Not yet. She and Sasha had gone straight home from Reclaimables. It was too soon to take on another case. Handling the Cross had left her feeling odd, as if she'd been displaced from the here and now and set down in another universe. She didn't like it.

She had needed time to herself before meeting Cissy

and Antonia at dinner. She'd locked the fake cross in her dresser drawer to give herself time to think about when—or if—she would pick it up again to allow the manifestation of a new client.

Chambers himself was probably just what he seemed to be: definitely out for a pathetic kind of vengeance; definitely a Bay Street case; definitely someone she hadn't needed to threaten the way she did.

The new client who had died clutching a fake Cross of Justinian? That was a different matter entirely. She was inclined to settle the White lawsuit by negotiating a settlement—using White's money, and not her aunt's. She wasn't at all inclined to take on another Angelus Street case—not so soon after the last one, despite Sasha's insistence.

She'd fallen into a deep, coma-like sleep on the couch in the living room of the town house on Factor's Walk before she'd gotten any further in her decision making. She'd wakened only when Antonia banged into the house from a shopping trip at six. Jerked from that deep, almost unnatural sleep, for a scary minute, she hadn't recognized her own sister.

Both of them scrambled to be on time for dinner with Aunt Cissy at B. Mitchell's. Since the restaurant was almost kitty-corner from their town house, they ended up being too early. They'd been sipping white wine for half an hour before Bree brought up her concerns about Prosper White. Antonia had exploded with indignation.

Her sister kicked her under the table to get her attention. "So? Are you going to tell her, or shall I?"

Bree looked at her cell phone to get the time. "Neither one of us is going to do a thing until I get a better handle on the facts. Anyhow, Cissy's late. Maybe she won't show up."

Antonia rolled her eyes. "She'll show up. When is she ever on time?"

"Like you can talk."

"I am extremely punctual," Antonia said firmly, which was true only when she had a theater commitment.

Bree grinned. This familiar squabbling was reassuring. For a moment, she felt totally herself again. "You're punctual with 'except-fors.' Except-for the dentist, except-for when you've agreed to meet me, except-for dinner."

Antonia kicked her under the table again. "Hush up. There she is." She waved one arm over her head and shouted, "Coo-ee, Aunt Cissy," to the marked displeasure of the power couple the next table over.

"Not a word about White and Chambers," Bree warned. "I mean it."

Cissy sat down in a swirl of Prada perfume. "How are y'all? Antonia, you're looking gorgeous, as usual. Bree, you're looking more peaked by the day."

She had changed for dinner into a tailored navy jacket, a green-apple silk turtleneck, and artfully worn jeans. "You need to put on ten pounds, and I never in this life thought I would say that to any woman." She leaned across the table and gathered their hands into hers. "And aren't I just the luckiest female this side of paradise? Don't you just love my Prosper?" She released them and sat back with a sigh. "This dinner's on me, darlins. I am just so happy!" The waitress hovered, and Cissy said, "A nice little Cosmopolitan for me. And one each for my girls. Now! You met with that awful Allard person, Bree."

Startled, Bree looked at Antonia, who shrugged, "not me." "Why would you say that, Aunt Cissy?"

"'Cause the little guttersnipe called me right after you left that trashy shop."

"He did?"

"He did. What do you suppose he wanted?"

Bree had a hunch. She didn't like it. She didn't like it at all. Wealthy divorcée Celia Carmichael made the "People about Town" column in the *Savannah Chronicle* on a regular basis. Her upcoming wedding to White had been news only last week. Chambers wanted money, and by now he undoubtedly had a pretty good idea of what her aunt could afford.

The waitress set the Cosmopolitans in front of them. Bree pushed hers aside. Cissy took a big sip, set the glass down, and said, "A private settlement, that's what."

"Oh my God," Antonia said. "The man wants money. I knew it. I just knew it. This is plain lousy, Bree!"

"Would you like to order a starter?" the waitress said, clearly wanting to linger. "No rush about it. I can see y'all need to talk."

"Artichoke cheese dip and fish tacos all around," Cissy said. "Unless you girls want something else? No? That'll be fine, then. You can bring it all at the same time, too. Thank you."

Bree waited until the waitress was out of earshot. B. Mitchell's was a big, low-ceilinged room with a bar across the long wall at the back and round tables set well apart from one another. As long as Antonia kept her voice down, it was one of Savannah's better spots for private conversation. "Did he mention a figure?"

"Fifty thousand dollars. Said I'd spend that much in legal fees defending poor Prosper, and I might just as well give it to him now unless I wanted my future husband's name drawn through the mud." Cissy bit her lower lip. Then she tossed back the rest of her Cosmopolitan.

"What did you say to him?"

"I hung up on the little bastard, of course."

Bree rubbed her face with both hands. "Okay," she said finally. "What do you want to do?"

"I thought I'd ask you," Cissy said, rather pitifully. "Chambers could get on the stand and tell all kinds of lies about Prosper, couldn't he?"

"Or all kinds of truths," Antonia muttered.

"What's that? What's that?"

Bree gave Antonia a shut-up glare.

"Nothing," Antonia said.

Cissy bit her lip, then turned in her chair and waved to the bartender. "I swear they make these drinks with as little vodka as possible. Another round here, please? Besides," she added in a braver tone, "it'd just about wreck my plans for the honeymoon. What if we had to come back to testify or whatever? I'm thinkin' fifty thousand's little enough to pay for peace of mind."

"I'm thinking that's crazy," Antonia said. "And why should you pay anything, anyway? It's White's problem. Let him settle it."

Bree had the same question. She searched for a tactful approach. "Does he have available funds?"

"Of course he doesn't!" Cissy snapped. "He's an artist! I thought that was understood, Bree. As for you, Antonia . . . Of all people, I thought you'd have some sympathy. I mean, with your life in the theater and all." She blinked away tears and then, when that didn't help, put the backs of her hands underneath her eyes to hold them back.

Antonia opened her mouth, and then backed off at Cissy's despairing look. "Of course, Auntie. Of course I understand. But if you just knew more about . . ."

It was Bree's turn to kick her sister under the table. Antonia glared at her. Bree jerked her head toward the door, and when Antonia stayed stubbornly in her chair, Bree drew her foot back to whack her again.

"Okay, okay, Bree. I get the message." She bounced up and wrapped Cissy in a fierce hug. "It's a pure shame, that's what it is. Y'all have to excuse me. I just remembered I promised to pick up some stuff for . . . somebody. Anyhow. Pack up my food, so I can eat it later, okay? I'll just be off now." She flipped her hair over her shoulder, then backed out of Bree's reach. "By the by, Bree's got something to tell you. Don't you, Bree? You get it on out of her, Aunt. Don't forget my tacos, Bree. There's not a darn thing in that fridge at home. "

Everybody watched as Antonia walked across the room and out the front door. But then, everyone always did.

Cissy stared over Bree's shoulder, her lower lip firmly between her teeth. After a long moment, she picked up her napkin, dabbed under her eyes, and sighed.

The waitress set the artichoke dip in the middle of the table, then the platters of fish tacos in front of Bree and Cissy. She looked at Antonia's empty chair. "Shall I wrap this third one up?"

"Might as well," Cissy said. "Take it away and keep it warm for her, if you would. We'll get it at the end of the meal. If there's ever going to *be* an end to this meal."

Bree waved the waitress away with an apologetic gesture. Cissy slammed her fist onto the table but not very hard. "I take it you're the one who's been elected to talk to me about Prosper?"

"Would that be okay with you?"

"Fine. Good. I'm ready. So you go ahead and tell me what y'all have wanted to say for the past month. You hate Prosper. Don't you. All of you. My whole loving family. You think he's after my money, and you think I'm too damn old and too damn foolish for any man to love me."

"That is just not true," Bree said firmly.

Cissy was in no mood to listen. "You know what? Y'all might be right. I don't care. I love him, Bree. And since the good Lord blessed both me and your mamma with more money than either one of us will need in a lifetime, and if I want to spend it on this man, who gives a rat's behind?" She stabbed the taco viciously with a fork. "Francesca's on the phone to me every minute, talking about a prenup. Your father squinches his eyes up like he's tracking down a fox after it's raided the henhouse. Even Antonia looks crosswise at me every time I talk about him. And you! You won't even call him by his Christian name!" She blinked away more tears.

Bree took her aunt's cold hands in her own. "We're looking out for you as best we can, that's all. We don't hate him, exactly. We just have some questions about how good he'll be to you. You don't need a man to make you happy, do—"

"You hush *up*!" Cissy shouted. She jerked her hands away. "Where's Francesca when I need her? You're no damn good at comforting, Bree. Not lately, anyway. Not since you moved to Savannah and got *hard*." She stood up, knocking the chair over in her haste to leave. "Do I need a man to make me happy? I purely do not. And if I do, what's it to you? And what do you know about it, anyway? Look at you, the way you're living. Like some cloistered nun. There's not one womanly thing about you. Do I need a man? Of course I do. What about love? What about companionship? What about *sex*?"

The power couple one table over got up in a pointed manner and moved to a table against the wall.

Five

"So you can't to go back to B. Mitchell's again, that's for sure," Antonia said with a cheeky grin twenty minutes later.

Antonia lay flat on the couch in their living room. Bree sat in the rocker next to the fireplace, still in her winter coat, Sasha on the floor beside her, the food from B. Mitchell's packed neatly up in a plastic bag. She'd come back to the town house and had been overwhelmed by the feeling of total dislocation.

Antonia sat up with a jerk. "She just slammed on out of there, Bree? After yelling all that out for everyone to hear? Without even a 'bye-howdy'?"

"It's not funny. And no, she didn't slam out for another twenty agonizing minutes. I agreed to meet White tomorrow at the Frazier and talk to him about an out-of-court settlement."

"Cissy's going to pay up?"

"Looks like it."

"Ugh. You're right, sister. It's awful. Poor Cissy. What are you going to do about it?"

Bree didn't want to do anything about it. She was tired, close to exhausted. Worse, the town house had a strange, foreboding atmosphere. The twenty-year-old couch in front of the fireplace looked unfamiliar. Her grandmother's sturdy rocking chair felt fragile. She was almost afraid to move in it. Maybe she hadn't recovered from the car accident that had broken her leg as well as she thought she had.

"Bree? You've got to find some way to get this bozo out of Cissy's life."

Antonia was right.

Was it her imagination? Or were the walls and ceiling veiled with a dirty mist?

An unaccountable depression settled over her. She wanted to be back in the Angelus office, where the angels formed a barrier between her family and things like Beazley and Caldecott. The town house, home to her family for generations, was alien territory to her now. She turned and looked up at the mirror over the fireplace, afraid that she would catch a glimpse of something that shouldn't be there.

She closed her eyes. She let her attention drift. The town house was at the end of a row of converted buildings that faced the Savannah River. Savannah had been the hub of the international cotton trade two hundred years ago, and the cobblestone embankments had carried warehouses, inns, and the offices of the shipyards. The buildings had survived pirates, slavers, the Civil War, and the Great Depression; Bree and Antonia's home had been the headquarters for slave auctions, and Bree was always faintly surprised that her dreams weren't troubled by the ghosts of the tormented victims. Maybe it was the echo of those poor souls that troubled her now.

She felt as if she were floating over the room, looking at it from a great height. She saw the narrow-planked pine floors. The floor-to-ceiling bookshelves that flanked the small brick fireplace. Double French doors that led to the small balcony that jutted out over River Street two stories below. In summertime, with the doors open to breezes from the river, the clangor from the street was a constant reminder that old Savannah was as vital as in her glory days. She'd known this place from birth.

Hadn't she?

"Bree!"

Bree jerked awake.

"You all right?"

"Fine." Bree stretched a little. Then she stood up. Sasha gazed up at her with anxious eyes.

"I think we should call Mamma," Antonia said. "Maybe she can come on down and shake some sense into her."

Bree bent to one side and laid her hand on Sasha's head. Bad enough that Cissy had a peripheral involvement in this case. She wanted both Royal and Francesca safe in North Carolina. "Not a good idea."

"What's the matter with you? She'll know how to handle Cissy. The wedding's in four days, and she's coming down for that. Why can't she come a couple of days early?"

Bree didn't say anything.

"Besides, you've got to tell both her and Daddy what happened today. Chambers called Prosper a thief, or as good as."

"I can do that over the phone."

"Better in person. We'll call a family meeting. With all of us sitting there, Cissy's got to see reason."

"You ever known Mamma to interfere? She's always let us make our own mistakes. Did they cut you off when you dropped out of school to chase after going on the stage? All they did was point out how much better off you'd be with a college education."

"I'm perfectly able to make decisions about my own life," Antonia said crossly.

"Exactly."

"Oh, never *mind*." Antonia scowled and bit at her thumbnail. "What a mess. That Chambers character's trying to extort fifty thousand dollars from her. I suppose you think we should all sit by for that?"

"It's not extortion," Bree said. She felt her confusion ebb as she concentrated on the legalities of Cissy's position. It helped to focus on the task at hand. She'd have to remember that. "He made a legitimate offer to drop the suit."

"Is she going to pay up?" Antonia swung her feet to the floor and sat up. "You'd best tell Mamma if she is. I mean, honestly. Fifty thousand dollars. That's a pile of money. If anyone can talk some sense into her, it's Mamma."

Bree thought about the woman she called mother. Of all the unsettling events that had occurred since she'd taken on Great-Uncle Franklin's celestial appeals practice, the most unnerving had been the discovery that she wasn't the child of Royal and Francesca Winston-Beaufort, but their niece. Franklin had been her father. And her own birth mother, a woman named Leah, had died as Bree was being born. She knew nothing at all about Leah, except for the talisman she had left her. A tiny gold replica of the scales of justice, enfolded by a pair of angel wings. Francesca had given her the talisman four months ago, when Bree reopened Franklin's cases. It was on a chain around her neck. She never took it off.

She got up and walked up and down the small living room. Something was wrong. Off. She felt it like a pressure at the base of her skull. She stopped at the French doors leading to their little concrete patio and looked out. The lights across the river were dim and insubstantial. She turned and stood in front of the fireplace. The antique mirror that hung over the white-painted mantel was clear at the moment, reflecting Bree herself, and behind her, Antonia.

That wasn't always the case. Nobody in the family seemed to know just how old the mirror was; Francesca seemed to think Franklin had found it at an auction somewhere. Just lately, Bree found that if she stared into the mottled depths, she could see the shadowy outline of a pale-faced, dark-haired woman looking back at her. Leah. It had to be Leah. The slender, waif-like creature who had married Franklin when he was fifty-five and she no more than the age Bree was now.

"I said, hey!" Antonia tossed a cushion at her. "You okay? You planning on sitting down and staying awhile? You haven't even taken your coat off."

"I'm fine. A little tired, that's all."

"Is your leg bothering you?"

Bree tossed her coat onto the couch and flexed her right leg absently. It was an unintended consequence of one of her most dismaying appeals cases. "Nope. It's fine."

"Are you upset by what Cissy said about you in the restaurant? Don't pay her any mind. All that stuff she said about you living like a nun? Well, you are, but so what? That's your choice, right? And she's like, thirty years older than we are, and she's got to be feeling that time is running out for her."

"At fifty-nine?" Bree said. "I don't think so."

"That generation gets all squirrelly about guys and hooking up, anyway," Antonia said. "So don't go all moody on me, okay? Time's not running out for either one of us. Honest to God, Bree, you're walking around with a cloud over your head and depressing the heck out of me. Cut it out."

Bree looked down at Sasha. He met the look with a sort of mournful reassurance and thumped his tail against the floor.

"Next time Hunter asks you out, you should go," Antonia said.

"Sam? What does Sam have to do with all this?"

"Just that he's a great guy, even if he is a cop, and you're over Payton the Rat totally, right? So maybe it's time to kick back a little. Give the work thing a rest."

"Give the work thing a rest, huh?" Bree said, suddenly fed up and in the mood for an argument. It helped to yell at somebody, and Antonia was handy. "And what the heck would *you* know about the work thing? You haven't worked a real job a day in your life."

Antonia shot off the couch, put her hands on her hips, and exploded. "Excuse me? This is me, ignoring the sarcasm and overlooking that totally unjustified slam because you've obviously lost whatever passes for your mind. You think stage managing isn't a real job? You think breaking my back six nights a week . . ."

"Between partying . . ."

"Making sure the lighting's on cue . . ."

"And sleeping with every good-looking bozo that calls himself an actor . . ."

"Not to mention the props!"

Sasha jumped to his feet with a bark. The phone rang. Bree picked up the receiver and yelled into it. "What?!"

"Bree?" Francesca's light, pretty voice came over the wire. "Bree, is that you?"

Bree sat down on the couch beside her sister. "Yes, Mamma, it's me."

"You two girls aren't fighting, are you?"

Bree glanced at Antonia. Her sister's face was flushed, and her eyes glittered. "Not really." Then, "How'd you guess?"

"You only get that tone in your voice when you're having a spat with your baby sister. And it's Monday night, so she's home." Then, anxiously, "Unless she's lost her job at the theater?"

"Nope, she's still employed. If you can call messing around in a theater employment."

"Bree, you are a total jerk!" Antonia yelled.

"Put me on speakerphone, honey."

Bree punched the button, and Francesca's voice flooded the small room. "The two of you cut it out right now, you hear?"

"This is *so* not my fault," Antonia said. "Bree started it, anyway."

"I don't want to hear about it. Not one word. What I do want to know is what in the Lord's name is going on with Cissy? She just called me, and she's all kinds of hysterical. What on earth did you say to her, Bree?"

"Nothing much. Not yet, anyway."

"Well, I wasn't going to come down until the day before the wedding, but I'm thinking I should come down tomorrow. Your father will head down on Friday, like we planned originally. "

"Yes!" Antonia said.

"Maybe we could talk Cissy into going up to Plessey, instead," Bree said. "Get her away from things for a while."

"Four days before the wedding?" Francesca's voice was mildly astonished. "I think not. But maybe I'll stay with Cissy, instead of y'all. She might feel easier talking about things without you two around."

"That'd be nice," Antonia said disingenuously. "The two of you can have a good heart-to-heart talk." The town house only had two bedrooms; as the youngest, she was relegated to the couch in the living room when her parents stayed over.

"Did you talk long?" Bree asked. "Did she tell you about the lawsuit?"

"She did. And I'm here to tell you girls she's not making a lick of sense. Not that she's made any sense since she met up with that man. It's getting worse the closer we get to the wedding."

"You've got to talk her out of marrying Prosper, Mamma," Antonia said.

"Your father and I have to be there for her, honey, which is something altogether different. We can express our doubts about the man if she asks us. Otherwise, we stay strictly out of it. You girls understand that; I know you do. Now. I'm driving down tomorrow, and I'm going straight to her place, so I won't see y'all until dinnertime. Why don't I meet you at that nice restaurant across from the town house? B. Mitchell's."

Antonia grinned at Bree. "Let's go for the crab cakes at Huey's instead, Mamma. You drive safe, now."

After further good-byes and assurances of love and affection, Francesca rang off.

Bree, who had settled into the corner of the couch, got up and shrugged on her coat.

"Where are you off to?" Antonia demanded. "I'm not mad at you anymore."

"I'm not mad at you, either. I'm just taking Sasha out for a walk."

"I already took him out for a walk when I got back from

the restaurant." She scratched Sasha under the chin. "Besides, that dog's so smart he can take himself for a walk."

"Well, I'm taking him out again."

"Fine."

"Fine. Antonia? Don't wait up."

Sasha at her side, Bree went out the front door and let it click shut behind her. She tested the latch: locked. She stood, looked around the concrete landing, and checked out the cobblestone street that ran past the building.

Sasha bumped his head against her hip. *Nothing there.*

"Something's wrong, though," she said. The night was chilly but mild for February. A fingernail moon rode a palmful of clouds. The daytime familiarity of the wrought iron fencing, the low walls of rough brick, and the hum of traffic on Bay was gone. She felt as if the air was pent up, waiting to explode. Some huge, anonymous pressure hemmed her in.

She hesitated. She could go to the Angelus Street office, and past the iron oak with its gaping grave. Or back to the Bay Street office and down to the basement to confront Beazley and Caldecott and tell them to leave her family alone.

And there was always Oglethorpe Square and the office of the Company's sixth member, Gabriel. She hadn't seen him for a month or more. Of all the Company, he was the one who stood between herself and physical attack from the Opposition.

But would Gabriel protect her family?

Just to her left, on Bay, a dark-blue sedan slowed down and stopped. A man got halfway out of the driver's side. Bree tensed. Sasha growled low in his throat. Then his tail began to wag.

"Is that you, Bree?"

"Hunter?"

He jogged easily up to her. Bree's sense of unease increased. She'd met Sam Hunter in the course of her first case for the Angelus Street office, when she'd been feeling her way, half convinced that she was in the grip of some persistent delusion. She'd had to solve a temporal murder before she could enter a plea for an overturn of her client's conviction, and Lieutenant Sam Hunter had been the Chatham County homicide detective assigned to the case. She'd liked him from the beginning; he was tall, broad shouldered, perhaps six or seven years older than she was, with an easy smile and a hard, keen intellect. She was halfway convinced it'd been more than liking when the car that came barreling down Bay Street a month ago had knocked her into the hospital.

He stopped and made a move to take her in his arms, then seemed to think the better of it. "You're looking kind of washed out, Bree. Everything okay?"

"Everything's fine."

He stooped to pat Sasha on the head. "I just called the house. Antonia said you'd gone out for a walk. I'm glad I caught you."

Bree didn't say anything. Her sense of unease was more urgent now. "What is it? What's wrong?"

Hunter's eyes were gray. They glinted silver in the light from the street lamps. "We've got a homicide. A dishwasher headed toward a late shift found a body in the parking lot next to your office building. I'd like you to come and identify it."

Six

Bree didn't ask which office building had a body behind it. No temporal ever found the way to the Angelus Street office. It had to be Bay Street.

"Who is it?"

"We're not sure who he is. We need you for an ID."

Bree hadn't realized her hands were clenched. He. Not Cissy, then. Not EB. And Antonia was safe inside the house, wasn't she? Sam had just spoken to her.

"He had his card in your pocket." He pulled out his cell phone and jabbed at the keypad with one finger. "It's a head shot. But it's not pretty. You ready?"

Bree nodded.

Beazley's contorted face flashed onto the screen. His yellowed teeth were drawn back in a snarl. Blood smeared the lower half of his face. She let out a long, puzzled sigh. "Yes, I know him."

"Well?" Hunter asked impatiently. "Who is it?"

"Beazley. I think his first name is Zebulon. I don't know him well, but, yes, that's him."

"Seems to be an attorney loosely attached to one of your cases. Can't raise either of his partners, and he doesn't seem to have any family to speak of. The most recent correspondence we found is with your office. He served a summons on one of your clients?"

"He's suing Aunt Cissy's fiancé, Prosper White."

"Can you come down to the morgue and make a formal identification?"

Bree looked up at the sky. The moon still swam among the clouds, slender and indifferent. The sense of something coming was almost a taste in the night air.

"I'll take you out for a glass of wine afterward." He shook his head, as if to get rid of something unpleasant. "You'll need it."

Bree's fingers curled into the thick fur at Sasha's neck. "Can I bring Sasha?"

He shrugged. "Sure. Why not. I'll take you down and bring you back."

"Okay, then." She followed him down to his car. He opened the passenger door for her and the back door for the dog.

The Chatham County Morgue—part of the City of Savannah's Department of Cemeteries—was located on Reynolds Street, a few minutes away. Bree checked the time as they pulled into the parking lot. Just going on nine, and the place looked deserted, except for a blue-and-white police cruiser parked at the entrance.

Bree hadn't had a lot of experience with morgues until she'd taken over the Angelus Street practice. She'd bet they smelled the same and looked the same countrywide, just like any other institution: hospitals, schools, and government offices. The floor was white ceramic tile. The walls were an institutional gray. Despite the pervasive reek of disinfectant, the place looked dingy and ill-kempt. She and Sasha followed Hunter down the narrow hallway to the viewing area—a small room with a thick Plexiglas window shielded by a drape.

Hunter's red-haired sergeant, Mellie McKenna, stood next to the window, her hands clasped behind her back. Her freckled face brightened as Hunter came down the hallway and then fell as she glimpsed Bree behind him. "Haven't turned up any next of kin, Lieutenant," she said. "Guy seems to have sprung out of nowhere. That home address on the driver's license? It's smack in the middle of St. Bonaventure Cemetery. Guy seems to have been a joker."

Without looking at Bree, McKenna let herself into the viewing room and pulled the drapes open. A body draped with a rubber sheet lay on a gurney directly in front of the window. A white-coated attendant stood behind it. McKenna punched at the intercom button on the wall, and her voice crackled into the hallway. "You ready?"

"She just needs to see the head, McKenna," Hunter said.

McKenna, seeming not to hear him, helped the attendant fold the sheet all the way back.

Despite herself, Bree gasped.

The body had been totally eviscerated. Some giant claw had ripped Beazley from throat to belly.

Seven

"Sure you're okay?" Hunter handed Bree a glass of Chardonnay and settled next to her on the couch. He'd driven her straight back to the town house after she'd signed an affidavit that the corpse in the morgue was known to her as Zebulon Beazley.

Antonia was out. Sasha was subdued. The town house still had the air of unreality that had driven her out into the street an hour before. She bent and ran her hand over the small Oriental rug beneath her feet. It had been her great grandmother's. She picked up the cloisonné vase that always sat on the coffee table. It was a relic from a relative who'd fought in the War Between the States. She'd been around these things all her life; and now? It was all in a kind of hyperfocus. She was intensely alert. The air hummed like wires in an electrical storm. "I'm fine," she said. "Just fine."

Hunter took his shoulder holster off, placed it on the coffee table, and put his arm around her. "Something's wrong. I wish you'd tell me about it. I know you're not upset about identifying the victim. You're getting to be an old hand at that. It's you in general. Ever since the accident. Physically, you recovered from that broken leg pretty damn quick. Mentally—I don't know. It feels like you're looking at things I can't see. Maybe you ought to give yourself time off."

Startled, Bree looked at him. He'd spoken lightly, but she could see the concern in his eyes. Slowly, she cupped his cheeks with both hands. Hunter wasn't a handsome man. His nose had been broken more than once. His features were blunt. He was thirty-five, but looked ten years older.

He cleared his throat. "I'm due some vacation time. I thought maybe the two of us could take off for a day or two. We could drive down to the Florida shore." He covered her hands with his own and drew them down to his chest.

The strangeness of the room ebbed, leaving her very aware of how close he was to her. How solid he was.

Hunter was always confident. That surety, that clear sense that he knew who he was and what he was meant to do, was one of the most attractive things about him. She felt it, clung to it, and the sense of utter dislocation that had plagued her from the moment she'd picked up the Cross at Chambers's store was replaced by a surge of affection for this man.

"Maybe you've had better offers? I hope not."

Bree smiled at that. Then she turned and kissed him. Really kissed him. It was warm and deep. She folded herself into his chest. His arms slid around her, a soft, steady insistence that made them feel like one person, not two.

She lay back, and he swung himself over her and looked down.

Hunter was real. The objects in the room became real again. Bree opened her eyes and looked over his shoulder, smiling, and her gaze fell on the mirror over the mantel.

It roiled with yellow smoke. She caught a tinge of sulfur. A smear of shadow appeared in the mirror's center. A horned figure, huge, dark, with its back to her. The figure turned slowly.

Sasha leaped to his feet, lips curled back over his teeth, snarling.

A thin stream of pustulant yellow oozed from the mirror and crawled across the floor. Bree's heart pounded. She pushed Hunter away. The thing in the mirror was huge against a vast plain licked with flame and dirty billows of smoke. Bree shouted, "Get back!"

Startled, Hunter leaped to his feet and whipped his hand to his chest, grabbing at the gun that wasn't there.

Sasha's growls ramped up to deep, ferocious barks. The mirror flared orange red, as if the horned figure had exploded into fire. A huge black hand tipped with talons passed over the surface.

The reflection that remained was of the room, the couch, and the back of Hunter's head.

"Sasha," Bree said. Her voice was hoarse. "It's okay." She sat up and put her hands to her hair. Her braids were loose, and she tucked them in. "Sorry. He's . . . not used to male visitors."

"I guess I should be glad of that." Hunter looked at the dog, perplexity fighting with annoyance. "You know me, Sasha. It's okay, buddy. Settle down."

Sasha trotted over to her and leaned his chest against her hip.

Not safe.

Bree stroked his head and looked up at Hunter. "I'm sorry."

"No problem." He extended his hand to the dog. Sasha acknowledged it, tail wagging. "It's a good dog's job, to look out for you. A little discrimination might be in order, though, Sash."

"No, I mean I'm sorry that . . ." Bree trailed off. Then she looked at her watch. "It's getting late, Hunter. And it's been a long day. Maybe you'd better go."

"I see."

"Hunter, I . . ."

"No. No. You look like you could use some sleep. And some food, maybe, too?"

"Sure." She blinked. "I guess I missed dinner. As a matter of fact, I brought some home with me from B. Mitchell's. There's a lot of it. Why don't we . . ." She saw the confusion in his eyes and her heart clenched. "Look. Let's grab the wine and sit down in the kitchen and eat. And maybe I can explain. About me. About the two of us. It's not that I'm not attracted to you, Hunter. I am." She smiled at him. "I guess you could tell."

He smiled back. "I thought I could, anyhow."

She bit her lip, thinking hard and fast. She couldn't give him the real reason. If she convinced him of the reality of Angelus Street, he'd be in danger. That one kiss and the appearance of the infernal figure in the mirror told her that. If she told him and he didn't believe her, she'd lose him. He wasn't the kind of man who wanted a crazy woman for a lover.

But Leah convinced Franklin.

Didn't she?

She could try the it's-too-soon-after-my-last-relationship

line, but Hunter would see that for the lie it was. She settled for a half-truth: "Antonia's due back any minute. I'd really like better privacy when we . . . I mean if we . . ." Then, hastily, "Let's have something to eat. It'll settle the wine."

The kitchen was at the other end of the hall to the front door. It was small, but Francesca had updated it with a blue-tiled center island and a fresh coat of cream-colored paint on the old pine cabinets. A small gateleg table sat by the window that overlooked the concrete courtyard. Bree settled Hunter at the table and turned the burner on. "It's fish tacos," she said. "That okay with you? If I take them apart and reheat them, they shouldn't be too squashy."

"Very domestic."

Bree made a face.

Hunter stretched his long legs out on the tiled floor, cradling his glass of wine. "Is that it? Are you afraid of losing your independence?"

"I think it is," Bree tried to look thoughtful. "Yes." Antonia was fond of afternoon talk shows, and she repeated something she'd overheard. "Of being swallowed up by a man. Of losing myself."

Hunter choked on his wine, set the glass on the table, and said, "Bullshit."

"Hey," Bree said indignantly. "That's a perfectly acceptable fear for women."

"For some, maybe." He leaned forward, his elbows on his knees, and stared up at her. "I can't think of a woman surer of herself, more independent than you. It's one of the things I love about you."

The word hung in the air. Bree made another face. "If I had a tennis racket, I could whack that word back at you."

"Now you've lost me."

"'Love,'" Bree said briefly. "*That* word. But you've got

that same kind of surety. It's why I . . . I'm so fond of you, Hunter."

"You ducked the word again. Pretty good volley." His gaze held hers for a long moment. She turned away, breaking the look, hoping that he read in her face what she felt in her heart: *Don't push it. Not yet. Soon.*

She separated the black beans from the rice and turned the fish in the skillet, and said, too casually, "Any leads on what happened to Beazley?"

He took a breath, as if to protest the obvious change in subject, then smiled easily. "Way too early yet. I haven't come across the firm before. Have you met him on a case? Somehow he didn't look the type to attend the monthly Georgia State Bar Association meetings."

Bree concentrated on the fish. "I was about to sit down with him over this suit he's bringing against Prosper White. Or was bringing. Maybe his partner will take over. I hope not. I hope the case died with Beazley." *If he is dead. Or maybe he was already dead. But if he was already dead, how could he run a temporal practice?*

Hunter pulled his notebook from his shirt pocket. "The other partner? Would that be Caldecott or Barlow? Bree? Are you with me, here?"

"Sorry. I forgot about Barlow. I haven't met him. Caldecott, yes. Not any more prepossessing than the deceased, I'm afraid to say." She thought a minute while she slid the tacos onto plates. "Now I remember. They represented the company that insured the car that broke my leg. They offered a settlement."

"So that's where you ran into him before." He seemed relieved. "Any merit to the current case?"

Bree shook her head. "I don't know." The summons was on file at the courthouse, so she wouldn't break client confidentiality if she told him about it. "I'll save you a trip to the records department and tell you. Then see what you think." She summarized the cause of action and then wound up, "I went to see Chambers, with Beazley's permission. The case feels like a grudge match, to tell you the truth. Prosper White seems to have made his reputation on exposing the Cross of Justinian as a fraud. Chambers claims the artifact he turned over to White was authentic. He says he got a fake one back." She put the plates on the table and sat down across from him. "I don't trust either one of them, but if push came to shove, I'd take Chambers's word over White's."

"Are we talking about a lot of money here?"

"Cissy says an original cross would be worth upwards of half a million and that Chambers is as mad about that as he is about losing his position at the university. She thinks it might be worth more to a collector, and I guess there's a fair number of those around. I'll get that verified, if I can. As for the 1952 cover of *Photoplay*, who knows? I doubt it's worth much all by itself, but according to White, it's an integral part of the collection and that adds to its value. I'll have to find an independent expert to verify that, too."

"You have your doubts about White?"

"I have my doubts about both of them. Chambers called my aunt and offered to settle for fifty thousand. If she wants to do that, I'll try and negotiate it down. Royal says it's always better to keep out of court if you can. He's right." She put her fork down. "How this could be connected to Beazley's murder beats me, though."

"Why should it be?"

She hesitated. *Because of the Cross and the new client I want to ignore. Because something forced Stubblefield to turn the case over to the Opposition. Because I've never felt this sense of estrangement from the mortal world before.* "Maybe it isn't. Maybe I'm just nervy on Cissy's behalf. The body was . . ." Bree searched for the right word. "Savaged."

"That it was."

"Have you ever seen anything like that before?"

"Nope."

"Any guesses?"

He raised his eyebrows. "Bear attack?"

"In Savannah. Right."

"Big cat of some kind? Panther?"

"There haven't been panthers in Georgia in a hundred years, Hunter."

He shrugged. He was making rapid work of the food. She poked restlessly at her own plate.

Hunter grinned at her. "So you won't buy a panther attack? Painter—isn't that what they call them here in Savannah?"

"In the Low Country, yes."

"If it wasn't a panther, I haven't a clue. Won't until the autopsy report's in, and . . ."

"The forensics are back," she finished for him. "Could you keep me in the loop?"

"You know I can't keep you in the loop. Are you going to finish that?"

She pushed the remains of the food around her plate and shook her head.

He took both plates to the sink, rinsed them off, and put them in the dishwasher, then put the sauté pan in the sink to soak.

Bree was used to stonewalling, not only from Hunter and the police, but the rest of the law-enforcement establishment in Savannah. Beaufort & Company itself was constrained by a set of celestial barriers that Bree had to figure out early on in her cases; her angels could only collect information available to the public, and their activities were limited to appeals work for the dead. "This isn't even my case," she said aloud.

"Exactly. And even if it were, you know better than to put your oar in." Hunter tossed the dishtowel onto the counter and crossed the floor. He was so close, she could feel the heat from his body. "I'd better be going."

It was a question. She hesitated. Sasha walked into the kitchen and sat at her feet, his body warm against her ankles, his head on her knee.

It's time.

She reached up and slid her arms around Hunter's waist. "You won't stay away too long?"

"Your call, Bree."

"Saturday, then."

"Saturday? Dinner at my place?"

"Dinner at Forsythe Park," she corrected him. "Aunt Cissy's wedding reception."

"Um." He made a face. "I might be on call that day."

She tilted her head back, smiling. "What is it about men and weddings?"

"Depends on who's getting married, doesn't it?" His kiss shook her deeply. She drew back. In silence, Hunter cupped her face with his hands and held her for a moment. He turned, and she followed him across the kitchen. He let himself out the back door.

She kept watch until his car disappeared into the distance.

The dog pressed his head against her side, and she heard the message again.

It's time.

Bree put her palm against her cheek, as if to keep the feel of Hunter's skin against her own. Sasha whined low in his chest. She drew a deep, sad breath. "Okay," she said. "Okay. It's time."

Eight

She unlocked the top bureau drawer and pulled it open carefully. The cheap little pine box sat on top of a pile of silk T-shirts. She picked it up. She didn't want to open it up in the living room because of the horned thing.

If she didn't open it up in the living room, it'd be a retreat.

Sasha at her heels, the box in hand, she sat on the couch and stared up at the mirror. It reflected nothing—not the couch or the living-room wall or the brass lamps on the end tables.

"I suppose Beazley's murder changes things."

Sasha thumped his tail, gently.

"It's connected, somehow, all of it. Beazley's murder, Prosper's case. And if I don't take on this client—I can't risk the family, can I?" She bit her lip. "I can negotiate a settlement with Chambers if I have to end up paying the poor guy myself. And with him out of the picture—there's no connection—none at all." She looked at the box that held the Cross. "Unless I take on this poor guy as a client. Which will keep up the connection, Sasha. Damn. Damn it all."

She bent her head over the box, snapped the lid open, and picked up the Cross. It was warm—hot—in her hand. A wisp of dark smoke rose into the air and dissipated.

"Miss Winston-Beaufort?"

Startled, she looked up. There was someone in the mirror. A young guy—perhaps Antonia's age—with long, fair hair curled over his ears. And sideburns?

His face filled the frame. She glimpsed moving water behind him. An ocean perhaps, or a fast-moving river.

"I'm Schofield Martin. I got your name from one of the souls here in the seventh circle. I was wondering if you could look into my case. I'd like to file an appeal."

Bree looked at Sasha, pleased that for once her communication with her clients was unimpeded by the Opposition. Her petition to Goldstein must have been approved.

"It'll help if I have more information, Mr. Martin. Where are you now?"

He looked over his shoulder, at something she couldn't see. "The seventh circle."

"And your conviction is for what crime?"

"Violence against Art."

She'd have to look that one up in the *Corpus Juris Ultima*.

"But I didn't do it." He grinned cockily at her.

Bree didn't say what she was thinking: *That's what they all say.* "And your sentence?"

"Totally unfair. Totally unwarranted. I was the victim of a conspiracy. The system set me up." He bent his head, so that his face filled the frame. He looked terribly earnest. "I was framed."

"I meant the length of your sentence."

Hopelessness devastated his face. "Eternity."

"Yikes." Celestial justice could be harsh. "I'm sorry to hear that." She didn't say what she was thinking this time, either: *The legal system in the Celestial Sphere isn't corrupt.* Unfair decisions based on cases where evidence hadn't been entered in fact happened occasionally—primarily due to unresolved events in the temporal world. That was how she herself got reversals in judgments. But deliberate abuses of the celestial system? Never. This guy must be guilty of something. She looked at the Cross in her hand.

"And what's your connection with the Cross of Justinian?"

The landscape behind Schofield Martin began to shift and swell. His eyes widened and rolled up. His image wavered. He flung one hand up in wild appeal and shrieked. "They're coming!"

Instinctively, she stretched her own hand out in response. The familiar stutter of black-and-white light spread across the mirror, and Martin blinked in and out of view like a figure in a silent film. She heard his voice, faint and almost lost in the swelling roar of sound. "Dig . . . Help me . . . Murder."

Martin plunged from view. The mirror went dark.

Bree tossed the pine box onto the coffee table and said, "Great."

Sasha nosed the box open. The Cross gleamed a little in the light from the reading lamp.

"I did pro bono work for Daddy's firm the first year I was out of school, Sasha. I've been conned more than a few times. Guys like that make a career of trying to game the system."

Sasha put his head on her knee and sighed.

"I know you think I should take this case." She stroked the dog's ears. "This is trouble. The phony Cross is mixed up with Chambers, who's mixed up with White, who's mixed up with Beazley, which is bad for Cissy." She resisted the impulse to fling the pine box across the room. "I don't like it. I don't like it at all."

She went to bed, and lay, sleepless, for a long time. When she did fall asleep, she dreamed of drowning souls, of being locked in a grave far beneath the earth, of suffocation. She woke to a grim and dreary dawn, which darkened her mood even further.

She'd made her decision, and her Company was just going to have to lump it.

Nine

Bree called a midmorning meeting at the Angelus office to begin the research on Schofield Martin's case. Ron had greeted her with fresh coffee and beignets; Lavinia with bunches of fragrant herbs. She had decided not to mention the visitation by the horned figure the night before. She didn't want any of the Company to have a reason to change her decision.

"Lavender's a cheery smell," Lavinia said comfortably. Her landlady wore her usual shabby wool cardigan and a print challis skirt that drooped around her ankles. Her mahogany face was surrounded by an aureole of wispy white hair. Bree had always placed Lavinia's temporal age in the mideighties, but with angels, you never knew.

She'd placed bunches of the dried herbs around the conference room table, and the crisp scent lifted Bree's heart.

Lavinia fanned a few sprigs out in a Mason jar and smiled at Bree. "You don't much like this new case, child?"

"I don't know enough about it, yet. Just the client's name. Although I've run across his type before." Bree didn't give in to the temptation to say what type; it wouldn't have been professional. Since what she was about to do wasn't professional, either, she figured she'd better occupy the high ground as long as she could. "I can't let this case involve Cissy. That's the main thing. I asked EB to set up a meeting with White at the Frazier Museum today. It's at eleven. If I can get Chambers off White's back, Cissy won't have any connection with it." She picked up a sheaf of lavender and brushed it across her lips, enjoying the scent. "You might as well know right away. If Chambers won't settle, which means Cissy's still exposed to Caldecott, we're going to turn down Martin's case."

Lavinia pulled her woolly sweater a little closer around her thin frame.

"I can't be the only celestial advocate out there," Bree said, as if Lavinia had raised an objection. "Schofield Martin has to find somebody else. I'm worn out. I need a break. Just a short one. I'm going to take some time off. I'm going away for the weekend."

Lavinia pursed her lips. She didn't actually say the words "whiner, whiner, whiner," and maybe she didn't even think them, but Bree felt guilty anyway. "Which weekend would that be, child? Your aunt's wedding is comin' along in a few days."

"The next available weekend. Guess what?"

"What, child?"

Bree dropped her voice to a delighted whisper. "I'm not going alone."

"Mercy," Lavinia said without surprise.

"I woke up as cross as two cats and went for a run along the river. The farther I ran, the worse this case looked. I refuse to get swamped by this job, Lavinia. I absolutely refuse. There's no reason why I can't turn this over to somebody else, is there? I'll prepare a summary for the next advocate. Then I'll take it to Goldstein and ask for a referral. The temporal system has a process for case referral. The celestial system must, too. Doesn't it?"

"What is time to the souls in the Sphere?" Lavinia asked rhetorically. She answered herself: "It don't exist, that's what. So I suppose Mr. Martin can wait for the next advocate to come along."

"Exactly," Bree said, although, since she was still confused about the metaphysics of the Spheres, she felt her confidence might be misplaced. "So I called Lieutenant Hunter and told him about my availability. For a weekend."

Lavinia's eyes were calm, deep, and expressionless. "That was a happy man you called, I think."

Bree blushed. Hunter had been very happy.

"You tole the others yet?"

"I will now."

Petru stumped into the conference room, a messy manila folder in one hand. Ron followed him, his iPad tucked under one arm.

"So," Bree said, as they settled themselves around the table. "What have we got?"

"I was not able to find a great deal of information about the artifact itself, as yet," Petru said ponderously. "But there is an account of an archeological dig thirty years ago near Constantinople."

"Istanbul," Ron said a little crossly. "It hasn't been Constantinople for years."

"Thirty years ago?" Bree said. "Hm. That's what Chambers must have meant when he said 'again.' He found the Cross once, and then lost it?"

"It appears so." Petru turned over the pages of the file one at a time and pulled a single sheet out. "Here is a newspaper story. It is primarily an account of Mr. Martin's death."

The story carried a photograph of a trawler. The name *Indies Queen* was just barely visible on the prow. A bright-white arrow was superimposed near the afterdeck.

GRADUATE STUDENT DROWNS ON DIG
Professors Claim Valuable Artifact Lost

A dig for Roman antiquities ended in tragedy yesterday when a young graduate student fell to his death from the Indonesian trawler Indies Queen. *Schofield Martin, a PhD candidate from the University of Georgia in the United States, apparently drowned while conducting routine duties. Archeologists Allard and Jillian Chambers, joint directors of the project, told authorities that Martin was in the midst of transferring a valuable Roman cross to the hold of the ship when he apparently slipped on deck and fell overboard. (See arrow for death site.) Rescue efforts were mounted immediately, but neither body nor artifact has as yet been recovered.*

"Not much to go on there," Ron observed. "Anything else?"

"An interview with Chambers in his local paper, upon his return to the United States immediately after the event. He vows to dedicate his career to the recovery of the artifact and the body of our unfortunate client." Petru placed a second piece of paper on the conference table. It was a photo of a younger, somewhat haggard Chambers. A thin, fierce-eyed woman stood next to him. The article was a few short paragraphs iterating Chambers's commitment to recovering the Cross. The photo caption read, *Professor Allard Chambers and wife Jillian.* Bree wondered at that. Jillian was a professor, too, wasn't she?

Petru smoothed his rough black beard with one hand. "There are few mentions of the professor's search for the artifact throughout the years. I did not bother to print them out as they provided little of substance to the case at hand—other than proving that the search continued. There were no results until eight months ago, when Chambers e-mailed his university that he had successfully recovered the Cross. But not, alas, the bones of our client. It may be worthwhile to note that the university had just notified those on the dig that the funding for these trips was to be cut."

"Oh, dear," Ron said.

"Yes. The professor had quite a motive for fraudulent representation."

"If he was the one who made the fake cross," Bree said. "White has a lot of contacts in the art world. He's more likely to have commissioned a fake, don't you think?"

Petru pursed his lips. "From my own time in Istanbul, I can tell you that there are many, many opportunities to have elegant copies made by those more interested in preserving historical continuity and the past than in the strictness of an actual artifact."

"It'd be easy to find someone to make a good copy?" Ron said. "If that's what you mean, why don't you just say so? Honestly, Petru. You'd think we bill by the word here."

Petru ignored him. "I then retrieved increasingly acrimonious communications between Chambers, Prosper White, and eventually, the university authorities who stripped the man of his position, denied him his pension, and cast him adrift to run the antiques store, Reclaimables. The correspondence is noteworthy for the passion with which Mrs. Jillian Chambers attacks all concerned." Petru closed the manila folder and tapped it. "No mention of the lad Schofield Martin at all."

"Did he have brothers and sisters?" Lavinia asked softly. "A mamma and daddy to mourn him?" She shivered a little, although it wasn't cold. Bree was concerned to see that she was looking faded. The soft gold light she carried with her was dimmer than it had been.

"I have not come across such as yet, Lavinia. The lad appears to have had a brother. He was a scholarship student. That I did ascertain."

"What about a report from the Turkish police?" Bree asked.

"That is here." Petru flipped to the back of the file and retrieved a yellowed parchment-like document. "It is in Turkish, of course. It is fortunate that I read Turkish. I made a translation for you, Bree. It is attached. I can sum it up, if I may. No witnesses. No foul play. No body. No clues. Disposition of case: accidental death."

"He's claiming he was murdered?" Ron said.

"Chambers told me that a good man died in pursuit of the Cross," Bree said. "If he was referring to Schofield Martin, he was wrong about the good part."

Ron raised his eyebrows. "You have taken against this client, haven't you? We don't know why he was condemned to the seventh circle, do we? For Violence against Art he said? An odd sort of felony, seems to me."

"Not to Signor Dante Alighieri, who catalogued many of the crimes that we appeal," Petru said. "I have researched Dante, also. The felonies range in degree from first to third: to wit, desecration of a work of art and artist; perversion of a work of art and artist; defacement of a work of art and artist; mutilation of—"

"Enough." Bree tapped the newspaper articles into a neat pile. "I'll take a look at the disposition of Martin's original case when I go and see Goldstein this afternoon. But it doesn't really matter at this point. We're turning him down."

Nobody moved, expect Lavinia. She crushed a bud of lavender between her thumb and forefinger. The sharp, welcome scent heartened Bree, and she swept the table with a smile. "Petru, if you could prepare a short summary of what we know to date, attach the exhibits, and draft a referral letter, I'd appreciate it."

"A referral to whom?"

"There must be somebody else. I was hoping that you guys might help with that. You were acquainted with my father and mother. They couldn't possibly have taken on all the clients who approached them for an appeal."

Nobody said anything. Bree raised her voice, hoping she didn't sound as defensive as she felt. "Well, did they?"

"Leah didn't take on any work when she was pregnant for you," Lavinia said. "That I do recall."

"There," Bree said, with relief. "So there must be a process for referral."

"Leah wouldn't have been offered any cases while she was pregnant," Ron said. "As for a process for referrals, there isn't anyone else. There's only one advocate at a time. We can't just walk away from this one, Bree. What about Beazley's murder?"

"What about Beazley?" Bree said sharply. "Beazley's murder isn't our concern, except as it affects Cissy. And if I can get Chambers to drop this case against White, Beazley's surviving partners aren't going get anywhere near my family again. We're not going down that road. Not this time. We're turning Schofield Martin's case over to somebody else, and that's that."

There was a short pause, heavy with silence.

Ron reached over and patted her hand. "There are many strands of time, and manifold realities. Mr. Martin can afford to wait, I suppose. "

"As for Mr. Martin?" Petru said heavily. "You have told him you are declining?" His eyes were black, and sharp with intelligence.

"Not yet, no. I thought about it overnight. I'll try and raise him again." She pulled the pine box out of her tote, where she had placed it before coming into the office. "I could try right now."

"Your reasons?" Petru said.

"Conflict of interest," Bree said promptly. "My temporal family is involved with this case." She didn't add her most compelling reason; once she'd made the decision to refuse Schofield Martin's case, the sense of unease, of being somewhere else, some*one* else, had gone away.

"Any conflict is peripheral, at best," Ron muttered. "Besides, your aunt Cissy was chairwoman of the Savannah Garden Club thirty years ago and nowhere near Constantinople."

Bree didn't ask Ron why he could place Aunt Cissy's whereabouts thirty years before; he was an angel, and that was that. "So if there are no objections . . ."

"It isn't *our* objections you have to worry about." Ron stuck his spoon in his coffee and stirred it one way, then another, with an annoying clatter.

"I'm sure I can make Goldstein understand."

"Goldstein's in charge of records. Goldstein's got noth-

ing to do with it. Think logically about this, Bree. The
CBA's the entity you have to be concerned with here."

"The CBA?" Bree pressed the palms of her hands
against her forehead. "Wait. Let me guess. The Celestial
Bar . . ."

"Association," Ron finished for her. "Yes. Maybe even
the ethics committee."

"*Not* good," Petru rumbled. "We should perhaps discuss
this further before you call Martin up and throw him to the
mercies of the enemy."

Bree flipped open her cell phone and looked at the time.
"Can't at the moment. I'm meeting Cissy and White at the
Frazier to discuss negotiating a settlement." She smiled at
them, feeling suddenly as light as air. "I'll be back around
two. If you have those documents ready, Petru, we can all
go over to the seventh floor and get this particular case in
happier hands than mine." She dropped a kiss on Petru's
head. "Don't worry. It's going to be fine."

The weather outside was buoyant. The sunshine was like
clean glass. The air was as crisp as lavender. Bree had
parked her little Fiat just outside the wrought iron fence
surrounding the Angelus office. She dug into her tote for
her keys as she let herself out of the gate and thought she
might take time to stop at Huey's for lunch after she'd
talked with Cissy. She was ravenous.

"Ms. Winston-Beaufort?"

Bree jerked upright. Caldecott stood in front of her car,
barring the way.

He looked awful. Although, to be fair, up close Caldecott always looked awful. From a distance, he looked like
an accountant, with a neat, compact figure flattered by his

inevitable pin-striped suit. It wasn't until you were face-to-face with him that he became unsettling. His eyes were yellow. The pupils were vertical, like a goat's. His skin was pale, paler than usual, and his fingernails had been bitten down to the quick. A spot of blood was smeared across one knuckle.

Bree wasn't sure how to address his partner's death. Nobody with any sense would be sorry that Beazley was dead. But the manner of his death had been horrible, and she had to address that.

"I was sorry to see that Beazley passed on in such a way, Caldecott."

He shivered, like a snake exposed to a chilly wind. "Yes. It was . . . unexpected."

"Are there any leads?"

"Leads?" Caldecott pulled his lips back in a rictus-like smile. His teeth were gray and pointed.

"The police have it listed as a homicide. Surely they must have interviewed you by now."

He shivered again, in that peculiar way, and ignored her question. "Zebulon's sense of humor was bound to get him in trouble one of these days."

"His sense of humor?" She waited, and when Caldecott didn't answer that, either, she stepped around him and unlocked the Fiat's door. "Yes, well. If you'll excuse me, I'm off to meet my client in the matter of Chambers versus White. You'll be available later in the day if my client is open to discussion?"

"My client would much prefer that his case be heard in open court. His desire for vindication is strong."

"Then he shouldn't have called Ms. Carmichael and offered to settle out of court." Caldecott's eyes flared. "He didn't tell you?" Bree's conscience stirred. Beazley and

Caldecott must have been friends. Of a sort. If nothing else, the death would affect the law firm's day-to-day operations. "I imagine you'll be pretty well occupied with, umm, arrangements in the next few days. A later time to discuss Mr. White, perhaps?"

"We're available at any time to carry on our client's business. I just wanted to alert you—Mr. Barlow will be taking over the professor's case. And there is one other—small—matter." His eyes darted to Bree's tote. "I'm afraid Professor Chambers was somewhat precipitate in turning over the artifact to you."

"The Cross of Justinian? It's a fake."

"Just that. And of no value to you. If you would return it, please."

Bree tightened her grip on the tote. Out of the corner of her eye, she saw a flash of silver-white. Gabriel? She hadn't seen Gabriel for a month or more. Caldecott, too, must have felt his presence. He winced, and stepped away from the car.

"I don't see what the artifact has to do with the matter at hand," she said pleasantly. "But I'll speak to Professor Chambers about returning the Cross to him."

"You'd do better," Caldecott hissed, "to return it directly to me."

The silver-white light flared, making the sunshine small. Caldecott held his hand against his eyes and tittered uneasily. "Of course, if you require the professor's permission, we'd be delighted to proffer a letter . . . We'll stay in touch, shall we . . . Until later, Ms. Winston-Beaufort . . . Good-bye . . ."

He faded away, leaving nothing but a faint smell of sulfur in the air.

Bree waited a long moment, hoping to see Gabriel.

A breeze rattled the dry branches of the iron oak over the Pendergast grave. The bright blue of the sky dimmed with gray. But Gabriel's light had faded, and the angel himself didn't appear.

Disappointed, Bree waited until her heartbeat returned to normal and then checked her cell phone: nearly eleven o'clock. She was going to be late.

She drove the few miles to the Frazier Museum. The day darkened with clouds from the west. She turned over the best way to approach a settlement with White and firmly refused to think about Caldecott and, worse, his dead partner's ravaged body.

The Frazier Museum was located on the west side of St. Bonaventure Cemetery. It had been created out of a French Provincial mansion abandoned to taxes. A large circular drive led up to the building itself; the drive led to a parking lot in the back. Bree left the Fiat next to Cissy's Audi and walked around to the front door.

The three-story building was an elegant rectangle built of gray stone. The center of the roof was composed of a series of skylights bound in bronze and surrounded by green tile. Bree liked the symmetry of the facade. Each story had six large paned windows, three on each side of the center. The frames were picked out in white. The azaleas on each side of the front portico were trimmed to knee height. The double-wide front door was made of mahogany, waxed to a high gloss.

Bree walked in and found Cissy in the black-and-white tiled foyer, bundled against the chilly morning in a soft mink coat.

Her aunt looked tired. She broke into speech as soon as she caught sight of Bree.

"I don't know what happened. It was such a gorgeous

morning, and now look at it—and Prosper's got his press conference scheduled in less than an hour. They're even talking snow. And it's cold." She lifted her chin defiantly. "So I got out my fur. I'd be glad if you didn't mention it to Antonia. You know how she tried to get me to join PETA, which I totally agree with except for mink. You ever run into a mink, Bree? A nastier creature doesn't live on God's earth." She snuggled her chin into the collar, and then peeked up at Bree. "You aren't mad at me, are you?"

"Of course not." Bree kissed her on the cheek. "How are you, Aunt Cissy?"

"All right, I guess. Didn't sleep too well. Your mamma's coming down to stay with me. She tell you that?"

"She did."

"Ought to come in sometime this afternoon. It's a long drive from Plessey. Said she wanted to give me a hand with the wedding arrangements."

"She's good at that sort of thing."

"Well, she is," Cissy said, as if Bree had posed an argument. "I told Prosper that. He thinks she's coming here to rag on him, but that isn't like Francesca at all."

"Is Mr. White . . . Prosper . . . here right now? Does he know that I'm here to discuss the best way to dispose of the lawsuit?"

"He's very busy," Cissy said evasively. "The TV people are coming to interview him about the decline of print media and the importance of preserving our print heritage for posterity. We're thinkin' maybe the History channel will pick it up. And Alicia's arranged for some investors to come in and make a bid on the *Americana* exhibit this morning. We're hoping to make that announcement to the TV people, too." Cissy gnawed at her lip. "Except that this business with that awful man Chambers might ruin everything. We stand to lose a ton of money if White isn't paid off. Except I'm not supposed to mention that, am I." She shook herself, like a little cat. "Anyway. Have you seen the exhibit yet, Bree? I surely wish you could have made it to the grand opening. It's wonderful, just wonderful. Here." She put her hand on Bree's back and propelled her through the foyer and onto the main floor. She waved at the girl behind the ticket kiosk, who'd half risen at their approach. "Drop your tote bag off, there. They don't allow bags in the museum. Then you come and look."

Bree got a ticket for her bag and followed Cissy onto the main floor.

Although the mansion dated from the early nineteenth century, the museum itself had been created a hundred years later. The entire interior had been gutted and rebuilt. The ceiling soared up all three stories. The skylights allowed natural light in every corner of the building. The center atrium was tiled in black-and-white marble. Stairs on either end of the room led to the second and third mezzanines. Mahogany railings were built into the open sides overlooking the atrium. The south side of the ground floor was given over to the *Magazine Americana* exhibit. At eleven o'clock on a Tuesday, a surprising number of people were there, most of them clustered in front of the glass-fronted display cases that held the magazine covers. A single security guard in the ubiquitous khaki stood chatting with the girl behind the ticket kiosk.

Cissy drew Bree partway across the floor, stopped cold, and muttered, "What's *she* doing here? She's supposed to be at the airport, picking up the buyers." With a determined set of her chin, she started forward again.

Bree didn't have to ask who "she" was. Prosper White was huddled in intense conversation with a striking girl.

She was tall and slender. Her dark hair was drawn back in a tight bun. She was dressed in a black pencil skirt, with a tight-fitting scoop-necked T-shirt. Elaborate gold earrings dangled from her ears. She had the sinewy elegance of a ballerina and a discontented lower lip.

"Prosper?" Cissy said as they approached—so timidly that Bree's heart broke a little. "Here's Bree to talk to you about that awful man."

The ballerina clone stepped between White and Bree's aunt. "You must be Mr. White's eleven o'clock appointment?" she said coolly to Bree. "If you'll just wait a moment, I'll escort you to Mr. White's office." She didn't address Cissy directly, but looked past her shoulder. "You'll probably want to go with Miss Winston-Beaufort, Mrs. Carmichael."

"It's *Ms*. Carmichael," Cissy said, with an air of having mentioned it before.

"Whatever. You wait there. Mr. White and I are finalizing the arrangements for the buyer's group."

"Aren't you supposed to be at the airport?" Cissy put one hand on the girl's shoulder, pushed her firmly aside, and nestled close to White. "I hope those poor people aren't standing around thinkin' they've been abandoned because Alicia forgot to pick them up."

"Of course I didn't abandon them." The girl's tone was sharp. She turned to Bree and said, "I'm Alicia Kennedy, Miss Winston-Beaufort." She extended her hand. Bree shook it briefly. "If you and your aunt would please follow me, I'll get you both settled in Mr. White's office."

"What about the buyers, Alicia?" Cissy demanded.

Alicia looked at Prosper and raised her eyebrows. White scowled. "The buyers have been taken care of, Cissy. We sent a stretch limo. I'd rather you not concern yourself. Sit in the office and wait for me." A chime came from the breast pocket of his suit coat, and he slapped at it irritably. "Damn cell phone hasn't shut up the whole morning. Go on, girls—shoo. I'll be there in a minute."

Alicia led the way to a door set behind the ticket kiosk, opened it, and stepped aside.

Prosper's office was simple, elegant, and hugely expensive. The window looked out over the circular drive. His large desk—of an exotic wood that Bree couldn't identify—was completely clear of anything but a landline and a dramatic marble sculpture of a lily. A stunning painting of two sisters—Bree thought it might be a Quilliam—hung on the east wall. The walls themselves were covered in gray damask. A round table, heavily carved with representations of the Chinese goddess Kwan Yin, sat in the northeast corner. A love seat in gray glove leather faced the desk. Cissy sat in it and patted the cushion beside her. Instead, Bree took one of the straight chairs at the Chinese table.

"Coffee?" Alicia said indifferently.

"Not for me, thank you."

Cissy shook her head.

Alicia's gaze slid over them both. "I'll get back to the floor, then. Mr. White may need me."

"I've a few questions before you go, Miss Kennedy. You've been named as codefendant in the suit brought by Allard and Jillian Chambers. Have you retained counsel?"

Alicia blinked. Her eyes were brown, rimmed with black liner. The lashes were heavy with mascara. "I thought you were taking care of things."

"I've agreed to represent your employer. Do you want me to represent you as well? I doubt that would be in your best interests."

She glanced at Cissy uneasily. "All I did was buy the copy of *Photoplay*. I didn't do anything wrong."

"Mr. Chambers feels otherwise. So may the courts."

"It's not my problem, is it?"

"It's very much your problem. I'm here to suggest that we attempt to negotiate a settlement with him. He's already made a demand. Fifty thousand dollars."

"So? Maybe you should pay him."

"How much can you contribute to the demand, Ms. Kennedy?"

"How much can . . . What?"

Cissy bit her lip and coughed.

"You're codefendant, Miss Kennedy. Equally liable for damages, under the law."

Alicia stepped back against the office door. "Me? You want me to give you money? You can't be serious! I . . ." She stumbled forward as the door flew violently open, and White stormed in.

His reflexes were good; Bree had to give him that. He steadied Alicia before she was halfway to the floor, and then shoved her onto the love seat beside Cissy. He glared at Bree. "That bastard's here! I just called the police. I want him out of my museum before he wrecks the press conference."

Cissy leaped up, more to avoid proximity to Alicia than anything else, Bree judged. "Who are you talking about, Prosper? Who's here?"

"Chambers—who do you think!" He went behind his desk and looked out the window. "Look at him. Damn it! He's called the media. Damn it!" He turned to face them, his face white with rage. "And Bullet Martin's just coming up the drive. Of all the frigging luck." His eyes narrowed and he pointed at Alicia. "You," he said spitefully. "This is all your fault."

Alicia burst into tears. White slammed both fists onto the desktop, closed his eyes, and took a deep breath.

Bree got up and went to the window.

The circular driveway was alive with cars and people. Chambers was center stage, no doubt about that, mostly because of the sign he carried. It was so big Bree could read it from her vantage point twenty yards away.

PROSPER WHITE ART THIEF

A skinny, fiercely glowering woman at his side carried a smaller banner. That was harder to make out, but it seemed to read PROSPER PROSPERS WHILE INNOCENTS STARVE. Jillian Chambers? It must be. The two of them talked at a glamorous blonde in a bright red suit. She held a microphone and looked bored. A cameraman with a Steadicam stood a short distance from them. Behind him was the Channel 5 news van. Behind that was an old yellow school bus with the legend CITY OF LIGHT MINISTRY in black letters on the side.

It took Bree a minute to figure out where all the people had come from. She recognized the security guard—who had an unfortunate resemblance to a garden toad—and the ticket taker. There were a few museum patrons who'd been looking at the *Magazine Americana* exhibit. Twenty or so other people, perhaps more, milled in the driveway. Most were dressed in shabby jeans, worn hoodies, unlaced tennis shoes, and tattered jackets—the homeless who frequented the streets of Savannah. Those poor people must have come in on the City of Light's yellow bus. That, she recalled, was the charity shop next to Reclaimables. Chambers was certainly resourceful.

A handful of people were very expensively dressed. Bree noticed a stretch limo parked discreetly off to one side. Had they come from there?

"The buyers are the ones dressed to the nines," Cissy said from behind her shoulder. "That man in the cashmere coat? With the lizard-skin cowboy boots? Charles Martin."

"Martin," Bree said, without expression. "Oh yes?"

"Prosper calls him Bullet. He owns the Houston Oilers. You know, one of the basketball teams from Texas?"

"So what the hell do I do now?" White demanded.

Bree turned around. White leaned against the far wall, arms crossed, his shoulders hunched.

Bree wished she'd brought Sasha with her. Sasha would have seen what she was seeing now: *guilty guilty guilty*.

But guilty of what?

"Wait for the police," Cissy said promptly.

"I can't leave Bullet Martin out there with that . . . mob. The man's worth thirty million dollars."

"Then go get him," Bree said mildly.

He pointed at Bree. "You! You're my lawyer. You go out and get him. I'm not going to dignify that . . . that . . . dem-onstration with any kind of statement." He drew himself up. "Or my presence."

"For heaven's sake, Prosper," Cissy said tartly. "You can't hide out in here, and you can't hide behind my niece. Why, you outweigh her by sixty pounds, and for goodness' sake, you're a man." She held out one gloved hand. "Come on, darlin'. You've got a press conference to give, and you're going to give it. I'll go with you. We'll show that little rat what's what."

Bree bit her lip so hard she almost yelped. She wanted to laugh. She wanted to yell, "Yay, Aunt Cissy." She couldn't do either, so she said, "I'll go out with you. I'd advise against making any kind of statement about Chambers. Keep cool. Don't respond to any provocation. We'll get Mr. Martin and bring him in here and maybe the TV people, too. The demonstrators can't get into the museum without a ticket, so don't sell them any, okay? Alicia, maybe you can take care of closing the premises for lunch, or something."

A few of the demonstrators had started a chant: "Thief! Thief! Thief!" White made a noise between a growl and a sob.

"I'm staying with Prosper," Alicia said.

Bree shrugged. "Fine. Whatever. I'll head out first, and you follow, okay?"

The main floor, which had been alive with people, was silent now. Everyone had gone out onto the drive to listen to the noise. Bree crossed to the front entrance, very aware of the click of her heels on the marble floor, and the press of the three people behind her.

She pushed open the front doors. The toad-like security guard stepped out of the way. The four of them stepped out onto the front steps. There was a momentary pause, and then a woman shrieked, "Thief!" A tomato sailed through the air and landed on White's Italian shoe. Another tomato sailed past Bree's ear. Somebody else shouted, "Get him!" and the crowd surged toward them, led by the blonde anchor, her microphone held aloft in her hand. She didn't look bored any longer.

Somebody moved Bree politely out of the way. White was surrounded—by Chambers, teeth bared in an unfriendly grin, by Charles Martin in his cashmere coat, and by a dozen others. Cissy clutched his arm, her face pale but unafraid. Alicia cowered behind his back.

"Thief!" Chambers roared.

The crowd pushed and shoved. Bree stumbled and then regained her balance.

White, furious, shouted, "Don't talk to me! Don't touch me! This is out . . ." He gasped, a huge, astonished, outraged intake of air.

He fell, sagging against the press of people.

Then Cissy screamed.

Ten

"Knife wound, most likely," the EMT said. "You can see the entry wound here, just under the sternum. Guy fell right away you said?"

"That was my impression," Bree said. "I didn't actually see him fall. Just felt the effect of it. Like dominos, if you know what I mean."

"You were three or four people away from him?" Hunter said. "He fell against them; they fell against you."

"Right. Anyhow, there couldn't have been more than a few seconds between the gasp and the fall."

"Dropped like a stone. Knife went straight into the heart, probably." The EMT zipped the body bag closed, and Bree wondered if she'd seen the last of Prosper White. She hoped so. "But don't quote me on that. Ask the medical examiner when the autopsy's done. Okay if we take him away now, Lieutenant?"

Hunter nodded. The techs pushed the gurney down the

front steps of the museum with an almost unnoticeable clatter. They lifted it effortlessly into the waiting ambulance.

Yellow crime-scene tape blocked off the circular driveway at both ends. The crowd that gathered behind it was larger than the mob of demonstrators had been. The Channel 5 anchor had been joined by two other media vans. The police response had been rapid; the media response, too.

Prosper White had been dead for less than forty-five minutes.

"I'd better see how Cissy's doing," Bree said. "Will it be a long time before I can get her home?"

Hunter rubbed the back of his neck. "Everybody at the scene's got to be searched, even though we got the knife. There are twenty-two people in there."

"Seemed like more at the time."

"May have been. It'd be helpful if you could write down brief descriptions of the people surrounding the victim. My guess is more than a few in the crowd slipped away before we got here. The security cameras should help some. And Channel Five was there, although we'll have the usual hassle over getting access to their tapes. Anyhow— we'll be a couple of hours, maybe. She holding up okay?"

Bree shook her head. "I don't know." She smiled. "You should have seen her, Hunter. She's got a backbone, Cissy does. White was scared green at the thought of facing the crowd. She told him to man up, and out he came."

Hunter glanced at the ambulance bumping gently along the driveway. "Yes," he said dryly. "He did."

"For God's sake, Hunter. She didn't have any idea that this was going to happen!"

"White might have, though. See what you can find out, will you? Did Chambers threaten him directly? Did the two men have any kind of face-to-face altercation? If they did, when was it?"

"Bree Winston-Beaufort, police snitch." She put her hand on his and squeezed it, lightly. "I doubt she knows anything, but she'll know how important this is."

The atmosphere inside the Frazier had changed. There was a hushed expectancy about museums that always pleased Bree in the past. That sense of pleasure ahead was gone. Somebody had brought out a number of folding chairs.

The witnesses to Prosper White's murder sat in clusters. They were discouraged-looking people. There was almost no conversation, expect for the flat official tones of the uniformed men and women taking statements and searching through purses, tote bags, and backpacks.

Bree scanned the group. Allard and Jillian Chambers weren't there; they'd been taken down to police headquarters almost immediately. She didn't see the members of Charles Martin's group, either; perhaps they had been processed and let go first. It was mostly the poor homeless and a scattering of unlucky museum-goers.

A uniformed officer stood outside Prosper White's office door. He straightened up as she approached and touched the rim of his hat. He seemed very young to Bree, and blushed easily. "Ma'am."

"I'm Brianna Winston-Beaufort, Ms. Carmichael's attorney."

"I know. Lieutenant said you can go right in, ma'am."

Bree tapped at the door, heard a muted "Yes!" and prepared to enter. The officer touched her shoulder shyly.

"How's the dog doing, ma'am?"

"Dog?" Bree cocked her head. "Of course! It's Officer Banks. You helped me rescue Sasha from that trap all those months ago. He's doing fine, thank you."

"And at the drowning a couple of months ago, ma'am. I was there, too."

"Yes," Bree said.

"You seem to run into murder a lot, ma'am."

"Yes," Bree said. "I'm working on reducing that statistic."

Inside, she found Cissy slumped dejectedly on the gray couch. Alicia Kennedy sat at the Chinese table. Behind Prosper's desk was the man who'd been identified as Charles "Bullet" Martin. He'd tossed his cashmere coat onto the desktop and reclined in the desk chair, his booted feet up on the desktop. He was sleek, well fed, with a shock of iron-gray hair. He had the kind of male looks that made it hard to peg his age. He could have been anywhere between midforties and midsixties. Bree nodded to him and took a quick glance at Alicia. Her dark hair straggled around her face. Her eyes looked bruised. She'd been chewing at her lip. She sat as if she'd been shot.

Everybody had red splashed on their clothes. Blood smeared the lapels of Martin's expensive coat. A huge stain marked the center of Alicia's black T-shirt. Cissy's mink was spattered with dried splashes of red. Tomatoes? Blood? It was hard to tell.

"Bree." Cissy had a handkerchief in one hand. She wiped her eyes, blew her nose, and scooted over so that Bree could sit down beside her. "This is the most horrible thing that's ever happened to me. Poor Prosper."

Bree put her arm around her. "I'm sorry, Aunt Cissy."

"I called Francesca."

Bree nodded.

"She's on her way. Course she was on her way already, but for a different reason. She was comin' to help with my wedding. Now she's comin' to help with the funeral."

"He wouldn't have married you," Alicia said, suddenly.

"And if he had married you, it's just because you're stink-ing rich. You're old. Old and stupid!"

Cissy shrank into herself. Bree got to her feet and walked over to Alicia. She didn't say anything. But she called on the same anger that drove her when she was best at her job. The anger was a pure, focused weapon. She knew that her face was white and cold. That her eyes were narrow points of ice. That a terrifying stillness possessed her body. She had, as always, the sense that she was both Bree-as-weapon and Bree-as-observer, standing outside herself, looking on.

Alicia paled and dropped her eyes.

There was a tap at the door, and Officer Banks opened it. "Ms. Kennedy? The lieutenant would like to take your statement now."

Alicia got up and edged past Bree to the door. She stopped halfway, turned, and with a sudden, vicious move-ment of her head, spat on the floor.

"Nice girl," Charles Martin said after the door slammed shut behind her. He grinned sarcastically.

"She's upset." Cissy smoothed her handkerchief, folded it, and tucked it into the pocket of her coat. "She was in love with him, you know. Prosper was going to fire her as soon as the *Americana* exhibit moved on to MoMA. He didn't trust her. Not one bit. Said the best way to get rid of her would be to ship her off with the show to New York." She gave a shaky sigh. "Jealousy—that's all it is."

Martin swung his feet off the desk and sat up. "I don't believe we've formally met, young lady. Charles Martin. Call me Bullet."

"Brianna Winston-Beaufort."

"Your aunt here says you're the best damn lawyer in the state of Georgia."

Bree smiled. "She's biased, don't you think?"

"Maybe." Bullet narrowed his eyes. "Says you're quite a hand at catching murderers."

"I'm a lawyer, Mr. Martin. I specialize in tax law."

"Nonsense," Cissy said sturdily. "She's solved four murder cases right in a row, Bullet. Most of them made the national news, too."

"Got a handle on this one?" Martin asked.

"Nope. Something like this is best left to the police."

"Should be a piece of cake for an experienced investigator like yourself." Something unpleasant moved behind his eyes. "Had quite the talent for attracting enemies, did our Prosper White. You'd have yourself a fistful of suspects, you decide to look."

"Including you?"

"Bree!" Cissy said. "Bullet came here to make a bid on the *Americana* exhibit for his museum in Houston, Texas."

"That I did." Martin slapped the desk with his hand and got to his feet. "If you'll excuse me, ladies, I'm going to go on out and check on the progress of Savannah's finest. Then I think I might punch a call in to my own lawyers back in Houston. Just in case." He cocked his forefinger at Bree. "Wouldn't want you to mistake me for the murdering son of a gun who dispatched Prosper White, would we?" His hand on the office door, he sketched a bow to Cissy. "Ma'am."

"Mr. Martin?" Bree said. She'd paused at the name when Cissy had mentioned it; now she remembered why.

He paused and turned around.

"Did you—that is, do you have any relatives named Schofield?"

"Schofield? Yes, ma'am. I surely did. My younger brother. Died more than thirty years ago in a tragic accident. Tragic. Now how did you hear about Schofield?"

Bree didn't answer for a minute. "I ran across him in some research I was doing for the museum. He was an archeologist?"

"That's what they tell me. Be seeing you again, Miss Winston-Beaufort, Miss Carmichael. I hope so."

He shut the door softly behind him. It reopened almost immediately. Officer Banks had her tote in one hand and a Barney's shopping bag in the other. "Lieutenant says you can have these back now."

Cissy took the Barney's bag and crushed it between her hands with sudden vehemence. Then, with an apologetic glance at her niece, she smoothed the bag on her knees and drew out a filmy black nightgown. "This would look wonderful on you, Bree. I've half a mind to give it to you." Her eyes filled with tears, but she blinked them back. "I won't be needin' this now."

Bree didn't answer. She'd emptied her tote onto the desk. The pine box with the Cross of Justinian was gone.

"What's the matter, honey? You look so grim."

Bree put her things back into the tote, one by one: legal pad, iPad, a set of Italian pens, lip gloss, brush, Mille Fleur cologne. She patted her jacket pocket. Her cell phone was there. So was her credit card and sixty dollars in cash. "This is important, Aunt Cissy. Did you and Prosper spend a lot of time together?"

"Every waking minute."

"So you've been in his house? Where does he live, anyway?"

"Of course I've been in his house. I found him a lovely little town house just off Washington Square. It's that new development that fronts Forsythe Park. He wasn't all that fond of older architecture. He loved Euro-Tech and the moderns . . ."

Bree went to the couch, sat down, and took Cissy's hand. "You know about this artifact?"

"The one that man says he stole? The Cross?"

"Have you ever seen it?"

"I don't believe so, no. What does it look like?"

"It's small. About this big." Bree held her thumb and forefinger apart. "It looks like solid silver, but it's quite light. The inlay is semiprecious stones—lapis lazuli, jasper, and coral."

"Those aren't semiprecious stones, honey. Those are just nice stones. Topaz, aquamarine—those are semiprecious stones. Diamonds, rubies, and emerald are the only gems you can legitimately call precious."

If there was one thing Cissy knew a great deal about, it was gems and jewelry.

"It's very ornate. Think. Did you ever see him with such a thing?"

Cissy shook her head. She bit her thumb. "Are you going to find out who murdered my Prosper?"

"It's better left to the police."

"That nice man you should be going out with. Lieutenant Hunter? Is he in charge of the case?"

"He is. And he's an excellent investigator."

Cissy sighed. "Good. It was that man Chambers. I just know it. I can't stand the thought of him getting off scot-free."

There was a sharp rap on the office door, and Hunter himself came in. He was accompanied by Sergeant McKenna and two uniforms. He carried a clear plastic bag that contained a boning knife. The inside of the bag was smeared with blood. He didn't look at Bree.

"Mrs. Celia Smallwood? You're known as Celia Carmichael?"

"You know very well who I am, Sam Hunter."

"We'd like to ask you, ma'am, if you recognize this knife?" He held out the plastic bag.

Bree was so stunned, it took her longer than it should have to register what was happening.

Cissy craned her neck at the bag. "Is that it?" she whispered? "Is that the . . ." She turned so pale Bree was afraid she would faint.

"Just answer the question, ma'am."

Bree jumped to her feet and knocked Hunter's hand aside. "Don't you dare," she said. "Don't you *dare*." She was so angry her head was swimming.

"What?" Cissy said. "What?"

Hunter looked at her. His eyes were opaque. She couldn't read them. She couldn't read them at all. "The knife comes from a set in her kitchen."

"It does?" Cissy said doubtfully. "That's one of mine?"

"Don't say another word, Cissy!"

"It's got a walnut handle. That looks like the set . . ."

"Cissy, *shut up!*" She turned on Hunter, furious. "You can't do this . . ."

"Ms. Carmichael, you have the right to remain silent . . ."

"This is insane. For God's sake, Hunter. Of all the stupid damn clichés! Of course she didn't kill him. She's been set up. You know why she's been set up, don't you?"

"No. I don't know why she would have been set up. If you know, you need to tell me. Right now."

Because someone wants me on Schofield Martin's case. Because I can't do it, won't do it.

And now I have to do it.

She closed her eyes and clenched her fists so hard her fingernails drew blood from her palms. She couldn't, wouldn't lose her temper. Not now. Not here. What she needed was control. Ice in her mind. Ice in her heart.

She smiled at Hunter. He flinched as if she'd slapped him.

Cissy trembled with panic. "Bree? Bree, honey?"

Hunter's voice was cool. "If there's anything I should know, tell me."

"No. You go ahead." *Bastard.*

He flinched again, as if he'd heard her thoughts.

Bree watched as McKenna recited the rest of the Miranda rights. She watched, helpless, as her aunt was handcuffed and led out of the Frazier Museum and locked into a police cruiser.

The TV cameramen were on them like leeches.

And she was damned if she was going to take Schofield Martin's case without a fight.

Eleven

"White's dead. And Cissy's been arrested." Ron sighed. "You *have* had a morning, Bree."

"I called my father. Royal, I mean. And then I came here." Bree felt as if she were speaking from a long way off. As if she were underwater.

"Good move." Ron glanced at Petru and then Lavinia. He put an imaginary cup to his lips.

"Hot tea," Petru said. "Of course. She has had a shock. I will be happy to brew some."

"Some of my hot tea would be better," Lavinia said. "Yours is just that Lipton, Petru. Not what she needs right now." She got to her feet with a grunt. "I'll go upstairs and bring it on down. Just the thing to warm her up." She went softly out of the room.

"Royal Winston-Beaufort will have Aunt Celia out of the holding pen before the sun has set," Petru said. He reached across the conference table and patted her hand clumsily. "You could not have gone to a better source. And this will free you to concentrate on the client."

Bree wanted to scream at them: *Did the three of you find some way to get Cissy arrested? How dare you! How dare you!*

She met Ron's wise and understanding gaze. His eyes were the color of the Caribbean Sea. He smiled at her, and the rage, the spite, the fury that consumed her since poor Cissy had been dragged off by the police ebbed a little.

"Sorry," she muttered. She scrubbed at her face with both hands. "It's not right to involve my family, Ron. It's not fair."

"The Opposition doesn't recognize right or fair," Petru said heavily. "Perhaps if you had agreed from the outset to represent Mr. Martin, things would not have come to this pass."

"Is that what this is about? My God!"

Ron drummed his fingers on the table. "Petru, for heaven's sake."

"No!" Bree was so angry she couldn't sit down. She walked furiously up and down the small conference room. "I won't be coerced. Coercion can't be part of the deal. I'm calling a meeting of the whole Company. All of us. Tonight, at Cianquino's place. Take care of it, Ron. Make sure that everyone's there. Gabriel included. There has to be a limit. I was born to do this, you tell me? Okay, fine. I'm in. But not my family. You guys have to understand that."

"All right." Ron took out his Blackberry and tapped rapidly at the keypad. "I'll tell Armand right now."

Lavinia edged into the room, a tray in her hands. "Sit down, child. This fury isn't going to help get your auntie out of jail or make things different than they are. Have some tea. We'll all have some tea."

Bree stopped short, put her hands together, and forced herself to be calm. "Okay. Okay. Thank you, Lavinia. It smells great." She sat, took a cup of the tea, and sipped at it. Her landlady grew herbs with a flavor unlike anything she'd ever tasted before. The scent had a trace of spice; the taste was of exotic flowers.

She sat down and looked at all of them.

The silence was profound. The air shimmered a little. The angels raised their hands, palms out. Bree closed her eyes and bent her head. Fatigue, anger, and depression slipped away from her, as if she'd shed a heavy coat.

She sat up. "Okay," she said. Then, "Thank you."

Ron put his Blackberry on the table. "The meeting's set for eight o'clock."

"And it is two o'clock now," Petru said. "What would you like us to do in the interim?"

"Cissy first. Why did they arrest her?" Any information that made its way into the public record was available to them. Ron would have checked on the evidence the police had for Cissy's arrest before she'd left the museum.

"The preliminary paperwork is in," Ron said. "It doesn't look good. The circumstantial evidence is pretty strong. She had means and opportunity." Motive, as all of them knew, was not a strong component of a police investigation. The police tended to leave motive up to the prosecutors. "The murder weapon is a walnut-handled boning knife from a matched set in her kitchen."

Bree pulled out her yellow pad. "Okay. So we check out who had a chance to steal it."

"A list of suspects would be helpful first," Petru said. "I can begin research on those who might have done this immediately."

"We'll get to that in a minute. What else, Ron?"

"She was at the scene, of course. Standing right next to him when he was stabbed. They've taken her coat to examine the spatter marks. That report hasn't been filed yet."

"There was blood all over her coat," Bree said. "All over everyone else close to him, too."

"They've taken a lot of clothes into evidence. From Charles Martin, Allard Chambers, Jillian Chambers, Alicia Kennedy. And some guy named Lloyd Dumphey."

Bree stopped taking notes. "Lloyd Dum-what?"

"D-U-M-P-H-E-Y. He's employed"—Ron's grin was a little sour—"as a paralegal at Beazley, Barlow & Caldecott."

"Somebody from Caldecott's office was there?" Bree digested this in silence. Then she nodded at Petru. "Ha! There's our list of suspects. Preliminary, anyway. Start with Dumphey, please."

Ron picked up his Blackberry. "Unfortunately, there appears to be an eyewitness."

Bree took in a deep breath. "Let me guess. Alicia Kennedy?"

"Yes. She says . . ." Ron squinted at the screen.

"Here, take these." Petru took his spectacles off. "These are readers."

Ron sighed and fitted the bows carefully over his ears. "Mortality isn't all it's cracked up to be."

Lavinia chuckled. "I could have tole you that, you asked."

"Let's get on with it, please," Bree said impatiently. "Could you read the Kennedy statement aloud?"

"There's a lot of not very pleasant stuff about your aunt. But the relevant part is this:

Mr. White and Mrs. Carmichael were fighting all week about paying off that professor. She didn't want to pay up. They had a big fight at the museum this

*morning. I walked in on them about nine thirty and
she was screaming at him like a fishwife.*

"That is *not* the Cissy I know," Bree said. "That's utter
nonsense."

*That niece of hers showed up about eleven and
told me I might have to pay up, too, which is utter
bullshit. Mr. White wasn't going to stand for that. He
came into the office about eleven twenty, and there
was another big argument, with Mrs. Carmichael
screaming at him again. Then Mrs. Carmichael told
Mr. White to go outside, where the protestors were
threatening him. He didn't want to go, but she forced
him. We all went out together, me, Mrs. Carmichael,
and that niece* (transcriber note: witness identified
Brianna Winston-Beaufort, Esq., as niece). *There
was a huge crowd of really angry people out there.
They all came toward us. Mrs. Carmichael was
carrying a big purse. She dug into her purse, shoved
me aside, and stuck the knife into Mr. White. He fell.
She raised the knife to hit at him again. I grabbed it
out of her hands and threw it down. Then I fell on top
of Mr. White, so she couldn't stab him one more time.*

Ron took the glasses off and handed them back to Petru.

"She's lying," Bree said. "And it's not hard to figure out
why. She hated Cissy."

"Will she tell the truth?" Lavinia asked. "That don't
sound awfully good."

"A good defense attorney can make mincemeat of Alicia's statement," Bree said with more confidence than she
felt.

"It's pretty clear why Lieutenant Hunter had to take her into custody," Ron said. "You can't be angry with him for that."

"No," Bree admitted. "I can't. I'm not."

"That's right," Lavinia said softly. "Save the righteous anger for the cruel and the liars. And spread mercy around like mulch in a weedy garden."

"Mulch," Bree said. "I'll try and do just that. But I think we should pull up a couple of weeds while we're at it. Petru, we'll need a case file. If you could begin with Bullet Martin and his family, we'll be able to get a better handle on the client. Then I'd like you to concentrate on the Cross of Justinian. You may have to consult sacred sources as well as the profane. I'm beginning to be mighty suspicious of this thing. Ron? You and I will have to pay Goldstein a visit tomorrow. My mother and father will both be in Savannah within the hour, and I have to get home. In the meantime, I need everything you can get from the police file, including the statements of both Allard and Jillian." Her cell phone shrilled, and she took it out of her pocket and flipped it open. "There's Mamma. I've got to go." She slung her coat over her shoulders. "I'm going to have to pay a visit to Caldecott and Barlow. I'm very interested in the mysterious Mr. Dumphey. I'll want to discuss that with Armand this evening before I do. I may need Gabriel with me. I'll see you all there? Tonight at eight?"

"May the Light travel with you," Petru said unexpectedly. "We will be there."

Twelve

"Oh, lord, lord, this is a pickle." Francesca sat in the rocking chair next to the fireplace in the Beaufort town house. Her red-gold hair was disheveled. She wore an elegant bronze silk pantsuit with a coffee-colored blouse. It looked as if she'd slept in her clothes. Bree had never seen Francesca like that before. "They wouldn't let me see my own sister, Bree."

"Try some of this tea, Mamma." Bree set a tray with the Limoges teapot and a cup and saucer on the end table beside her mother. She sat on the floor at her mother's feet. Sasha came and settled heavily at her side, his head on her knee.

"Smells good." Francesca took a cautious sip. "I don't believe I've ever had anything like this before."

"You remember my landlady, Mrs. Mather."

"That nice old African-American woman that visited you when you broke your leg? I do."

"She grows her own herbs and spices. This is her mix."

"She ought to package it up and sell it. She'd make a fortune." She drained the cup, and a little color came back into her face. "I'm not going to be staying with you two. As soon as they let Cissy out of that place, I'm moving on to her house. She'll need me for a bit. Your father called Lewis McCallen to represent her. Somebody from his office is supposed to be getting her out right now." She looked restlessly at her watch. "Why does it have to take so much time?"

"It's just after three, Mamma. She's been in the holding pen—I mean the place where they keep the new people—a little over four hours. That's not too bad."

"You and Antonia are so like us."

"We are?"

"You surely are. We used to fight like a couple of cats. Drove your grandmother Carmichael stark ravin' mad. Or so she said. But I'd do anything for my sister. Anything."

"I know you would, Mamma. We all feel that way."

"Just like you'd do anything for Antonia."

Bree reached up and smoothed Francesca's hair away from her face. "You bet I would."

"Where is she? Antonia, I mean."

"At the theater?" Bree looked around, as if expecting to see Antonia materialize at the sound of her name. "You didn't call her?"

"Me? I thought you did."

"Uh-oh." Bree grabbed for her cell phone. "I thought you did. That means she's going to hear it—"

The front door slammed. Antonia marched into the room, eyes narrowed to brilliant, glittering slits of blue.

"From somebody else," Bree said. "Hello, Antonia."

"I would like to know, I would just bloody well like to know, why I have to hear of a family tragedy from a bald, fat, smirking stagehand who should have died from sheer, unmitigated nastiness before he was born." She dropped her duffle bag to the floor with a thud.

"You shouldn't have, darling." Francesca got up and wrapped her arms around her youngest child. "I thought Bree called you. Bree thought I called you. It was an honest mistake."

"I am always the *last* to know anything in this family."

"Antonia," her mother said firmly. "This is not about you. This is about getting Cissy out from under this horrible mess."

Antonia kicked her bag a couple of feet along the carpet and flung herself on the couch. Francesca sat down beside her. "I told you," she said grimly. "I told you all Prosper White was a disaster waiting to happen. Nobody pays any attention to me in this family."

"Well, we're paying attention to you now, honey. Bree, give your baby sister some of that nice tea."

"I'd rather have a nice glass of wine," Antonia said bluntly.

"What a good idea, honey. It'll settle us all down. I'll have a glass of wine too, Bree dear."

Bree looked at her dog. "What do you think, Sasha? Should I get my family tiddly?" She went to the kitchen to get the bottle and two of the largest wineglasses she could find.

"We'll all go into the kitchen," Francesca said. "I'm not having you drink wine without something on your stomach, Antonia."

After a certain amount of motherly tsking over the lack of anything but yogurt, Cheerios, and an aging log of cheddar cheese, Francesca settled them at the table and began to put together an omelet.

"Did Daddy find out anything more about Prosper White?" Antonia drained her first glass of wine and reached for the bottle.

Francesca cracked the eggs against the ceramic bowl with an expert flick of her wrist. "You'll have to ask him."

"Did he use an investigator?" Bree asked.

Francesca paused while she whipped the eggs, and tipped them into the pan. "Yes," she said at last, "we did. But if you tell your aunt, I'll have your guts for garters."

"Mamma!" Antonia said. "As if we would." Then, "But if it's anything really bad, it might make her feel better to know what a rat he was."

"Let it alone, Antonia. It's water under the dam. Let's concentrate on where she is now." Francesca set a plate with a perfect, puffy omelet in front of each of them and then sat across from Bree. She looked better. Activity— especially where it concerned her daughters—always took Francesca out of herself.

"What are you smilin' at, Bree?"

"You, Mamma."

"You still going to be smiling when you tell me just how much trouble my sister's in?"

"Maybe not so much," Bree admitted.

"What kind of evidence have they got? And don't you try and fudge the facts. I've been married to your father for thirty years and I've about heard it all."

"They quarreled that morning, in front of the museum staff. The weapon seems to be from her kitchen. She was standing next to him when he was killed. There's spatter patterns of blood on her coat."

"She was wearing that fur, I expect," Antonia said darkly.

Bree picked up her fork and put it down again. "Unfortunately, there's also a highly prejudiced eyewitness."

"Alicia Kennedy," Francesca said. "That little witch. Cissy was worried about her. Thought she had a crush on Prosper. Am I right? I thought so. Eat your omelet." She clasped her hands together and stared down at the table for a long moment. "This doesn't sound good."

"She didn't kill him," Bree said.

Francesca started to wring her hands. "You sure about that?"

"Mamma!" Antonia stared at her, shocked.

"Had to be asked," Francesca said steadily. "Cissy's got a temper, and she's impulsive. Bree? What do you think?"

"I'm sure. She didn't . . ." She hesitated, searching for the right way to explain. "There was no aura of violence about her, Mamma. That's the best I can do. Cissy's pretty well-grounded, in her way. She doesn't have the kind of crazy edge that could push her into an impulsive act of violence, and she seemed to genuinely love Prosper. Besides, this murder was planned. You just don't carry a knife around in your pocket on the off chance you're going to run into a chicken that needs boning. And anyway, she'd bought a new nightgown for her honeymoon that morning. If she'd been planning to kill White, she'd have bought a new black suit. Don't you think?"

Francesca smiled a little. "So who did kill the son of a gun?"

"A fair number of people had good reason." She glanced up at the kitchen clock. Nearly six o'clock. "As a matter of fact, I've got to start to look into it right now. You two going to be okay if I go out for a bit?"

"I've got to get back to the theater," Antonia said. "Why don't you come with me, Mamma? It's time you got a good idea of what I do."

Francesca bit her lip. "I want to wait here."

"It's unlikely to be today, no matter who Daddy hired," Bree said. "She's going to be held over for arraignment. The best we can hope for is tomorrow afternoon."

"Then you come on with me, Mamma. I'll get you a front-row seat for the show. It's *Pygmalion*. You've always liked Shaw. Then we can go out to Huey's after, and I'll introduce you to the cast."

Francesca's hands went to her hair. "Let me freshen up a bit. You come with me, Bree. I'm all unsettled."

Bree followed her into the small bathroom and watched as she brushed her glowing hair.

"You're looking a little peaked, honey. I was thinking maybe you and I could take a weekend off. Maybe go on up to that nice spa near Asheville."

"I'm all right," Bree said absently. "But you're on for the spa weekend. As soon as this is all over. Tell me something. You and Daddy spent some time with White, didn't you?"

Francesca made a face. "He was after us for a donation to that damn museum of his. So yes, we did. For Cissy's sake."

"There's a piece of jewelry that's connected to his case. I'm not sure how, just yet. It's a cross. It looks very old. Silver, inlaid with lapis, coral, and jasper. About this big." Bree held her forefinger and thumb apart. "And very ornate."

Francesca put down the brush. "What?"

"A cross. It's called a pectoral. It may have once been

attached to a silver chain. It dates from the Holy Roman Empire. The first Christian emperor, Justinian?"

Francesca knew something about antiquities. "Prosper White never had anything like that that I ever saw. But your birth mother did. Leah. She was a volunteer on a dig out in Istanbul more than thirty years ago with Scholield Martin and Terrence Kennedy."

Thirteen

Armand Cianquino lived six miles outside Savannah at Melrose, a cotton plantation built by a notorious slaver in the early nineteenth century and converted into apartments by a banker from New Jersey in the latter half of the twentieth. The huge, old place faced the Savannah River. It was built in the Southern Colonial style. Its broad verandahs, gracious oaks, and extensive rose gardens usually delighted Bree.

Not this evening.

The setting sun left sullen tails of orange in the western sky. A few stars poked through the oncoming blanket of dark. The moon was a wan splinter of light. Bree pulled into the graveled driveway and sat for a moment in the darkened car.

She had an orderly mind. She had a gift for detachment. Both traits were crucial to her success as an advocate in the temporal and supernatural worlds.

Leah had a cross like the one in this case.

"This," she said to Sasha, "has thrown me for a loop."

Francesca had been bewildered at the intensity of Bree's questions. No, she hadn't seen the Cross since; it wasn't in Franklin's effects after he died. Leah had worn it until she became pregnant with Bree. Then she began wearing the necklace she had left to Bree: tiny gold scales of justice cupped by a pair of wings.

Bree had that necklace on now. She touched it. It lay against her breast.

Sasha butted his head beneath her hand. She cupped his ears and smoothed the silky fur over his skull. She had called this meeting of the Company, and she was determined to get answers.

First, she would think this through.

Then she'd ask coherent, logical questions.

She wasn't a praying woman, but she prayed now, briefly, for courage and compassion both.

Armand's apartment was one of two on the ground floor of the sprawling old house. Bree had never seen any of the other tenants. Maybe there weren't any live ones. Local legend had it that Melrose was haunted by ghosts, although Bree had never seen either the beautiful slave murdered by the son of the original builder nor the suicidal lover of a pirate chief. Armand Cianquino would have been a match for either.

Armand had taught the history of law at Bree's former school. He'd been respected as a historian, feared as a professor, and retired with honors after a long, successful career. Like Bree, he had held another, secret profession. He was the director of Beaufort & Company. He had been director of the Company when Leah and Franklin had done what she did now. For all she knew, he'd been director dur-

ing the first case cited in the *Corpus Juris Ultima*: Lucifer
v. Celestial Courts (Year One).

There were lights in the ground-floor apartment overlooking the river. The Company was assembled there,
waiting for her.

A line from an old movie drifted into her head—Roy
Scheider as the obsessed choreographer staring into his
bathroom mirror each morning: "It's showtime, folks!"—
and Bree repeated it to herself under her breath.

"Come on, Sasha."

She let herself into the foyer. The pine floor was highly
polished as always. Fresh lilies sat in the vase on the credenza underneath the stairway, filling the air with scent.
She knocked on the door and waited, hearing the whirr of
Armand's wheelchair over the wood floor. He opened the
door.

"My dear. And Sasha, too. Welcome."

Old habits of respect were hard to lose. Despite her fury
and her concern, Bree bent and dropped a kiss on his head.
"Professor." She wanted to say he was looking well, but he
wasn't. Age laid a heavier hand on him every time she saw
him. He looked exactly like the old silk screens of Confu-
cius, the Chinese sage.

"Just leave your coat on the couch. We needn't stand on
formality, do we? We're meeting in the library, as usual."

She tossed her coat on the white leather couch and followed him across the room, Sasha at her heels. His living
room was spare. The white leather couch faced mullioned
doors that overlooked the river. A reading lamp curved
over the back of a comfortable recliner. There were no
rugs, to allow for the unimpeded movement of the wheelchair.

The library was located at the far end of the living room.

The doors were made of rosewood, heavily carved with ornate spheres and the Scales of Justice. The wrought iron fence surrounding the Angelus Street office featured the same design. Bree pushed both doors inward, then stepped back to allow Armand to roll through.

The library never changed. The glass doors directly opposite the entrance from the living room opened onto the terraced gardens outside. A fireplace had a roaring fire against the evening chill. Except for an oil lamp at each end of the long table in the middle of the room, the fire provided the only light in the room.

The long east and west walls held books: books of all kinds and of all descriptions. Editions of the Koran sat side by side with translations of the Torah. There was every possible translation of the Christian Bible. Hand-stitched volumes of the Hindu Vedas were tucked between books on religions Bree had barely heard of.

The long table in the middle of the room was heaped with strange and exotic objects. An ancient sword lay underneath a jumble of bowls, trenchers, pieces of armor, and a couple of knives in short scabbards. A huge bronze birdcage sat in the middle of the table. The door was open. Bree greeted the brown owl inside. "Hello, Archie."

"Go home," Archie said. "Go home, go home, go home."

Bree was never sure if the familiar greeting was aimed at her or if the bird was expressing a desire to be elsewhere. One of these days she'd ask him.

She pulled out one of the heavily carved chairs grouped at the table and sat down. Sasha cocked his head at Archie and wagged his tail. Archie shrieked at him. Armand rolled to the head of the table.

They sat silently for a long moment.

Three of the four unoccupied chairs began to fill with

columns of light that whirled and spun like noiseless fire-works. Green. Blue. Violet. The lights coalesced into vaguely human forms.

"I, Rashiel."

"I, Dara."

"I, Matriel."

Ron, Petru, and Lavinia shimmered and became flesh. The fourth chair—Gabriel's chair—disappeared in a brief flash of silver. When the light returned, the angel himself stood behind it. He was tall, and the flickering from the oil lamps and the fireplace made him seem taller still. He was beautifully built, with the shoulders and chest of a boxer. He gave her a cocky salute.

Armand lifted both his hands in what may have been a benediction. "There has been a significant temporal event since we last formally convened. I believe it's this event that has brought our advocate here."

The owl clacked its beak. "The key. The key."

"Patience, Archie. Bree. You asked that we meet. Perhaps we can take care of your concerns first."

Bree stood up. She had one severely tailored black suit she used in court. She wished she had it on now instead of her skirt and sweater. She also wished she'd taken the time to make notes. She said, formally, "I came to request clarification on the rules of conduct that apply to my position as the current appeals advocate." She waited, but nobody said anything. She cleared her throat.

"First. A client has requested that I represent him. Taking his case on might endanger my own family. I'd like assurances that I can turn down such requests."

"You may, of course," Armand said. "It is a matter of your own conscience."

"Second. If I do take on his case, does the kind of protection I have"—she nodded at Gabriel—"extend to my family members, too?"

"As far as physical threats are concerned, absolutely. There is, however, a caveat. We cannot protect you or anyone else from temporal actions. We cannot, for example, extricate your aunt from her current difficulties."

"Third," Bree paused and bit her lip, almost afraid to bring the relic into the open. "I'm tired. Perhaps that's why I'm feeling so uncertain. So . . . dislocated. As if I'm somewhere else instead of here."

"You have doubts," Armand said with great kindness. "About your mission? The Company? About yourself? We cannot help you with that. It's part of the human condition."

"Doubts." Bree thought about this. "Doubts about what I'm here for? No. I was fated to do what I do. Doubts about whether I can continue? Some. It's a tough job, and I wasn't fully aware of the kinds of sacrifices I've had to make. Other kinds of doubts?" She hesitated. "Yes. For instance, I'm not sure you're telling me everything I need to know. I want to know about this Cross of Justinian. It's got some kind of horrible power. Is it dangerous?"

Archie clicked his beak and cried, "The key!"

Lavinia said, "Oh," very softly. Although she didn't move from her chair, Bree felt the soft touch of her fingers against her cheek. "All you have to do is ask us, child." She turned to the others, her face sorrow filled. "It's us she's having doubts about, Armand."

"I'm in the middle of a scary case. It involves my aunt, whom I love very much. Not an hour ago, I learned that it may involve my birth mother. I'm out of my depth. I don't know what kind of help to ask for. I don't know what kind of help you can give me." She looked at Armand. "Professor. I'm a temporal. You seem to be a temporal, although of a special kind. You others . . ." She looked directly at them, one by one. "This case is heading beyond celestial juris-prudence into something else. You're angels. *Why can't you fix this?*"

Sasha pressed himself against her knees.

"This business of this . . . artifact. And Leah." Bree's lip quivered. She clamped it between her teeth, then managed. "You know about that?"

"At the time of her death, Leah had in her possession the key to a gate that should never be opened," Gabriel said.

"The Cross of Justinian?" Bree said. "It's a key?"

"There are several keys." Armand passed his hand over his mouth, troubled. "But you think that the artifact known as the Cross of Justinian is one of them?"

"Is it?" Bree demanded.

Nobody answered her.

"I don't know anything about the relic. It's supposed to be a fake. But somebody stole it from my bag this morning. Why would anyone steal a fake? And how can it be a key? A key to what?" She looked at them again, one by one. Then she said firmly, "I want some answers."

"I will attempt to explain," Petru said. "This"—he struck the oak table—"is formed of matter! I am formed of matter. The same matter. Divine energy transforms matter into you, dear, Bree, and me, and this table, and that bird." He pointed at Archie. "It is all the same. And! It is all very different!"

"Not me," Archie said, fluffing his wings indignantly. "I'm special."

"A little humor is often thought to be a good thing," Petru said with mild disapproval. "But you see my point. All things are created of the same matter. All things are different."

"I don't think Archie was joking," Ron said. "But we all see your point."

"I don't need a lesson in celestial metaphysics," Bree said. "And *I* don't see the point. I don't even see the relevance of what you just said, Petru."

Petru seemed unoffended. "It is highly relevant. The key is matter. It can take many forms. It may have taken the form of the Cross of Justinian. It may not have. Ha! Now, if you will permit, Director, a replica of the Sphere would be very helpful to illustrate further explanation."

Armand nodded. He cupped his hands. A glowing ball of light appeared between them, hovering just over the table top. The bottom of the ball was a black so deep that the eye was lost in it: the Dark Sphere. The top—the Crystal Sphere—was an achingly pure, celestial white.

"I will begin with why the Company cannot 'fix this,' as you put it." Petru stroked his beard, got to his feet, and began to pace up and down. With a stab of affection, Bree realized her friend was in his pedagogical element. She glanced at Ron, who winked at her.

"As you know, there are spheres within the Sphere. What you do not seem to know is that only angels are directly involved with those in the temporal world. There are celestials far above us in the angelic hierarchy who would, indeed, be able to *fix this*. But there is no route for them to do so." Petru paused, and passed his hand over the crystalline brilliance at the top of the Sphere.

"At the very top is the Light, the Lord, Allah, Buddha, Jesus . . . temporals have given the Light many names. They have cloaked the Light in many manifestations, given the Light many temporal attributes. But there is only One, fixed, eternal, and indestructible. It is the very stuff of the universe.

"There is a ladder that stretches between the life that is Light and the nothingness of the Dark. The ladder connects the six Spheres. We are born, each of us, in the very center of the ladder. All life, temporal and celestial, is a journey on the ladder. There are those who choose to climb up. There are those who choose to climb down. Each rung is a struggle. There always comes a time in the struggle when one says: 'No more. It is too difficult. Here I must rest. I must stop. I must stay. I cannot go on.' Wherever one is in the journey, it is there that one stays. That is the path of Souls.

"The ladder connects the Spheres. What *are* these Spheres that are the objects of our journey? The Light is the very top. The Apex. The goal to which most souls aspire. A very few souls have reached this top and become one with the light. Allah, Jesus, Buddha, and a few mighty others. The great religions of the world celebrate the achievements of these few.

"Below the Light is the First Sphere. Those souls that remain in the First Sphere have been called Seraphim, Cherubim, and princes of Thrones. These beings are the guardians of the Light, and their task is praise. Their gaze is directed upward. They do not look back. Their concerns are only with adoration.

"Those that stop at the Second Sphere are Dominions, Powers, and Virtues. They are overlords. Their gaze is directed *across* the span of the Sphere and its many universes, both temporal and celestial. Their task is to assure that the celestial journey continues." Petru paused and looked at his companions. "There is only one of us here, I believe, who reports directly to the Second Sphere, or has even seen those who inhabit it."

Still standing behind his chair, Gabriel bowed gravely at them.

"The Third Sphere is where *we* reside, dear Bree. The Angels, Archangels, and Principles. We are members of the Company and the Courts. Sensiel, Matriel, Rashiel, and I, Dara, and our angel brethren are directly involved in the affairs of humankind. We angels are limited to the past and present behaviors of those in the temporal world. We cannot see into the future. That is above us. We cannot see into evil. That is below us. This is why we cannot 'fix it,' as you have asked. We are not sure what 'it' may be. We are here to aid, support, and fight on your behalf. But the character and direction of the task is up to you. It is, if you will pardon a descent into the homely, the job of being human."

"I say hooray for a descent into the homely," Ron grumbled gently. "Honestly, Petru. You will go on and on."

Petru settled his spectacles more firmly on his nose. "I am boring you, dear Bree. I apologize."

"No, no, not at all. This helps a lot. Please go on." She smiled, her heart lighter than it had been all day. "And on and on, if you need to."

Petru resumed his pacing and his lecture. Bree thought she heard a tiny sigh escape from Lavinia. "Now, you may ask, what of the Dark Sphere and those who journey—not upward, but *downward*? What of those who voluntarily give up the essence of Light, atom by atom, to journey down the ladder to a final and eternal emptiness?" He pointed his forefinger dramatically at the floor. "Again! They occupy spheres within spheres.

"At the very end is nothingness. The Sixth Sphere. Eternal death. The black of nonbeing.

"In the Fifth Sphere are those who were—long ago— Seraphim, Cherubim, and princes of Thrones. These beings are no more. They have become as Beelzebub, Lucifer, and Astroth. They gave up life in the Light for death in the

Dark. They do not praise the Dark, but damn it, eternally and without ceasing. They do not concern themselves with anything but that, thank God! We do not have direct dealings with them.

"The beings in the Fourth Sphere were once Powers, governors of Dominions, and Virtues now made Sin. They interfere but rarely in the temporal world, but when they do, chaos and revolution reign. I am afraid that the problem you came here to lay before us may be a matter of interest to them. I hope that I am wrong.

"We share the Third Sphere with fallen angels of our kind. It is these demons, imps, and monsters who make up the Opposition. It has been their task to interfere with the lives and deaths of temporals."

"The topology of the Spheres in a very large nutshell, Bree," Ron said. "Well expressed, Petru. If a little lengthy."

"I don't understand what this has to do with the key and the Cross of Justinian," Bree said. "Although I'm grateful to have this all explained more clearly to me than it has been in the past." She couldn't keep the acid from her voice.

"You never had doubts this severe before this, child," Lavinia said softly. "You just went ahead and did what you had to do. You got guts, that's for sure."

"May I continue?" Petru said.

"You can tell me about my mother's key?"

"Somewhat. Your patience, please." Petru raised his forefinger in the classic lecturer's pose. "There are gates along the way, to keep the Dark at bay. There are keys to these gates. Leah had one of the keys in her possession. It is not known how she obtained it. It is not known what form it took. What we do know is that she released it as she died and that it has not been found since." He sat back. "It is certainly possible the key is in the *form* of the Cross of Justinian."

"Aha! That would explain a lot," Ron said. "The Opposition's after it."

"What happens if they get it?" Bree asked.

"Oh, my," Lavinia said. "It would let a bunch of folk out that shouldn't be out. That Pendergast, for example. He slipped out of the gate, crossed the bridge, and goodness knows what he's been up to since that grave went empty."

"Where does that leave us?" Bree said. "Are we supposed to get the key and what, return it? Use it? Destroy it?"

"Matter cannot be destroyed," Petru said. "It can only be formed into something else. But the energy it would take to transform such a key is considerable. Far better to get it and return to one of the gatekeepers. It would be safe there and subject to the laws of the Crystal Sphere. Much better for us all."

"And what does my mother, Leah, have to do with all this?"

Armand raised his eyebrows. "Your father, Franklin, is involved, too, I think. We don't know, my dear. The answers to those questions are up to you to discover. It is our job to help you do just that."

"Dangerous for her." Gabriel sat with his arms folded, a slight frown on his face. "Something got at Beazley. A nephiliam, if I'm any judge. We never did catch who killed Franklin in that fire. Wouldn't surprise me if that was a nephiliam, too. Had all the marks."

Bree looked at Petru, who nodded gravely. "A nephiliam is a failed Power, from the Fourth Sphere. The offspring of humans and angels—the results of rape in a long ago war. Very fierce. Very much out of our league, you might say. We have few defenses against it. Gabriel is our best hope if it comes to a battle. But even he may be tested beyond his strength." He turned to Gabriel. "I do not mean to disparage you, my friend. You understand that an objective view of the enemy is itself powerful ammunition."

"It would be an interesting challenge," Gabriel said. "But I'm ready for it. If Bree is."

Nobody said anything.

Bree thought of Beazley's body, of the dreams she'd had of the fire that had consumed her father, Franklin. She directed her question to Gabriel. "Do you think this nephiliam is behind my parents' deaths?"

"If the key is involved, almost certainly."

"Do you know who it is?"

"I could hazard a guess. I won't know for certain until I meet it. It would help to have a name. Each of the Powers has a specific character."

Everyone turned to Petru.

"I do not know, at this point. A great deal is hidden from us, Bree, as you may surmise. But, just as Gabriel is ready to do battle with his sword, I am ready to fight with my scholarship."

"And I," Armand said.

Lavinia didn't move from her chair, but Bree felt her caress on her cheek.

"We're all with you, Bree," Ron said. "You haven't had to call on it yet, but I've got some pretty impressive weather to field when we need it. And Lavinia, of course, has the birds of the air and the beasts of the field. What more could an army ask for?"

Bree bit her lip. Not to fight at all? Was that an option? She met Armand's grave gaze. She wanted to shout: "What do *I* have, against all these terrible things?"

"More than you know," Lavinia said. "Think about this,

child. In the last four months, you never asked once: Why me? Why am I the advocate, and not some other poor soul? When I was laying there in the slave ship on my way to the auction house all those years ago, I never asked 'Why me?' either. It's how it is. You play the cards you been dealt.

"What I did know is what you know deep inside you. I got the will. You got the will, too, Bree. You have the *will*. It should be enough."

"What do you wish to do?" Armand asked mildly. "Your initial question, I believe, was whether you had the option to turn down a prospective client. You do. You asked what protection is available to you and yours. Petru has just told you. Ron has told you. Gabriel has told you. You have the might of lightning and the power of the sea. You have the beasts of the field and the birds of the air. You have Gabriel's sword and your own, considerable will. If that will has flagged in the face of all that a temporal life has to offer? That's to be expected. This won't be the last time." His thin lips quirked upward. "Unless, of course, it *is* the last time, and you decide to renounce the position and choose a temporal life, with all the joys and sorrows that is heir to. That's your choice, and yours alone."

Bree stared at him.

Armand paused, as if waiting for an answer. When she said nothing, he went on. "You asked what connection your family has to this case. We don't fully understand that yet. It appears that Schofield Martin once possessed the Cross. He was killed while handling it. Prosper White, too, is dead. And he had it in his possession to assess it, however briefly."

"But the relic White had was a fake," Bree said. "Chambers gave it to me. He said it was a fake."

Petru tugged at his beard. "The artifact Chambers threw

at you was a fake. Perhaps. The artifact that is missing from your bag was a fake. Perhaps. Beyond that, we know very little."

Bree closed her eyes, to shut out the sight of the Company. She folded herself into the chair and made herself as small as she could. She put her hands over her ears, the better to focus on what she should do. She imagined herself utterly, entirely alone. For a long while she sat there, waiting for an answer.

Archie's shriek pierced her isolation. "So," Archie said. "Do you go home? Do you go home? Do you stay and fight? Stay and fight?"

She blinked. The light of the angels' spirits dazzled her, and she waited until her eyes adjusted to their shapes. "We need to find out. Don't you all think so? So I'll take Schofield Martin on as a client. And we'll take it from there."

A crystalline light rose slowly in the corners of the room, spreading like a great, soundless rush of sparkling water. It spread across the walls, the books, the bodies of those in the chairs around the table. It spilled upward, bathing them in a serene and joyous peace. Bree's bone-deep weariness faded. The ache in her chest ebbed. She breathed in the scent of sun and meadows starred with flowers.

"*Hola!*" Archie screeched. "One for all!"

"And all for one," Lavinia said softly. "To the Company."

Bree swept her gaze around the table and nodded her agreement. "The Company."

Fourteen

"You're not very late, dear." Francesca was curled into the rocking chair by the fireplace, a book open on her lap. "Did you accomplish what you set out to do?" She looked at Bree over her reading glasses. "You must have. You look rested, thank God, and not so . . . exhausted. Almost back to normal. What happened?"

"I think I got a handle on the case."

"Your father frets until he sees the way, too. Well, I'm glad you're feeling on top of things, honey. We were all a little worried about you." She stroked Sasha, who had padded over to greet her. "Although I always feel that Sasha will look out for you. Even if he's only a dog."

Bree glanced at the clock on the living room wall. Less than an hour had passed since her trip out to Melrose. Lavinia's voice echoed in her mind: What is time to an angel?

"Were you dozing?" Bree gave her a hug.

"I must have been."

"You didn't stay for Antonia's play?"

"No. No. Shaw is such a talky playwright. But it's an excellent production. And the technical staging is superb. Antonia's very good at her job." She rubbed her forehead. "If I could just feel a little settled about Cissy . . ."

"Any word?"

"Your father called. McCallen rustled up a judge. She'll be released in a bit."

Bree raised her eyebrows. "So soon? I'm truly glad of that. But it's going to raise a ruckus."

"Preferential treatment for the wealthy? You're right. And what kind of good liberal am I, that I don't give a damn? Not when it's my own sister."

Bree moved restlessly around the room. She felt keenly alive. She was ready to take on the world, and if the world wasn't ready, she'd settle for the Chatham County judicial system. "I feel the same way, Mamma. It'd be different if she'd had a hand in all this, but she didn't."

"I was just waiting to hear that she's on her way home." She patted her cell phone, which sat on the end table. "Soon as your father calls, I'm going to head on over there. I'm glad you got back before I had to go."

"Would you like me to drive you over? You can pick up your car tomorrow."

"No, no, thank you, darlin'. God knows what we'll all be doing tomorrow. Although you and your father ought to get together at some point. Why don't we plan on breakfast at Cissy's about eight?" The gentle tones of her cell phone ring sounded. "And there he is." She picked it up.

Bree stared at the mirror over the mantel, thinking of the horned thing. Was there a way to summon it up? Could she confront it, send one of the Third Sphere demons back to Hell, and leave her home a refuge, the way it used to be?

Sasha barked. She brought her attention back to her mother.

"I'm on my way." Francesca had her lambs' wool coat over one arm and her umbrella in the other. "Daddy says he'd like us all to meet at Cissy's house, eight o'clock tomorrow, if that suits you. She's got one of those ankle bracelets, poor thing. So distressing. We'll have breakfast ready. Bring Antonia if you can. She can distract Cissy while you and the other lawyers talk."

"I'll ask EB to come, too. It'd be good to have someone to take notes."

"Now I do like that secretary of yours. How is she getting along with that GED?"

Bree realized that her whole family—her whole temporal family—had accepted EB's presence without one question about Ron and the Angelus Street office. "She's doing really well. As soon as she gets that diploma, she's going to start at one of the community colleges. She's bound and determined to become a paralegal."

"Isn't that a wonderful thing."

"Yes." Bree eyed Francesca a little mischievously. "You're not going to ask about Petru? Do you think I should ask him to give EB pointers?"

"Who, dear?"

"Petru. Petru Lechta. You met him at the party you gave me at 700 Forsythe three months ago. He didn't stay very long. He fades early at cocktail parties."

"Who would that be? One of your older lawyer friends here? Is he married?"

"He has a sister. Rose."

"A single gentleman, then." Francesca slung her handbag over her shoulder with an absentminded air. "EB's a widow, isn't she? I hope he's nice and older than fifty. Walk me out to the car, dear."

Bree walked her mother out to her car. It was turning colder. Rain clouds hung heavy and swollen over the river. But it felt safe—unlike the threat of the night before. She looked for the flash of silver that meant Gabriel was nearby but didn't see it. The Cross was gone—and the lack of it cheered her up enormously.

Francesca belted herself in and held her cheek up for a kiss. "Sleep well. See you in the morning. Now look at that. Who's coming to visit at this time of night?"

Bree recognized the Crown Victoria. Suddenly, it was a little harder to breathe. "It's Lieutenant Hunter. You drive on, Mamma. I'll talk to him."

"Sam Hunter, huh? Well. Tell him I say hey-howdy." Francesca looked up at her mischievously. "You get to bed early, now. Nothing like a good night to make you feel terrific in the morning."

"Mamma!"

"Bree!" she mimicked. She pulled the driver's door closed and drove off into the humid night.

Bree waited for Hunter by the front door. He had only a sport coat on to protect himself against the cool air. "Come on in where it's warm." She held her hand out and tucked it under his arm and drew him into the front hall. "Thank you for coming by. You've heard that Cissy's been released on house arrest."

"I heard."

Bree shut the front door and went ahead of him into the house. He didn't follow. She turned to him. "Sam? Are you coming in? I can open a bottle of wine, and we can maybe send out for something to eat. Mamma made me an omelet, but I'm starving."

"I can't stay."

"You can't . . . Oh." She examined his face. She should have known immediately why he had come. She walked slowly back to him where he stood by the door. "Oh, *damn*."

"The case against your aunt is a good one."

"So there's no fraternizing with the suspect's family?" She leaned against the wall, her arms folded under her breasts. "She didn't do it, Sam."

"I don't think she did."

"But there's a ton of media attention."

"Yeah." His face was a little stern. "It might have been better if your father's high-powered attorney hadn't pulled as many strings as he did to get her out so quickly. But there you are. I suppose if it were my mother's sister, I'd try the same thing. You don't make a big deal of it, Bree, so I forget how influential your family is."

"I don't make a big deal of it because it doesn't matter, day to day."

"Except under exceptional circumstances. Like your aunt being arrested for murder."

"You aren't going to go all . . ." She waved her hands in the air. "I don't know. Huffy on me? I can't help who I'm related to."

"There's not a good feeling in the department about this."

"I don't expect there would be. This is just a temporary thing, right? This not seeing each other? Especially," she added, feeling rather pitiful, "since we just *started* seeing each other."

"I don't know," he said.

"You don't know?"

"I don't have to tell you how long things like this can drag on. You're a witness. I'm the arresting officer . . ."

"Stop."

"Okay."

They stared at each other.

"We're going to handle this just fine," he said.

Bree said suddenly, "What this is, is a big-time motive to find out who really killed Prosper White."

"For me, it certainly is. And before you challenge me to a race to see who can find the real murderer first, I have to remind you that you're an officer of the court and not a member of the Chatham County Police Department."

"I know that."

"So you'll keep your head down and let the department do its job."

"I hear you loud and clear."

"Which is *not*, as I hear it, a promise to leave it alone."

"No," Bree admitted, "it isn't." She slid her arms around him, underneath his sports coat. "Maybe I can divert your attention?"

"Maybe not. That sounds like a key in the front door."

Bree grabbed his wrist and looked at his watch. "Damn. It's too early for Antonia." She scowled as her sister let herself in. "But it's Antonia, after all. What are you doing back from the theater so early? It's not even ten thirty."

"Exigent circumstances, my director said. I had to Google 'exigent' on my Blackberry. It means extreme or perilous." Antonia began to divest herself of her hoodie, her scarf, her boots, and her various parcels, which she left in a heap by the front door. "I think he doesn't like all the attention coming my way because of Cissy. I don't like it myself."

"Don't leave all that stuff there. Somebody will fall over it. And I know what 'exigent' means."

"Then you'll know that Tony's right. It's better that I'm home during a perilous emergency. How's our aunt? And you . . ." She directed a glare at Hunter. "You're the jerk who arrested her. What are you doing here?"

"I was just leaving."

"Good!"

"Not good," Bree said. "Leave us alone for a minute, Antonia."

"If I don't, will he arrest me, too?" Antonia tossed her head and sidled by them both. Bree waited until she heard her sister clattering in the kitchen.

"So, Hunter." She slid her arms around him once more and kissed him. It was a long kiss but not long enough. She buried her face in his shoulder. He smelled like cold air and damp wool. "You won't forget me, Hunter, while all this is going on?"

"I can't forget you. Sometimes I wish I could."

Antonia was at the kitchen table with Bree's morning yogurt in front of her when Bree came in some minutes later. "Fraternizing with the enemy."

"Don't joke about it, okay?"

Antonia darted a shrewd glance at her. "You look awful." She made a face and said, apologetically, "Couldn't help but overhear. But things are like, temporarily off?"

"That's right."

"That sucks, Bree."

"It sure does."

"Sorry. It's a mess, isn't it?"

"Couldn't be messier."

"You and Daddy going to fix this?"

"We're going to try."

"Can't ask for better than that." Antonia yawned, suddenly. "Gosh. I'm pooped. What's on for tomorrow?"

"Breakfast at Aunt's. Mamma's in charge. Lewis Mc-Callen will be there."

"He's the lawyer who got Cissy out of jail tonight?"

"Yes. He's going to give Daddy and me some direction on what we can do to help from here."

"The media's all over this one, Bree. Have you seen any of the broadcasts?"

"No. But I'm not surprised. That anchor—Fairfax, I think her name is—was right there when it happened, with the cameras rolling. As long as she keeps to a strict account of what she saw, and doesn't speculate, Cissy should be okay."

"Good luck with that," Antonia grumbled. "Every talk show in Georgia's going to be after her. Talk about a career booster. The murder occurred right on camera, even though you couldn't exactly see what happened. What a scoop."

There was a small television tucked under the cupboard over above the long counter. Bree debated whether to turn it on. It wasn't worth it. It was late. She was tired. She had a tense day coming up tomorrow.

And she was going to try something she wished she had tried months ago, when she had first learned that Leah was her birth mother. She wanted Antonia to go to bed. She had to be alone.

"I'll take a look at the TV in the morning. Unless you want to. You could tape anything you thought was out of line. If there is anything, we might be able to get an injunction to keep her from trying this case in the news."

Antonia brightened. Bree realized, with a pang of conscience, that her sister was dying for a way to contribute to the case. "I can do that. Which do you think would be better? Computer or the TV?"

"Computer, without question. You can do it in your room. With the door closed, so you aren't distracted. It's an important job. You might even want to use your headphones."

"So I can focus. I'll do that. I'll stream the news videos and bookmark them."

"Make a DVD and turn it over to McCallen, in the morning," Bree agreed.

"I'll get started right now. You want to come and help?"

"I want to go to bed," Bree said with an air of frankness. "I'm beat. And you're better at the networking stuff than I am."

She waited until Antonia shut the door on her room and then placed her hand over the talisman at the base of her throat. Her clients came to her through relics and objects present when they died. Leah had been wearing this when she had passed on to whatever kind of heaven waited for her. Why hadn't she tried this before now?

At her feet, Sasha whined and thrust his cold nose into her hand.

Don't.

"Why not, Sasha?"

The dog looked up at her, his eyes a deep golden brown.

Why did dogs always look so mournful? Even Sasha, who wasn't mortal but something more than that.

Don't.

Bree slipped the necklace over her head and held it in her hand. The scales and the wings were smaller than her thumbnail. She closed her hand around it. She concentrated on the images she thought, hoped, *knew* must be her birth mother. Pale face. Silver eyes. Dark hair. A tender, haunted expression barely glimpsed on the deck of the ship in the painting *The Rise of the Cormorant.*

Nothing.

Nothing.

After long moments, Bree opened her hand and looked at the small gold pendant.

Sasha's tail thumped against the kitchen floor.

Bree got up and got ready for bed. She took a shower, letting the hot water wash away the day's horrors, the day's triumphs, the day's defeats. She got into bed and lay staring at the ceiling. On some nights lights from the surface of the river danced in the window. Tonight was such a night, and for a long time, she stared at them.

She fell asleep and plunged into the dream, the dream that had tormented her sleep for years, a dream she thought was gone, banished by the work she did for the angels on Angelus Street.

She was drowning, and those around her were drowning, too, in a sea as vast as time. A furious wind whipped the waves to skyscraper heights. Shrieks of terror, shouts of pain, groans of terrible fear pierced the noise of wind and water. She had fallen from a great height into the ocean, and she plunged down, down, down to the black horrors that waited at the bottom. The water rushed into her, filling her throat and finally her lungs.

The Cross was below her, just out of reach. She struggled, kicking, hands outstretched in furious appeal.

Then, blackness.

She woke again, to a place she knew to be a grave. She was suffocating, smothering. There was no air. Desperate, she inhaled and sucked in dirt and bones and a slime-like mud that gagged her. The smell of

*death, of earth's corruption was a tangible, touchable
thing. The universe vibrated in her eyes, in her ears,
and she gasped for air that never came.*

Bree sat bolt upright in bed, shrieking.

The door to her room burst open. Antonia flipped on the
light. Her eyes were black with fear. "Hey!" she said. She
rushed to Bree's side and grabbed her. "Hey!"

Bree choked, gagged, and vomited dirt onto the sheets.

Antonia grabbed at the phone beside the bed. Her voice
was surprisingly calm. "I'm calling 911. Then I'm going to
clear your throat. You take it easy, sister. Just quiet.
Quiet . . ."

Sasha leaped onto the bed, and Antonia batted at him.
"Not *now*, Sasha."

"No." Bree coughed and coughed again. The room
steadied. The air thinned. She could breathe. "No emergency. I'm fine. Honestly." She sat up, and brushed her hair
away from her face. She smiled at Antonia. "It's okay. Really. Just one of those dreams, you know? The kind I used
to have."

"But the sounds you made and the dirt . . ."

Sasha licked Antonia's hands, his tail wagging. He
whined—a comforting sound—deep in his throat. Slowly,
Antonia put the phone back in the cradle.

"Really, sweetie, I'm okay." Bree cleared her throat. Her
voice was hoarse. "I'm just going to get up and get a glass
of water. Okay? Let's go into the kitchen." She swung herself out of bed. Seaweed coiled around her ankles. She wore
sweats to bed these days. The bottoms were soaked with
sea water.

Sasha barked.

Antonia shook her head, as if to get rid of flies. "Bree?"

"Right here," Bree said.

"You okay?" Antonia looked around, as if unsure as to why she was standing in the middle of Bree's bedroom.

"I'm fine."

"I thought I heard you shout in your sleep."

"I was having a bad dream. But I'm fine now."

"Oh." Antonia patted Sasha on the head. "I'll bet he was lying on your belly. You really shouldn't let him sleep with you."

"You're right."

"I'm going back to bed now."

"See you in the morning."

Antonia didn't forget to turn out the light when she left Bree's bedroom.

But she'd forget the rest of it.

Fifteen

Cissy had a housekeeper named Lindy who came in by the day. With Francesca's help, she'd created a lavish breakfast. It was too bad that the only person in the mood to eat it was Antonia.

Bree and Antonia arrived at the dignified old house just off Washington Square a little before eight. Their aunt had bought the house just after her divorce from Ash Smallwood, and she worked off a lot of her postdivorce angst bringing it back to its former glory. Built just before the War Between the States, the house was a mix of Southern Plantation and Southern Gothic. Wide verandahs completely enclosed all three stories. Cissy had replaced the rotting white clapboard, repointed the four brick chimneys, and hired a landscaping team that turned the gardens inside the wrought iron fence into a lush and fragrant Eden. Inside, the house was lavishly comfortable, with cherrywood floors and oriental carpets.

Francesca had set the breakfast in the Palladium-styled conservatory attached to the back of the house. Bree and Antonia walked in to find their father and mother, Cissy, and the attorney Lewis McCallen seated at their aunt's round glass-topped table.

"There you are." Francesca bustled to her daughters and kissed them both affectionately. "We've got some of that nice smoked ham and shirred eggs. I want you two to eat up before we start your meeting."

Cissy was dressed in a cream-colored silk pantsuit with a turquoise blouse. The bright color made her look sallow. She shoved back her chair and stuck out her leg. "How do you like my new ankle jewelry, Bree? I'm going to make it the new fashion accessory in town." She wriggled her foot. The ankle bracelet reminded Bree of the kind of boot the police put on illegally parked cars, only smaller.

"I'll be the first to go out and get one on *my* ankle," Antonia said loyally. She sat down at her father's left. Bree took a chair on his right. Royal paused in the careful dissection of his grapefruit half. He was a tall man and thinner than he had been the last time Bree had seen him. Had it only been a month? There was more gray in his hair than she remembered, too. He spent a lot of time outdoors at Plessey, and his face was tanned and wrinkled with too much sun. "I'm sorry I didn't get over to see you two last night."

"No problem, Daddy." Antonia set aside the grapefruit sitting on her plate and reached for the eggs and ham.

"He and Lewis here were slaying dragons, busy gettin' me out of the slammer," Cissy said brightly. She stretched forward and fiddled with the arrangement of white roses and ferns set in the center of the table.

Her aunt didn't look good. She'd pinned her hair up in a

careless French twist. Her face was drawn, as if she hadn't slept. There were circles under her eyes, imperfectly concealed by smears of makeup.

"We're happy to slay any number of dragons on your behalf, Celia," Lewis McCallen said gallantly. He had proposed to Cissy several years before. Bree wasn't entirely sure why her aunt had turned him down. He was nice-enough looking—balding, middle height, about Cissy's own age—and a truly brilliant litigator. Cissy had dismissed him as stodgy, but Bree had seen him in court and witnessed his passion for his work firsthand.

Bree cut into her grapefruit. "That had to be some kind of record for setting up an arraignment, Lewis. She was in by one and out by ten. You must have been wielding a mighty big sword."

"I rousted Judge Farber." Lewis nodded at Royal. "With your father's help, of course. And it was a deck of cards, not a sword. Farber was losing a bridge tournament at the club and was only too happy to have an excuse to bow out." The housekeeper came in with a carafe of coffee, and he held out his cup. "Thank you, Lindy. The prosecutor's office wasn't too happy about it."

Bree smiled. "I'll bet Cordy Blackburn gave you an earful." Assistant district attorney Cordelia Blackburn was smart, assertive, and set on becoming Georgia's first African-American female governor. Bree was certain she'd do it, too.

"Both ears. She would have added a kick up the backside if I hadn't jumped out of the way just in time." He set his coffee cup carefully back into the saucer. "They appear to have a pretty tight case. There's no flies on that lieutenant of yours, Bree. Sam Hunter."

"He's good at his job."

"Runs a tight ship," Lewis said. Then, with a vagueness Bree knew to be deceptive, "Word on the street is that you and he are an item."

"On the street?"

"Local media," Lewis said. "This Felicia Fairfax? The local anchor? I didn't catch the news last night myself, but my partner Jim Santo did."

Antonia swallowed a spoonful of shirred egg and waved her hand in the air. "She was there at the scene, Fairfax was. She reported that you and Hunter were 'very close.' It was all over the news last night." She beamed at McCallen. "I made a DVD of all the news clips I could find. The major networks carried the story, too." Antonia rolled her eyes at McCallen's frown. "Not good, huh? I was just trying to help, Daddy."

"Very good, Antonia. We might be able to use it to get an injunction against the local news stations. You did a fine job."

Antonia glowed. Francesca had been right. Antonia's natural ebullience seemed to make everyone feel better, including Cissy.

"Glad I could help. But Hunter's a peach. There's no way he believes Aunt Cissy did this. You've met him, Mr. McCallen, right? You like him. It's not so bad, is it?"

"Depends," McCallen said thoughtfully. "How long have you two been seeing each other, Bree?"

Bree gave him a measuring glance. One of the things that made Lewis so good at defense was his complete focus on winning. If Hunter's relationship with her could be used to cloud the integrity of his investigation, McCallen would do it.

Royal said easily, "We're keeping Bree out of this, Lewis."

McCallen raised his eyebrows. There was no way of

mistaking the implacable warning in Royal's voice. He held up his hand in a placatory way. "Of course, of course."

"They aren't seeing each other," Antonia said. "At least not while the investigation's going on. Hunter came over last night to dump her."

"That's me," Bree said sourly. "The dumpee."

"Well!" Francesca said brightly. "Are we all finished with breakfast here? Lewis, maybe you and the others want to go into the library with Cissy. Antonia, let's you and me go shopping."

"I don't have any money to go shopping, Mamma."

"We'll look for an early birthday present."

"But I thought you wanted me to keep Aunt Cis—ow!" Antonia bent down and rubbed her knee. "Okay, okay. Can we go out to the Tybee mall?"

"Whatever you want, darlin'." She got up, hauled Antonia out of her chair, and gave her husband a kiss. "We'll see y'all later. Sister? We'll be back in time for lunch with you. When you finish with Bree and these men, I want you to go straight back to bed and catch yourself a good nap. Come along, Antonia."

The two of them left, Francesca trailing the scent of Tea Rose.

Royal patted his suit-coat pocket, in an automatic search for a pipe he'd given up years before. "Your mother said that Mrs. Billingsley would be along to take notes, Bree."

Bree glanced at her watch. "She'll be here at nine. Another couple of minutes. She has a great-grandson to get to day care in the mornings. "

"Let's go into the library, then," Cissy said. "It's always easier to talk business in there." She craned her neck to look through the archway into the hall. "Lindy? You there?"

There was a faint response from the kitchen.

"We're going to be in the library. You bring coffee and tea in, if you get a chance." She smiled brightly at them. "There, now. We're all set."

She led the way to the front of the house. The library was on one side of the front foyer; the living room on the other. The double doors to both rooms stood open. Bree caught a glimpse of the living room. Cissy's nineteenth-century furniture had been replaced with leather and steel. The occasional tables were glass. "You redecorated since I was here last, Cissy?"

"I did. Prosper just hated the French. All that furniture in there was Empire, if you remember."

"He hated everything French?" Lewis said. He followed them into the library, which was traditionally furnished in leather, forest-green damask wallpaper, and dark oak. "How can you hate a whole nation?"

"He said they have a cluttered mentality." Cissy sat down in a large leather recliner to the right of the desk and propped her feet with up a sigh. "He had a lot of decided opinions, Prosper did." She didn't seem to realize she was crying.

Bree rummaged in her tote for a pack of tissues and handed them over.

"Thanks, honey. He wanted to redo this room, too. We were going to tackle it after we got back from the honeymoon."

The front doorbell chimed. Bree heard the murmur of voices from the foyer, and EB came in. She carried a shiny brown briefcase. Bree greeted her with a smile. "Morning, Mrs. Billingsley."

"Good morning, Ms. Winston-Beaufort."

"You've met my father, and Aunt Cissy, of course. This

is Lewis McCallen. He's senior partner with McCallen &
Santo."

"Big defense firm out of Atlanta," EB said. "Yes, indeed. Glad to meet you, sir."

"Mr. Royal here speaks very highly of you, Mrs. Billingsley. Why don't you sit at the desk? It will make it easier
to take notes. That's a fine briefcase you're carrying. I hope
it's chock-full of yellow legal pads. We have a lot to get
through this morning."

Bree bit her lip. Mr. Royal? She was never more aware
of the generation gap than when men of McCallen's generation met women of EB's age and color.

EB cast a sympathetic look at Cissy's ankle bracelet.
She nodded gravely at Royal. She assessed McCallen for a
moment as she settled behind the big desk. With a rather
pointed air, she opened the briefcase and took out her laptop. "Y'all shoot," she said.

"First thing," Cissy said. "No matter what you saw on
TV last night, I didn't do it, EB."

"No, ma'am," EB said with emphasis. "Even if Prosper
White *was* a lyin', cheatin', gold digger."

"Is that what they're saying?" Lewis said alertly. "The
media? Jim Santo's sending a clip by FedEx this morning.
I haven't seen the news."

"At breakfast, Antonia told us that she downloaded a
bunch of local stuff last night," Bree said. "I didn't get a
chance to ask her if she thought the media was trying the
case in public. You've got a DVD player, don't you, Cissy?
Or we can run it on EB's computer."

EB snorted. "I'll put in on my computer, but you don't
need to see it to believe it. If by media you mean that
blonde woman's who's the local anchor, you bet they are."

"Felicia Fairfax," Bree said.

"Said she saw the killing with her own eyes," EB said. "Although she didn't say she saw who did it."

"We'll take a look later on," McCallen said grimly. "But one of the first moves we're going to make is to try and shut the lady up."

Bree sighed, took a yellow pad out of her tote, and began to doodle.

"Knew all about the lawsuit with Professor Chambers, too." EB pressed her lips together and shook her head disapprovingly.

"Fairfax is trying to infer a motive, then," Lewis said. "One of my least favorite places to try a case, the media. I'm thinking about filing for some kind of gag order, at least locally."

"Might be a good idea to do that right now." Royal hadn't settled into a chair. He stood at the window, looking out at the street. "Be an even better idea to clear them away from the street outside, but we've got a snowball's chance of that."

"They're out there already?" Cissy said. She gnawed at her lower lip. "Oh, my Lord."

"They were gathering just as I came up," EB said. "One of them yelled 'Hey!' at me, but I just kept on coming in."

McCallen stood at Royal's shoulder and watched the activity in the street. "Good for you, Mrs. Billingsley. I don't need to tell any of you in this room how dangerous it could be to give them a statement. Any kind of statement." He turned to Bree. "What's the status of this Chambers versus White case?"

"Chambers can sue the estate, of course. I'm hoping he'll think better of it."

"The whole legal thing would go away if the museum

just agreed to give the magazine cover back to him and his wife, wouldn't it?" EB asked.

"Maybe," Bree said. "But Alicia Kennedy is alive and well, and she's a codefendant . . . It's possible the estate could be held responsible for damages, especially if Alicia Kennedy is broke. And there are Prosper's heirs, whoever they might be."

"That would be me," Cissy said.

All three lawyers in the room looked at her.

"We had wills drawn up," Cissy said. "We're each other's heirs."

Royal frowned and patted his pockets for his pipe. "When did you do this, Cissy? And who did it for you? The wills didn't go through my office."

"Mine, either," Bree said.

Cissy hunched her shoulders. "Prosper didn't want to involve anyone in the family in our affairs. He said y'all had a prejudice against him. He was right, too. You kept hammerin' away at me about a prenuptial agreement, Royal. And you didn't like him from the get-go, Bree. Prosper said it was time to start keeping our business to ourselves."

"So, who drew up the wills for you?" Royal asked gently.

"This new law firm in town. We signed the wills just before we came up to see you, Bree, the day that process-server dragged us all into this. It was that poor man who got killed the day before yesterday. It was in the papers. Mr. Beazley?"

"What?" Bree said.

"And his partner, Mr. Caldecott? They've got an office in your building Bree. In the basement." She hugged herself, as if she were cold. "I have to say I didn't like the looks of the paralegal who witnessed the will for us. Mr. Dumphey? Kind of a creepy character, if you ask me. So was Beazley. The offices weren't very nice, either. I never did meet that partner Barlow."

Royal put his hand on Bree's shoulder. "What's the matter, Bree?"

"Nothing, Daddy."

"She's probably cold," Cissy said. "I know I am. I hope my furnace isn't getting fidgety."

McCallen looked at Bree. "You know this firm?"

She scribbled furiously on her yellow pad. Was there a way to get Caldecott disbarred for conflict of interest? Beazley wrote the wills. Caldecott represented Chambers in a lawsuit against White. No conflict of interest regarding Cissy. Maybe a nice big one as far as Caldecott was concerned, if he took over Beazley's clients. "Met up with them a few times," Bree said cautiously. "They keep a low profile. Can't say a great deal about their reputation."

"I'll ask Santo to get them checked out. Do you have a copy of the will, Celia?"

Cissy looked around, as if expecting to see the will on the coffee table or the desk. "I don't believe I do, no. It's with Prosper's things, I expect."

"I'll get it," Bree said. "Aunt, I'll need a power of attorney from you, if that's okay. You're an executor?"

"Yes. And Beazley."

"Beazley's an executor?" Lewis said. "You're kidding!"

"He's dead," Bree said flatly. *I hope.*

"It's a conflict of interest," EB pronounced. "Right? Firm can't handle the estate *and* sue the estate." She tsked. Her expression was pleased.

Lewis scratched his cheek. "Maybe. A lot depends on

the nature of partnership agreement between the two of them. But we can sure make a noise about it." He turned to Bree. "So we can assume that you can effect a reasonable resolution of the Chamberses' claim? This Caldecott will have to do one of two things: Turn the executor duties over to someone else or refer the claim for damages."

"Right," Bree said. "At the very least, I can bring a motion on Cissy's behalf to renounce the coexecutorship and leave Cissy as the sole executrix. As far as the lawsuit is concerned, Caldecott needs to drop it and hand the case back to Marbury, Stubblefield."

Cissy sobbed. "This is horrible. I'm going to lose Prosper's lawsuit, and his name will be dragged through the mud. Nobody's going to believe either one of us is as innocent as lambs. Not while I'm accused of . . ." Tears started down her cheeks.

"Nonsense," Bree said briskly. "The civil and criminal are totally separate. You haven't been convicted of a thing, Cissy. And you won't be. You just let me handle this." She felt her father's gaze on her again. "It's no problem, Daddy. Easier for me to handle the smaller stuff. You're going to be all tied up with the defense."

"The defense. Yes." Lewis clasped his hands behind his back and began to pace up and down the room. Cissy's eyes followed him wistfully. "I'm thinking our best bet here is to present an alternate theory of the case."

"You think the circumstantial evidence is that strong?" Royal asked.

"We may find that the security tapes are exculpatory in and of themselves, but I doubt it. It was quite a melee at the scene, wasn't it, Bree? Lots of people around? Pushing and shoving?"

"Yes, it was."

"My guess is that it was hard to see what was going on, which we can use to our advantage." His gaze drifted past Cissy as if he didn't see her. "Cordy Blackburn didn't bring the tapes up at the arraignment, and she would have if the evidence was clear and unambiguous. We'll get to view the tapes, but it'll be some time before we actually can take them apart."

Bree made a note to herself. There were a number of advantages to having angels on her side at the Angelus office; if a piece of evidence was going to end up in the public domain, they had access to it right away. She could view those tapes herself this afternoon. And Petru always had the latest dissection software. If the tapes had evidence of who had really stabbed Prosper White, they'd find it.

"As far as the eyewitness testimony"—McCallen flicked his fingers—"pshaw."

Bree smiled, despite her worry. "Pshaw?"

"Easy to discredit, these days. We'll run Miss Alicia Kennedy up and down the flagpole. Santo's got the background investigation on her rolling already."

"I'm gettin' real curious to meet this Mr. Santo," EB said.

Cissy, huddled miserably in the corner of the big leather recliner, lifted her head. "Me, too, EB. Sounds like Superman."

"As for White himself"—McCallen paused and glanced at Royal—"you can send that on over to us?"

"On its way," Royal said.

"Send what?" Cissy demanded. "You went ahead and did what you promised not to do, didn't you, Brother-in-Law? Investigated him." She drew a deep breath. Her face was bright red. "I hate you," she said furiously. "I *hate* you."

"Aunt!" Bree protested.

Royal was compassionate, but it was clear he wasn't sorry. "Had to, my dear. I apologize for the necessity."

"Better to know, Ms. Carmichael," EB said comfortably. "Even if he hadn't been sent on to meet his Maker, you'd want to know what sort of man he truly was . . . If it was me . . ." She corrected herself. "*Were* me, I'd be right grateful that my brother-in-law was looking after me that way Mr. Winston-Beaufort is. You would have found out whatever it is sooner or later. Nobody sayin' don't marry him. What they're sayin' is: This is the guy. Marry him if you want. Better to know what you got, don't you think?"

Cissy sniffed, blew her nose, and slumped against the leather cushions. Bree didn't think she'd ever seen anyone more dispirited. "Maybe," she said softly. "I suppose you're right, EB. I would have married him whatever they said about him."

"Our pastor always says, 'Perfect love casts out fear, but perfect understanding gives you a head start on the buggers.'"

"Isn't *that* the truth," Cissy said. It was the first spark of genuine animation Bree had seen in her since the tragedy. "You have some smart pastor, EB."

"Shall we go on to our other suspects?" McCallen said sternly. "Who've we got? Allard Chamber had a grudge, but he was going to get his day in court. I don't see a strong motive there. Alicia Kennedy—jealous love." He clapped his hands together. "Got any ideas for me, Bree?"

"Charles Martin," Bree said. "Known as Bullet. What do we know about him?"

"Bullet?" Cissy tucked her blouse neatly into her waistband. There was a little color in her cheeks. "That Alicia went on and on about how rich he was and how much he depended on Prosper for his collection."

"You've met before?"

"Oh, yes. Prosper and I went out to Houston a couple of weeks ago. And he was here for a little donor party I gave two weeks ago. I was a little surprised when Alicia told me he was coming to the Frazier to see about making a bid on the *Magazine Americana* exhibit. He wanted it as a permanent exhibit for his Bowie Museum. But his real interest is the same as Prosper's. Roman antiquities. The Christian ones."

"Really," Bree said.

Royal looked at her, his gaze sharp and concerned. "This means something to you?"

"It might. I'm wondering how much of this case can be traced back to a Roman artifact from the first days of the Holy Roman Empire."

Royal drew his brows together. "What's this?"

Bree explained, then concluded, "Chambers accused White of substituting a fake relic for a real one. As a result, Chambers lost his tenured position at his university because his department thought he was engaged in fraudulent research. He claims he lost his pension, too, although I'm sure that's a bit of hyperbole." Bree stared at McCallen, thinking hard. "I'm not as sure as you are that Chambers didn't have a compelling motive to kill White. I think he's a very strong suspect. The question is, why now? If Chambers was angry enough to plan this murder—and it was planned, the theft of the knife from the kitchen here is proof of that—why at this particular time? I can see why the murderer chose the press conference as a venue; there were a lot of people there to begin with, and Chambers made certain that the crowd was even larger by trucking in the homeless people from the City of Light shelter. I like

Chambers as a suspect. I like him a lot. I agree with you about presenting an alternate theory of the case. It's always a good tactic. But we're going to have to investigate the three likeliest suspects right away. Alicia, Chambers, and Bullet Martin. If I could see that file you have on Prosper White, Daddy, it'd help a lot."

"Excellent suggestions, Bree," McCallen said smoothly. "I'll take them under advisement, of course. You're going to have your hands full settling this lawsuit on Cissy's behalf. Not to mention getting her out from under this Caldecott's executorship."

"The more I think about it, the more I realize that a little triage would be good here, Lewis. I'll get my staff started on the background investigations right away."

McCallen frowned. "Juries don't like complicated cases, Bree."

"Juries like the truth, Lewis."

McCallen gave her a broad smile. "Wrong. A mistake, I may add, that many untried defense lawyers make with their first cases. I think we all agree that experience is what's needed here, Royal."

EB slapped her hand down on the desk. It was a large hand and it made a large noise. "Our firm," she said with great authority, "has solved four of the biggest murders to hit this town in twenty years. Who you callin' inexperienced?"

"My goodness, EB," Cissy said. "She's right, of course, Lewis. I told you my niece is the best lawyer in Savannah."

McCallen's face was red, but his expression was bland. "Indeed, Cissy."

"Maybe this case doesn't have to go before a jury." Bree stood up. She had a lot to do. "I've got to go. Lewis? EB and I are here to help. You're welcome to use the Bay Street office. Atlanta can send the documents to EB, and she'll print them out for you. She's an excellent assistant."

EB cocked her head in a considering way. "We'll get along just fine, me and Mr. McCallen."

McCallen gave her a sour smile. "I do believe we will, Mrs. Billingsley."

Sixteen

"I think we've got everything the cops have got, at least so far," Ron said. "Do you want to go over this stuff now? Or do you want to go see Goldstein first?"

"I am on the Internet, searching for background data on the Cross," Petru said. "I am not having much success, but I will persevere. Would you like to see what *I* have so far?"

"I don't know," Bree said. "I need to think."

The three of them were in Bree's office. Petru sat in the recliner, his cane at his side. Ron leaned back against the wall, arms folded.

Bree sat at her desk and looked at the neat stacks of paper in front of her. If she turned her head, she could see the painting of *The Rise of the Cormorant* over the fireplace through her open office door. She'd glanced at it on her way in. There were more drowning souls in the fiery ocean than there had been the day before. There was no pale-faced woman shrouded by the rigging.

"Bree?"

Bree turned back to her desk. "Sorry. Didn't mean to lose focus. I can't afford to." She looked up at him. "There's so much at stake. Except that it's all personal. I suppose that in the great scheme of things, with all that happens in this world every day, it's not so much. Is it?"

Petru may have been smiling beneath his beard. It was always hard to tell. "John says: 'No man is an island, entire of itself. Each man's joy is joy to me. Each man's grief is my own.' Wise words, I have always thought. The great scheme as you call it, dear Bree, is made up of many matters such as these."

"That doesn't help," Ron said crossly. "What's on the action list?"

Bree flipped a page on her yellow pad. "I need to interview the Chamberses. I have to get that bloody Cross back, and I haven't a clue as to who's got it. I've got to get to Bullet Martin before he goes back to Texas. And Cissy has to get that damn ankle bracelet off. The woman's humiliated in addition to being squashed flat with grief over that jerk Whitc. I'm feeling . . . messy. Maybe it's my hair." Bree hadn't taken time to braid her hair that morning. She'd wakened late after her terrible nightmares. She'd bundled it up in a knot at the top of her head, and it was falling down. "Maybe it's that condescending son of a gun Lewis McCallen. You know what's bothering me the most?"

Petru nodded. "The presence of Mr. Caldecott as your aunt's executor."

"Right." She tossed the yellow pad aside. "I'm feeling pushed. I like order, Ron. You know that. At the moment, I'm not sure where to start."

"Order and method," Ron said. "Optimize the use of the little gray cells."

Bree looked blank.

"Never mind. When you retire from all this, you'll find time to read." A DVD sat on top of the first stack of material. Ron tapped it with his finger. "This is a copy of the footage from the surveillance cameras. There's also the footage from Channel 5. I'd start here. We need to know just how strong the case against your aunt will be."

She brooded for a long moment. "You don't think she really did it, do you, Ron?"

"No. But you never know with mortal juries. They can be swayed. Cordy's a terrific prosecutor. Word on the street is that she wants to handle this one herself."

"I am going now, to prepare a file on the relic." Petru heaved himself to his feet with a grunt. "I will prepare a summary. Ron will also. This will help you decide where to plunge in first." He stumped out of the room.

"I ought to be tired," she said. "I had another of those dreams last night."

"I'm sorry." Ron voice was warm with sympathy.

"I don't feel tired, though. That's odd, don't you think?"

"I rarely feel tired," Ron said simply. "That will happen to you, too. It's very nice, not being heir to everything that ails the flesh."

"You need reading glasses, though."

"Yes. This temporal body's aging. At a slower rate than a mortal's would, but aging it is." He tapped the stack of files he'd placed on her desk. "Time, now. Time's not something I can halt or change. We don't have a great deal of it, at the moment. Do you want to look at the evidence that supports your aunt's arrest?"

Bree slipped the DVD into her laptop and booted it up. After a moment, the facade of the Frazier appeared on-screen.

"The surveillance cameras are motion-activated," Ron said. "There's four cameras. Two in the front, one in the parking lot, and one on the west side of the building, where the delivery entrance is. What you're seeing now is the beginning of the demonstration Chambers staged at the front. I'll take the time this afternoon to go over the tapes from the other sides of the building. We need to know who slipped away when the going got tough."

Allard Chambers drove a battered Ford Fiesta into view. The yellow school bus from the City of Light Thrift Store and Grocery was right behind him. Allard got out of the driver's side of his car, then went to the passenger side and opened the door. Jillian got out. She jerked away from Allard's supporting hand, put her hands on her hips, and surveyed the front of the museum.

The camera was angled about 45 degrees, so Bree's view of Jillian was distorted. She was painfully thin. She wore a long, baggy print dress that looked as if it was made of cotton and a puffy ski jacket. Her feet were in thick socks and heavy sandals. She carried a paper bag over one arm, the kind with paper handles.

The doors to the yellow bus opened silently, and people began to stream out onto the driveway. Jillian gestured at them, and they lined up at the side of the bus. Jillian went down the line, dipping into the shopping bag.

"What's she giving them?" Ron said.

"Tomatoes, squishy fruit, whatever," Bree said. "The parking lot was a mess." She leaned back in her chair. "Look at her posture, Ron. She's clearly the organizer here."

Allard pulled the two signs from the back of the Fiesta and leaned back against the car, glancing frequently down the driveway.

"Waiting for Channel 5, I bet," Ron said.

He was right. As soon as the Channel 5 van pulled up and Felicia Fairfax got out with her microphone and her cameraman, the protestors went into action. Allard handed the smaller sign—the one that read PROSPER PROSPERS WHILE INNOCENTS STARVE—to Jillian. He hoisted his sign up. His mouth moved. Jillian prodded the homeless people lined up at the bus with her sign, and they began to chant in unison.

"They're saying 'thief, thief, thief,' " Bree said.

The stretch limo pulled around the yellow bus and parked directly in front of the museum steps. Charles Martin got out, along with several other people.

Bree stopped the DVD. "Do we have a list of who came with Martin?"

Ron pulled a manila file off the top of the stack. "Four people: Martin's assistant, along with a member of the Bowie Museum board in Houston and her husband. Martin's girlfriend is the one in the sable hat."

"This is in black and white."

"Sable as in fur," Ron said. "Don't tell Antonia. Anyhow, the only person who'd met White before was Martin. Everyone else seems to be along for the ride."

"Good. We'll set them aside as suspects for the moment," Bree tapped the Play button, and the footage moved forward. "And there's the four of us, coming out of the building."

They both watched as Bree came out of the front doors. She was several steps ahead of the others. Cissy crowded on one side of White; Alicia clutched his opposite arm.

"I don't look skinny," Bree said. "No matter what anybody says."

The security guard and the girl from the kiosk came out

behind them. The guard stopped, looked at the crowd, and put his hand on his pistol. Martin caught sight of White, lifted his hand, and started toward the front steps.

Jillian lifted her sign. She shouted. The crowd of homeless people surged behind her, and they rushed the steps.

"There," Bree said. "Look. It's Martin who moved me out of the way."

She saw herself stumble a little. White was completely surrounded by the crowd.

"Look!" Bree said. "Cissy's been pushed to the side. There's at least one head between her and White."

"It's Alicia Kennedy."

White went down in a melee of bodies.

Bree stopped the DVD and reran it. She reran it again. And again.

The actual killing wasn't visible. Bree didn't know whether to be glad or sorry.

"The Channel 5 people were too far away to get anything," Ron said. "Look. The camera guy never left his post in front of the news van."

She let the rest of the video run. There was a short moment of chaos, once White was down. The recruits from the City of Light raced for the safety of the bus. The security guard talked frantically into his cell phone. Fairfax pushed closer to the body. Cissy fell to her knees. Alicia Kennedy threw herself across White's body. Charles Martin stood still for a moment, then pulled out his cell phone. The Chamberses, husband and wife, stumbled back and stood together. Jillian clutched Allard's arm, her eyes wide. Allard looked shocked. The jackets they both wore were spattered with dark splotches. Bree saw herself move people away from White's body, then lift Cissy to her feet and turn her over to Charles Martin. She knelt at White's side and pulled open his suit coat.

She remembered knowing instantly that he was dead.

"Ugh." She hit the Stop button, then Replay.

"Are we looking for something specific?"

"A little toad-like guy. Do you see anyone who resembles a toad?"

Ron bent over her shoulder. He smelled like sunshine and peppermint. "Our toad would be?"

"Mr. Dumphey."

"Ah. Dumphey of Barlow & Caldecott?"

"The same. He's listed as a witness in the police reports. Aunt Cissy's met him; hence the description. The only possible place he could have come from would be the bus."

Ron shook his head, pulled out another manila file folder, and opened it up. "I've got the names of the bus people. No Dumphey here."

"Wait a minute." Bree stopped the DVD and zoomed in on a face. "Would you say that's a toady sort of face?"

"The security guard."

"Yeah."

Ron flipped a couple of pages in the file. "Here he is. Lloyd Dumphey. Employed as a security guard, part-time. His first day on the job was—"

"Don't tell me. Yesterday?"

"You got it."

Bree drummed her fingers on the desk. "Well, well. You know, Ron, there's no rule that says villains like Caldecott have to be smart. And a good thing, too. If nothing else, I have a strong hunch where the Cross is. Would you make an appointment for me, Ron? With Mr. Caldecott and his paralegal. No. Strike that. I'm going over there right now."

"Maybe you should take Gabriel with you."

"Against Caldecott? That'd be using a nine-pound hammer to drive a halfpenny nail. And Dumphey? Did he look like a demon of the—what did you call it? The really vicious guys. The nephiliam class?"

Ron's brightness dimmed, and he said soberly, "You don't want to joke about them, Bree."

"Okay. I won't. But I'm going over to see Caldecott and his little toady buddy right now."

"I'll go with you."

"Nonsense. Why waste the energy?" Every time her angels appeared in the temporal world outside the Angelus Street office, it took a little of their mortal life span from them. She was already concerned about Lavinia, who seemed to be fading before their eyes.

"At least take Sasha with you."

"That I can do."

She was out marching down Bay Street in minutes. It felt good to have a clear, unambiguous job to do. Halfway down Bay, Sasha caught up with her. He cocked his head at her in what seemed to be a worried way but trotted along obediently beside her.

The lobby to the Bay Street office was lightly crowded with people going to lunch. Bree thought about heading up to her own office first but decided it'd be better to tackle Caldecott before he, too, headed out to lunch.

"Unless he isn't in at all," she said to Sasha when they were headed to the basement in the elevator.

I don't know.

"And Dumphey?"

He's there.

"And what's-his-name. Barlow?"

No answer from her dog.

The elevator door slid open. Bree stepped out into the short hallway. The entire Bay Street building had undergone a complete renovation some months before Bree had moved in, and it had been a large and expensive task. One builder had gone bankrupt in the middle of it, and the second had cleared out of Savannah just before the place had reopened. Neither builder had felt the basement needed the kind of attention that had been paid to the upper floors.

The walls and the floor were faced with twelve-by-twelve industrial ceramic tile. The color was a sickly yellow. Bree had to admit the color might be due more to the cheap lighting than the actual tile. Sixty-watt bulbs were placed at ten-foot intervals along the ceiling. Bree marched past a janitor's closet, the furnace rooms, and a supply room before she came to the door labeled Barlow & Caldecott Attorneys-at-Law Suite 0. The bottom half of the door was battered mahogany. The upper half was rippled glass, just like her own office door on the sixth floor. Even the font of the lettering was the same. She put her hand on the brass door knob, threw it open, and strode in.

Her first thought was that she couldn't imagine Cissy in the place. A waist-high room divider made of dented and splintered particleboard closed off the paralegal's desk from the waiting area. Two orange plastic chairs with bucket seats had been placed on either side of a rickety end table. Red plastic roses in a cheap vase sat on top of it.

Her second thought was that somebody had heard her coming and had scuttled off behind one of the office doors that led off of the little lobby. One door was labeled Barlow. The other, Caldecott. A faint smear of glue beneath Barlow's sign picked out the ripped-off letters: Z. Beazley.

Bree rapped on the lintel of the main door and said, "Hello," very loudly.

A faint scratching behind Caldecott's door was her only response.

"Caldecott!" she said. "I want to speak with you."

"Not here," came a muffled voice. "Out to lunch. Come back later."

Bree looked down at Sasha. "Dumphey?" Without waiting for an answer, she went to Caldecott's door and pulled it open.

The security guard from the Frazier huddled behind the battered oak desk. Face-to-face with him, Bree decided that he did look like a toad. It wasn't so much his physical appearance—which was unprepossessing—as the way his head poked out from his hunched shoulders. She resisted the impulse to holler, "Stand up straight." Instead, she glared at him. "Mr. Dumphey. I'm Brianna Winston-Beaufort."

He looked at her spitefully. For a second, she thought he might spit. "I know who you are."

"Then you'll know what I've come for."

His eyes were small, beady, and black. They darted from side to side. "I don't know what you're talking about. Mr. Caldecott isn't here. Mr. Caldecott's out to lunch. Come back when Mr. Cald—"

Bree leaned over the desk and grabbed him by the collar. She had never been able to rely on the abnormal strength that had come to her after she'd assumed Franklin's practice. Or at least, she'd never actually tried to summon it up. She did so now. She pulled Dumphey over the desk and dumped him at her feet. "You took something from my tote yesterday," she said pleasantly. "It doesn't belong to you. It was given to me for safekeeping. I want it back."

"I don't . . ."

Bree hauled him to his feet. He was shorter than she was. She raised him off the floor until she could look him in the eye. "Give it to me."

"Mr. Caldecott won't like it."

She shook him. He gurgled a bit. "Mr. Dumphey. I don't know if you were the one who killed Mr. White yesterday. If you did, I'll find out. If you had anything at all to do with that crime, I'll find out. But what I want from you now is the Cross, and if you don't give it to me right this minute, I will hold you like this until you turn purple and faint dead away. Got it?"

He nodded in a strangulated way. Bree noted with mild interest that his face was turning red. "I'm going to set you on your feet. Then you are going to retrieve the Cross from where you stashed it and hand it over to me. Got that?"

"Yes," he said.

She set him on his feet. He put his finger around the inside of his shirt collar and loosened it. Bree focused the power of her considerable will on him.

Dumphey thrust his hand in his pocket and pulled out the pine box. Bree took it and opened it up. The Cross shone a little in the shadow. She dropped dropped the box in her tote. "I'll want to see Mr. Caldecott shortly," she said.

"He's not here."

"Then Mr. Barlow will do."

"He's not here, either. They're gone. They left yesterday."

"When are they due back?"

"I don't know."

"Leave a message for them, please."

"Can't do that, either," he said fretfully. "If I'd been able to leave a message, I could have told them . . ." His eyes darted toward her tote.

"That you stole this from me?"

He shuddered. He had small, oily hands. He clutched her sleeve. "Lissen," he whispered. "Lissen. Can you do me a favor? Please?"

Bree fought down her distaste. "What sort of a favor?"

"Don't tell him I got it. Don't tell him you took it. I can just say . . . I can just say I didn't get a chance to grab it. Please. Please."

Sasha nudged her knee. Bree patted his head. "This is the second time this week I've behaved badly," she said to Sasha. "I'm turning into a bully." She eyed Dumphey. "I apologize for scaring you. And of course I won't tell Caldecott."

"Not Caldecott," Dumphey hissed urgently. "Barlow. You can't tell Barlow."

"Okay." She reached out and adjusted his ratty tie, which had come partially unknotted in the unequal struggle. "I'd like you to take a message for me, and I want to be sure you deliver it one way or another. Mr. Beazley was an executor of Prosper White's estate. Mr. Caldecott represents Allard and Jillian Chambers, who are suing Mr. White's estate. Partners in a firm can't do both and still practice in the state of Georgia. He needs to give one of those clients up. I'm suggesting that he turn over all executor duties to Celia Smallwood, who is currently coexecutor. That's the simplest way out of his current difficulties. Whatever he decides, I want an answer." She gave Dumphey a farewell pat on his shoulder. He staggered under the weight of it. "Soon, Mr. Dumphey. Soon."

Seventeen

EB looked up from her computer as Bree walked in the door. "There you are. I was just about to call you. You got Sasha with you? Good."

"Is Lewis McCallen here?"

"Nope. We aren't fancy enough for him. Walked in. Took a look around. Said he'd do better in his suite at the Hyatt. Wanted me to come along to give him a hand. Said he couldn't count on the secretarial services from some temp agency."

"Oh, dear," Bree said. She tried to squash her immediate reaction: dismay and resentment in equal parts. "That'd be a great opportunity for you, EB. Lewis McCallen is the best criminal defense attorney in the state. His partner's even better. You'd learn a lot."

"So he told me." EB tried to look indifferent. It didn't work very well.

Bree knew EB was flattered by the offer. Bree cleared

her throat with some difficulty. "It's okay, you know. If you want to go."

EB's smile was a little smug. "Anyway. He brought by the investigator's report on Prosper White's background. Your daddy hired some firm out of New York City to do it."

Bree tossed her coat on the floor and sank into the visitor's chair. "Did you read it?"

"Sure did." EB handed over a three-ring binder.

"Anything we can use?"

"There surely is. You'll see. I used that yellow high-lighter."

Bree looked at the first page index: "Family/Early Years"; "Academic History"; "Employment History"; "Financials"; "Criminal Record"; "Marriages/Relationships"; "Businesses, Failed"; "Businesses, Successful"; "Known Associates." She flipped immediately to "Criminal Record": two bad-check convictions and a ton of parking violations.

"Look at the marriages. Man had a past," EB said disapprovingly. "I checked the names in the report with the witnesses you talked about this morning. There's one name that jumps out at you like a pig in church."

She flipped to the marriages. White had been married twice before. Yellow highlighter splashed across the second name. "Whoa," she said. "White was once married to Charles Martin's sister? And she died?"

"White inherited the whole shebang. She was rich, too." EB frowned as heavily as Bree had ever seen her. "Killed in a car crash. That man was in the car with her. He walked away. She didn't."

Bree's heart constricted. For a moment, she needed to breathe. "He was Aunt Cissy's heir."

"Yes, he was. And he used some low-life lawyers nobody'd ever heard of to do it, too. That ought to tell you something. How long you think your auntie would have lasted after they got married?"

"It's bad, EB."

"Not as bad as if he weren't horizontal in the county morgue this very minute."

"True. So. Charles Martin moves up on the suspect list."

"There's more," EB said. "It's about those Chamberses. You see that index tab for academics? It's green. Prosper White was a student of Allard Chambers more than thirty years ago."

"He was?"

"Chambers flunked him. The class was called Roman Antiquities—AD 400 to AD 1000."

Bree flipped through the pages. The investigating team had done a thorough job, although not as thorough as Petru's. White's school transcripts were there. The course description was there. EB had highlighted Chambers's name. A short description of White's exposure of the fake cross was there, too. Petru needed to see this. It offered some very promising leads. "I'm going to take this report with me, EB. If that's okay with you."

"Sure is. I got an e-file from those investigators. Made checking off our suspects' names a lot quicker. Why anybody uses paper nowadays is a mystery to me. You want to know what else?"

"There's more?"

"Uh-huh. That there report's not the only thing that made my eyes pop open this morning. Things are moving on this case at a pretty good clip. Way things are going, I'll bet you'll get this murderer locked by Thursday. Friday at the latest. Which is why I told Lewis McCallen thank you very much but no thank you after I thought on it. I'm staying right here makin' sure you crack this case."

Bree suppressed a whoop of relief. "You did?" Then, meekly, "I'll do my best."

"I'll see to that. Anyhow, that Chambers called you. Wants to talk settlement, he said."

"About the *Photoplay* cover? Did you tell him he needs to go through his lawyers?"

"Said he fired his lawyers."

"Ah. Excellent. We need documentation of that. He's got to march on down there, give them a formal letter, have them acknowledge the letter, and give a copy to us. He's also got to pay his bill."

EB drew her brows together. "I didn't know about havin' to pay his bill. I told him to send an e-mail, keep the answer, and forward it on to us." She took a sheet of paper from the printer tray. "Thought that'd be enough."

Bree read it. Chambers's e-mail to Caldecott was brief: *I do not want the firm of Barlow & Caldecott to represent my interests in the matter of Chambers v. White, Kennedy and the Frazier Museum. Please forward the case file to my business address.* Caldecott's reply was briefer: *Acknowledged.*

"That do?"

"Probably." The chance that Caldecott would make an issue of retaining the file was slim. But a good advocate reduced the chance factor to zero when she could.

On the other hand, the day was getting better and better. She had the Cross back. Charles Martin's motive to murder White was looking strong. If Caldecott was out of her aunt's orbit, the field would really open up. She could interview the Chamberses without running into ethics violations. "I have to talk to Jillian and Allard as soon as I can about their involvement in White's death. The settlement can wait. Besides, I'll need more solid verification that

Caldecott's off Cissy's case than this e-mail before I can offer him any money. And we haven't gotten him dismissed as coexecutor of her will yet, either."

"I'll take care of both these things. I'll go right down there to Caldecott's office and get whatever we need."

"No!" Bree said. "I'll do it."

EB looked startled. Then she looked hurt.

"I don't want you anywhere near those guys."

"All right." EB straightened a stack of papers that didn't need straightening. Her dark skin was a little darker than usual. "Professor Chambers asked you to call him as soon as possible to set up an appointment. You going trust me to do that?"

"Don't get all ruffled with me, EB. Have you actually met Caldecott? Or Dumphey?" Bree brushed irritably at her hair, which was falling into her eyes. "They're creeps."

"I can handle creeps. I've been handling creeps all my life. What kind of paralegal am I going to be if I can't? You only let decent folk into this office, you're going be waiting a long time for business."

"You've got a point. Okay. But you don't need to go down there. E-mail them. Copy in Allard and Jillian Chambers. When we've got absolute verification, let me know."

"All right." She watched as Bree got up and began collecting her stuff. "Where you going now? I'm not finished with you. I've got the Dunleavy lease ready for you to look over. And Ms. Blackburn's office called. They want you to come in and answer some questions from the police. As a personal favor to her, Ms. Blackburn said."

"Could you tell Cordy I'll drop by in about an hour, if that's convenient?"

"I'll do that, sure."

"And try and track down the Chamberses. Both of them.

I'd like to see them as soon as possible. Tonight, if not sooner. Just go ahead and set up a meeting time; then text me. Okay?"

"I can do that, as long as you take the Dunleavy lease with you. It'd be good, we could find the time to keep the regular business going. That's going to be around long after we get your auntie off."

Bree snatched it out of her hand. "This is me, taking the damn lease. I'll read it, okay? As soon as I get half a chance. And EB?"

"What!"

"You tell Lewis McCallen the next time I see him, I'm going to snatch him balder than he is already. The nerve of him, trying to swipe my staff."

Eighteen

The Celestial Courts were on the seventh floor of the six-floor Chatham County Municipal Building on Montgomery. It was six long city blocks from Bay, but Bree decided to walk. As she crossed Martin Luther King Jr. Boulevard, she became aware that Sasha was gone and that Ron swung easily along beside her.

"I got the Cross back."

"So I hear."

Bree looked sideways at him. Angels knew what they knew. "I have a ton of stuff on White's background for Petru. There's some very promising leads. Did you know that Chambers had White in class thirty years ago? Flunked him, according to the college transcript."

"That's very interesting." Ron looked satisfied. "I took a look at the some of the other footage from the surveillance cameras. We've got a nice clear shot of Chambers and his wife trying to slip out by way of the parking lot in the back.

One of the lieutenant's minions grabbed them. Foolish, really, on their part. It might be easier to crack this case than the others." The crossing light at Market Street turned red, so they stopped. "I take it we're headed over to the Celestial Hall of Records to pick up Schofield Martin's closed-case file?"

"Yes. I haven't had a chance to try and raise him again yet. I'll try it when we get back to the office. Did I tell you he came through pretty clearly at first? I think that petition I filed requesting more direct interviews with the clients must have been approved."

Ron looked doubtful. He stood aside to let Bree go into the big concrete building ahead of him. Bree wasn't sure if he was visible to the throngs of people in the lobby or not, so she fell silent. She passed through the metal detector, waved to a couple of on-duty cops who were friends of Hunter's, and wedged herself into the elevator. When the car reached the sixth floor, she hung back, smiling at the blonde attorney who held the door open so that she could exit first. "Forgot something. I'll have to go down again."

"You said the same thing the last time I rode up to the sixth floor with you."

Bree, who had been trying to decide if she could risk tackling the Chambers interview without a definitive response from Caldecott, came to attention. "Hey! It's Karen Rasmussen, isn't it?"

"And the time before that." The door bumped rudely into Karen's hip. Bree knew her from the monthly meetings of the Georgia State Bar Association. She was a new member of Cordy Blackburn's staff. "What is it you keep forgetting, Bree?"

"Coffee, this time. I bought some from the machine and left it there. On the top. Of the machine."

A quiet chuckle drifted past her ear. So Ron was still with her.

"I've got a pot in my office. It'll be a lot fresher than the junk from the machine. Why don't you come by? It'll save you a trip. I . . . Ooof." She stumbled outside the car. The doors closed. The elevator continued on its quiet way up.

"That wasn't very nice, Ron."

"It was a very gentle shove."

"Yeah. But she couldn't see you, right? So I'm the only one in the car. She's going to think I pushed her out. Thanks a ton."

The car swayed to a halt. They stepped into the hallway. A large emblem on the wall had a bronze image of the scales of justice surrounded by angel's wings. The letters that circled the seal read:

Celestial Courts

The directory beneath listed the rooms for Justice Court, Circuit Court, the Court of Appeals, the Appellate Division, the Hall of Records, and the Detention Center.

The seventh floor looked exactly like the other six floors of the Municipal Building. The walls were off-white. The doors were made of steel and painted bridle-brown. The floor was laid with sixteen-by-sixteen tiles in a terrazzo pattern that didn't show dirt. But the air was different, in the way that club soda was different from water. And the ambient light seemed brighter. It glowed with colors better than sunlight.

Ron opened the door to the Hall of Records and stepped back. A part of Bree always worried that Goldstein would bow to the pressures of his celestial governors and computerize the Hall of Records and that the Hall of Records itself would change. But he hadn't, not this time at least. The place still looked like a monastery from the Middle Ages. The walls were made of huge blocks of cut stone. The vaulted ceilings soared to a soft darkness. The stained-glass windows let multicolored sunlight in. The recording angels stood at their oak daises, wings folded neatly under their rough monk's cassocks, quill pens busily scratching at parchment.

Ron clicked his tongue in annoyance. "I see Goldstein still hasn't got the IT guys in."

"Efficiency isn't everything," Bree said a little primly.

"True."

She followed him to the huge back wall, which was filled with small wooden cubicles containing rolls of parchment. Goldstein stood behind the chest-high oak counter. It looked like he was eating yogurt. Ron sauntered up and folded his arms on the counter. "What *is* that stuff, Goldstein?"

"What does it look like?"

"Yogurt."

"It is yogurt." He patted his belly, which was round and occupied a larger portion of his monk's robe than it had when Bree had seen him last. "Thought this body ought to lose a few pounds." He smiled. "Hello, Bree. It's good to see you here. We heard you were thinking of passing on this client."

Bree glanced at Ron, who blushed a little.

"But I see you've changed your mind." He bent down and pulled a roll of parchment from beneath the counter. "Here it is. Schofield Martin versus Celestial Courts. Sentenced to eternity in the seventh circle for the theft of a sacred relic, conversion of a sacred relic for malign pur-

poses, consorting with nephiliam, suicide, theft of intel-
lectual property, and I don't know what all. You ask me, it's
going to be hard to find grounds for appeal here."

"He claims he was murdered." Bree unrolled the parchment. "And he says he was tricked."

"You think you're going to find evidence of—what's the
mortal term—'entrapment'?" Goldstein's eyebrows, which
were as thick as caterpillars and bushy black, rose almost
to his tonsure.

"If by entrapment, you mean that someone on our side
set him up, of course not," Ron said. "But the Opposition
could have tricked Martin into doing what he did—
whatever it was. And the Opposition can be pretty sneaky
about testimony. Throw in a defending attorney who's
maybe new at the job, and I wouldn't be at all surprised if
the right questions didn't come up on Judgment Day. Per-
fection is only found at the highest levels of the Sphere."

There was a murmur of agreement from the monks behind them, as if this was a mantra often repeated.

Bree, absorbed in the case notes, made an exclamation
of disgust.

"True," Goldstein said. "What is it, Bree? You look
balked."

"There's no description of the sacred relic in here. Just a
citation from the *Corpus Juris Ultima*. Ron, if you can
send the citation on to Petru, it might help him on the hunt
for what it looks like." She bit her lip. Balked? She was
more than just balked. She was frustrated. This case was
all about the key. The sooner she got a handle on the key,
the sooner she could begin to clear this up. What if the key
wasn't in the form of the Cross of Justinian? How would
she know? If it was, who or what would turn it back into a

key? If it wasn't . . . what then? Bree made her hands into fists so she wouldn't clutch at her hair. "Balked, frustrated, annoyed, and in the dark. Let's get moving, here."

Ron took out his Blackberry, cast a glance at the case number, and tapped at his keyboard.

"May I see?" Goldstein asked.

Bree spread the roll of parchment on the countertop. Goldstein read for a few minutes, tugging thoughtfully at his lower lip. "The relic is the key to the eighth circle of Hell. It says so right here."

"But it doesn't say what it *looks* like," Bree said impatiently.

"What it looks like?" Goldstein rubbed the bald spot on his head. "You mean does it have a form that temporals can identify?"

"Of course that's what I mean. What else would I mean?"

"That's an impossible question. It has no meaning. The key is . . . well . . . the key. It can 'look'"—at this point, he wiggled his forefingers on either side of his head, which infuriated Bree—"like a can of tuna. It all depends. What's important is what it's made of. The sacred keys are made of concentrated, *con*secrated energy."

Bree rolled the parchment up, knotted the ribbon twice around the scroll, and tied it in a double knot. "Damn it all." She ignored the rustle of disapproval from the angels behind her. "Well. At least we have grounds for appeal, right there. My client may not have known that he had a sacred relic."

"These things are hard to mistake, Bree," Goldstein said a little stiffly.

"Schofield Martin is—was—is—a mortal. A human being. We human beings live in a concrete universe, Goldstein. We name things. We have shapes for things. We are not equipped to understand or identify formless objects of—what did you call it?—concentrated, consecrated matter. I'll bet my client didn't have a clue that the Cross could be holding energy that made it a sacred key." She tucked the scroll into her tote. "Ron? Why don't you go back to the office? Take this background report on Prosper White while you're at it. It'll save Petru some time."

"You know better than that, Bree," Goldstein said. "After all, what is time to an angel?" He smiled benignly at her. Bree resisted the impulse to whack him over the head with the parchment. "I'm going down to see Cordy Blackburn." She scowled. "Just for the moment, I've had it up to here with angels."

Nineteen

"Ms. Blackburn's not here," Karen Rasmussen said coldly. "She had to leave for a deposition."

"I'd better set up an appointment, then. I know how busy she is." Bree set her tote on Karen Rasmussen's desk and pulled out her iPad.

Karen cleared her throat in what could only be described as a marked manner.

"Oh! Sorry." Bree blushed, removed her tote to the floor and tapped the iPad screen. "Does she have any time tomorrow?"

"I have no idea. I am not her secretary." Karen swiveled in her chair to her desktop computer and began to type.

Bree smacked her forehead with her palm. "Of course you're not. I'll just go along and find her."

"You do that. And when you do that, you'd better check with *your* secretary. You forgot more than your coffee downstairs. There are some people here to see you. They've been poking their noses into the offices up and down the corridor for the past ten minutes. Why you can't set up your own meetings in your own office is beyond me. Have you forgotten where that is, too?"

"Karen, I didn't shove you out of the elevator."

"No? An act of God, perhaps?"

"Maybe you just sort of lost your balance?"

"You. Put. Your. Hand. On. My. Butt. And pushed. I felt it distinctly."

Bree stuck her hands in her suit-coat pockets. "I'm sorry we had this misunderstanding."

"Yeah, well. Forget it."

Yes. Forget it. Bree concentrated hard. She'd been able to pull Dumphey over his desk; maybe she had the angelic ability to erase memory, too.

"If you're going to be sick," Karen said, with spurious sympathy, "the bathroom's down the hall. Now, if you don't mind, I've got a brief to write." She bared her teeth in an insincere smile. "Unless you want to push me out of my chair, too?"

"Of course not. Honestly. I'm not sure what I'm apologizing for, but I am well and truly sorry."

"Fine."

Bree waited. Karen's fingers flew over her computer. "Um, Karen?"

"What!"

"These people you said were here to see me?"

"In the waiting room. Out front."

The district attorney's office occupied the whole of one floor in the Municipal Building, and the waiting room was large. Bree walked down the hall and pushed open the double glass doors to reception. The place was crowded with potential witnesses, defense attorneys, messengers, cops, and perpetrators. Jillian and Allard Chambers were tucked in a corner, almost concealed by a potted plant.

Bree's cell phone vibrated in her pocket. She pulled it out; the text message was from EB:

CHAMBERS AT DA OFC 2PM. (sorry).

The "sorry," Bree assumed, was because she hadn't texted Bree sooner.

Chambers caught sight of her, jumped to his feet, and waved. "Athena! Over here!"

Bree wound her way through the crowds.

"This is my wife, Dr. Jillian Chambers."

Jillian had the bones of a beautiful woman: high cheekbones, an elegant aquiline nose, and slender, well-shaped hands. She was thin to emaciation. She wore her thick gray hair in a braid down her back. It was in need of a good shampoo. Her eyes were black and bright, with an almost avian quality. She moved in a series of awkward jerks, elbows out, knees splayed. She seemed almost feral, like an ibis or a crane. Bree felt she'd fly away if startled.

"I've been meaning to meet you, Dr. Chambers."

She extended her hand with a slight air of bewilderment. Bree shook it, carefully. Her voice was hoarse and not unattractive. "Allard says you can help us."

"I'm not sure about that," Bree said. "I would like to talk to you both though." She turned to Allard, who was gazing at Bree with something like despair. "You've both decided to fire your current lawyers?"

"You're talking about Caldecott?" he said impatiently.

"Yes. We have. I copied your assistant on the e-mail."

"That's not quite enough, I'm afraid. Have you received the case file?"

"I'm sure it's on its way."

"And have you settled your bill with them?"

He rolled his shoulders uncomfortably. "I'll work it out with them."

"Then we can't discuss the suit you're bringing against White's estate. Not yet. I can tell you that my aunt is executor of the estate, and amenable to a fair offer to settle. But I would like to talk with you and Dr. Chambers about your past relationship with White. Right now, if you have the time."

"Allard says you can help us," Jillian repeated. "We need money. Your aunt's rich. She's going to marry White. She owes us."

"Prosper's dead, Jillian," Chambers said gently. "He was killed yesterday, in front of the Frazier. You saw it on the news."

Jillian's eyes widened. "We were there."

"Yes, dear, we were there."

Bree looked down at her feet. She was overwhelmed with a sudden, fierce pity. Chambers touched her arm. "The doctor gave her something for the shock. You know. White getting stabbed right in front of us like that. I think it might have been too much of whatever it was."

Jillian's behavior didn't look like a drug overdose to Bree—but who knew?

"Jillian, dear. Would you mind sitting down again for a moment? I have something to ask Ms. Winston-Beaufort, here."

Jillian's eyes narrowed. She drew her teeth back. "Is she another one of your sluts, Allard?"

"Jillian. Please." He took her arm and guided her back to the chair. She sat down, feet together, hands in her lap, and glared fiercely at Bree. Chambers ignored the curious glances from the people around them. He drew Bree apart from the crowd, all the while keeping an eye on his wife. He blurted, "I think the police are going to arrest her."

"For White's murder." Bree didn't make it a question.

"We need your help, Ms. Winston-Beaufort. I've checked around. You've been involved in the successful resolution of four murders. Can you help us? Can you take on her case if she's accused of this crime? I promise I'll drop the lawsuit against White's estate if you do."

Bree sighed. She looked at the desperate figure huddled in the corner. "Okay," she said finally. "Just to be clear, here. You're representing yourself, pro se."

"That's correct." He smiled wanly. "My Latin's still up to snuff. That means 'for self'?"

"Yes. And you will drop the suit against White's estate if I agree to represent Jillian against any charges brought by the state of Georgia in the matter of Prosper White's murder." Which, Bree thought grimly, was bound to happen sooner or later.

"Yes."

"Then I'll ask my assistant to draw up a stipulation of discontinuance. Celia Carmichael will sign it. You will sign it. That should take care of the matter."

"Thank you." He moved, as if to grab her hands. Instead he said again, "Thank you."

Bree wanted to ask if Jillian had killed White. She didn't. A successful defense was sometimes based on what the defense didn't know. "I'll need to talk with her. When did she take this drug?"

"A couple of hours ago. She wouldn't eat anything this morning. If I got something into her stomach, I think it would help."

"We can do that." Bree took him by the arm, and guided him back to his wife. She smiled at Jillian. "I missed lunch,

Dr. Chambers, and I'm famished. There's a wonderful restaurant in the market very close by. Savannah Seafood
Company. Famous for its crab cakes. May I take you and
your husband there?"

"We both like crab cakes," Chambers said heartily.
"And I know the place you're speaking of. It's got quite a
reputation. She'll eat something there. I'm sure of it."

"Good. Why don't I meet you both there in about half
an hour? I have a couple of matters to clear up here."

She waited until Chambers had steered his wife into the
hallway and into the elevators. Then she found her way to
Cordy Blackburn's office. Cordy had a new assistant, a
good-looking guy who couldn't have been more than a year
out of community college. Bree darted a quick, surrepti-
tious look at the nameplate on his desk. "Hey, Gavin," she
said. "Bree Winston-Beaufort." She reached across his
desk and gave his hand a friendly squeeze. "Nice to see you
again. Cordy's not in?"

Gavin rose to his feet, clearly trying to remember where
he had seen her before. "No, ma'am."

"Darn. She asked me to check on the arrest warrants for
the Prosper White murder. Has the warrant for Jillian
Chambers been issued yet?"

"Ah." He glanced nervously at his computer. Bree
smiled, trying for the exact expression Ron, Petru, and Lavinia had when they wanted to be particularly reassuring.
If she didn't—like the Shadow—have the power to blur
men's minds (or make them forget they'd been shoved out
of an elevator), at least she might be equipped with the angelic equivalent of a good dose of Prozac.

"I don't think we've met before, Ms. Winston-Beaufort."
He set his jaw. "And I'm sorry, but information relating to
ongoing cases is confidential."

So she could scratch that particular angelic advantage, too. "Of course it is. Then if you would, please set up a meeting time for me."

"Ms. Blackburn's schedule is pretty packed. Winston-Beaufort, did you say? Oh. Sure." He scowled, much like a threatening puppy. "Ms. Blackburn's been looking for you."

"And here I am. What about tomorrow, early. I can meet her for breakfast at Huey's at seven, if she'd like."

"She's big on breakfast meetings," Gavin said gloomily. "I mean, like, early. Half the time I gotta be there, too." He tapped at his keyboard. "Nope, seven A.M. is not a good time for her. She can squeeze you in at seven P.M. Here in her office. You sure this can't wait until sometime next week? I've missed dinner three nights in a row already."

"Seven tomorrow night is fine. Thank you. Put a note in the file—I'll bring some dinner with me."

"Just so you know, we hate pizza."

She smiled at him. "Got it."

Bree went out of the Municipal Building and across the street to the market with a feeling that events were unfolding at a satisfactory clip. She texted EB:

CHMBRS V WHITE DROPPED. S. CHMBRS RETAINED US RE WHITE MRDR. TELL MCCALLEN TO CK W. DA RE DRP CHRGS CISSY.

Savannah Seafood Company sat at the very edge of the downtown market. Like almost all of the buildings in historic Savannah, it had been remodeled over and over again during the past two hundred years. Unlike all but a few of the old parts of the city, the building had always been a venue for seafood. In the early eighteenth century, it'd been a packing plant for cod, whitefish, and other food drawn from the Atlantic. It was still a market for fresh fish and shrimp, but the front half of the building had been converted to an excellent restaurant. The narrow-planked pine floors were slightly sticky with the city's omnipresent humidity. A row of mullioned windows on the west and north ends of the room let in the daylight. The tables were well spaced so that you didn't feel you were joining the table next to you for lunch. It was a good place for an interview with her new clients.

The Chamberses were seated at a back table. Jillian sat against the wall. Allard sat at her right. Bree took the chair directly across from her, so she could look into her face when they talked.

"We ordered the chowder," Allard said.

"Good choice." Bree looked up at the waitress who hovered, menu in hand. "I'll have the chowder, too. And sourdough bread, if you would. Thank you." She settled herself back in the chair. "I'd like to know everything about your association with Prosper White. From the time he was a graduate student in your antiquities course thirty years ago to the moment he died in front of you at the Frazier Museum."

Twenty

"I think Jillian Chambers killed Prosper White." Bree's voice was high with strain. She sat at the head of the conference table. Petru was at her right, a thick pile of printouts in front of him. Ron fussed with the tea tray. Lavinia herself was in her usual spot at the far end, running a currycomb gently along Sasha's back.

Bree was wound as tightly as a violin string. Jillian Chambers had been arrested for the murder of Prosper White shortly after her lunch at the Savannah Seafood Company. Bree had spent the remainder of the afternoon with a distraught Allard and an unsympathetic prosecutor.

It was dark outside. A quarter moon rode in the sky above the live oak sheltering Josiah Pendergast's grave. Shadows pooled among the graves in the All-Murderers Cemetery.

Petru shook his head gloomily. "A bad business."

"A very bad business," Bree agreed.

"Your auntie's cleared," Lavinia said softly.

"Yes, thank God. They dropped the charges early this afternoon."

Petru nodded. "The spatter patterns on your aunt's coat were mostly tomato. They showed she was farther away from White's body than either Charles Martin or Alicia Kennedy. The fingerprints on the knife were not your aunt's. There were two sets only. The housekeeper's and Jillian Chambers's. And Alicia Kennedy, after refusing a lie detector test, recanted her statement. This Lewis Mc-Callen is very good at his job."

Bree wondered why she was bothering to debrief when her angels seemed to know everything anyway. She knew that the immediate access of the Company to facts revealed during the investigation was limited to the here and now, but it was still unsettling.

"The charge is premeditated murder," she said.

"Because of the attempt to set your auntie up as the killer? By using a knife from her kitchen?" Lavinia shook her head. "Oh my, oh my."

"Academics are notoriously underpaid," Ron observed. "It probably didn't occur to Mrs. Chambers that your aunt hadn't touched a kitchen utensil in twenty years. I'm sure she thought that Cissy's fingerprints would be on the knife."

"Aunt Cissy cooks," Bree said. She was a little nettled at the assumption that her aunt was an overprivileged member of the upper classes. Although it was true. "But you're right. If Jillian took the knife and if she took the knife with the idea of implicating Cissy in the murder, she may have just assumed Cissy's prints were on it. But who knows?" She sighed. "The poor woman's nuttier than a fruitcake, to put a well-known clinical diagnosis on it."

"You are thinking a plea by reason of unsound mind, perhaps?" Petru asked.

Bree got up and stared out the window. "I don't know. I didn't ask her if she did it. Allard thinks she did. I just . . ." She realized that she was clenching her fists so tightly that her fingernails drew blood from her palms.

"It is the mark of a fine advocate, to believe in her client's innocence," Petru said.

"Thanks, I guess." She sat down again. "Okay. Let's go over what we have here. The Chamberses lost everything when they lost their positions at the university. The Prosecution's got one heck of a motive."

"You want to start with the hard part," Lavinia interrupted quietly. "Best get it over with."

"Leave me alone!" Bree snapped. She took a deep breath. "Just let me back into it, okay? I'll get to it." She willed herself calm. Then, with another deep breath, she began with the lunchtime interview with Allard Chambers and his wife.

"Up until six months ago, Allard Chambers was a professor of archeology with an emphasis in the field of Roman antiquities. His PhD thesis topic concerned artifacts from the court of the empress Theodora and her husband, Justinian. Justinian was the first Christian emperor in Rome. Theodora urged him to convert. She was a remarkable woman. Very beautiful, according to contemporary accounts, and very smart. She started life as a courtesan, with lavish tastes, and she brought those tastes to the throne. She commissioned a number of Christian artifacts; jeweled crosses were a particular favorite. Thirty years ago, Chambers got a grant from his university to conduct a dig for those artifacts in Istanbul during the summer term. At the time of the dig, Chambers taught a seminar for graduate students; there were five or six in the class—Allard doesn't remember how many. Three accompanied him on the dig—Prosper White; Schofield Martin, Bullet Martin's younger brother; and Terrance Kennedy, who would later father a would-be archeologist, Alicia.

"There was a fourth grad student with them, a volunteer looking for a short vacation from law school.

"Jillian also went with them, of course. She and Allard had married in graduate school. Did I tell you guys how beautiful she must have been then? You can see the remnants of the beauty in her now. Although it's been distorted—almost destroyed—by her illness." Bree paused, and worried her lower lip with her teeth. "She's suffered from bipolar disorder for years. She was treated through the university, but Chambers claims that when he lost his position, he lost his benefits and his pension, too. Their current medical insurance doesn't offer much coverage for psychiatric disorders."

"Bree, dear," Lavinia's voice was soft but insistent.

"I'm getting there!" Bree shouted. "Just let me get there in my own time." She scrubbed her face with both hands. "Sorry. I'm sorry." She breathed deeply and forced herself to go on.

"The dig was successful as far as relics went. They recovered some pottery, a few earrings, and part of a statue of Christ. And the Cross of Justinian. It wasn't so successful from the people side. The first signs of Jillian's illness began to show up. She had periods of extreme lows—sleeping too much, not eating—followed by weeks of extreme highs. She lost her inhibitions during the highs and had affairs with both Martin and White. Late one night, after a lot of wine, I guess, a quarrel developed between Martin and White, over the provenance of the Cross, Allard says, although it's easy to guess that jealousy was behind it, too. Anyhow, Chambers ordered Schofield Martin to take all of the stuff they'd dug up to the hold of the *Indies Queen* for safekeeping. Martin went onboard during a storm and was swept overboard. The Cross disappeared. Martin's death put that summer's dig to an end. After the Turkish police investigated, everybody went home.

"Except for the student on sabbatical from law school. She disappeared, too." Bree looked at her friends around the table. She was crying now. The tears fell from her cheeks onto the table. "You know who it was, because Allard told me this afternoon and you knew, you knew as soon as he said it.

"It was Leah.

"My mother. Now I think she might be involved in Schofield Martin's murder."

There was a soft click of dismay from Lavinia. Petru cleared his throat with a heavy annoying hack. Ron poured himself a cup of tea but didn't drink it.

"You are upset," Petru said.

"Petru's a charter member of the School of the Blindingly Obvious," Ron said. "If there's something we can do for you, just say so."

"Spit it out child," Lavinia said. "You'll feel better."

Bree mopped her eyes with the back of her hands. "I'm tougher than this. I didn't even know Leah. She died when I was born. The only mother I've ever known is Francesca, and she's terrific at it."

"Your own blood . . ." Lavinia said. "Natural that you'd have feelings about it."

"It's what I don't know that's scaring me, Lavinia. What did you call it, Ron? The School of the Blindingly Obvious? Try this on. The Cross may be the key to a gate to

Hell. Martin had it. He's dead. He died in the kind of storm at sea that's given me nightmares ever since I was little. Leah was on the dig. She's in the nightmares I have about the sea. She had the Cross right here in Savannah. It's obvious she knew what it was, isn't it? Did she kill Martin for it? No matter how justified she may have been, no matter how important the key is to the Sphere—am I going to plead Schofield Martin's case only to discover Leah is a murderer?"

The silence in the room was total.

Lavinia was the first to move. She got up, wrapped her woolly sweater more tightly around her frail body, and tugged at Bree. "Let's go see."

She led Bree to the fireplace, where *The Rise of the Cormorant* sat over the mantel. The lamps in the room were on, but the painting outshone them like a dull, throbbing bruise. Lavinia rose to her tiptoes, to get nearer to the painting, and held her palm out.

The quiet, violet glow that characterized her as Matriel, the Angel of the Beasts of the Field, the Birds of the Sky, the Fish of the Ocean, spread over the ship and the souls crying out for help in the water. The light obscured the scene, then, like a cloud, moved on.

"Look there," Lavinia said.

The pale-eyed dark-haired woman had moved out from the rigging. She was stretched over the side of the ship, both hands reaching down.

"She's helpin', not hurtin'." Lavinia patted Bree's back with a soothing, circular motion. "You don't have to be afraid of what you're going to find out. She was a good person. A strong person. If you have faith in that, then things are going to come out for the best."

Bree stared at the painting, willing the figure to look up.

"This painting doesn't lie. It's a camera, like. Just shows what is. Your Leah is not a murderer, Bree. No advocate has ever killed, except in defense."

"Got it." Bree mopped her eyes with the back of her hand. "It was a shock, is all. To find out she was connected with this. Schofield Martin was murdered while stowing the Cross on the ship. Leah disappeared from the dig, and the Cross was in her possession before she died here in Savannah. Did she kill Schofield Martin thirty years ago?"

"So you got yourself two cases where family runs smack up against your duties as an advocate."

Bree's chuckle was a little watery. "Well, one's disposed of, anyhow. Cissy's safe."

"I think Leah's safe, too. You're going to find out, aren't you? No matter what?"

She didn't answer.

Lavinia drew Bree down to sit beside her on the leather couch. Her hands were light, almost insubstantial. "You was probably feeling mighty strong. Maybe a little bit proud of what it is you do here? Like you could take on the mortal world and a little bit beyond that, too? Natural enough, those feelings. It's good sometimes to remember that pride goeth before a fall. Balance," she added thoughtfully. "It's always about finding your feet in the right place. Anyhow, you set your grief and worry aside and get to the bottom of this case. We're going to go back in the conference room and set up the investigation like we always do."

"All right." Bree mopped her eyes again. The skin on her face felt raw. "I feel about twelve years old."

"That's just fine, honey. We all need to go back to being little children now and again. Now. I'll go bring down some more tea. You get that Ron started on setting up appointments."

When Bree walked back into the conference room, Ron and Petru were sitting side by side, staring into Ron's laptop.

Petru greeted her with a nod. "You are all right, then. So. Shall we continue?"

Another good thing about angels: There was never a need to talk about it.

"Ronald obtained this new software to take apart the images on this surveillance film. It is not working too well. I am unable to determine whether or not Dr. Chambers is guilty."

"The software's working just fine," Ron said. "The actual crime isn't on the disk. I've sorted out the various heads, arms, and legs in relation to White's body, and we're still back to four people. Alicia Kennedy, Charles Martin, and the Chamberses. Any one of the four could have reached Prosper with the knife."

"So we start with the murder weapon." Nobody was going to bring up her fit of nerves, and for that she was grateful. "Who took it from Cissy's kitchen? When did it disappear? Ron, if you could interview Lindy, the housekeeper, it'd be good to get started down that road."

"Oh, my," Ron said.

"What do you mean, 'oh, my'?" Bree stopped herself and said, "Oh, my. You can't help me on this part, can you?"

"It is a Bay Street case," Petru said. "We are sorry. We were able to . . . what the expression is—push the envelope—which is an expression that does not translate into any of the other languages I speak, so I may not be accurate . . . We were able to support this case before because of the familial attachment."

Ron shoved his chair away from the table. "If you're

trying to say that we got some leniency to help when Bree's aunt was involved and now we can't, then just say it, Petru."

"We cannot," Petru said regretfully. "Only if it involves Schofield Martin. I do not see how that can be."

"Let's give it a whirl and find out." Bree took the little box containing the relic out of her pocket and set it on the table. "I'm going to call up Martin."

"You know, I don't think I've actually seen you do this before," Ron said.

Bree flipped the lid up with her thumbnail. The Cross looked small and unimportant. She picked it up and held it in her palm.

———⟨⟩———

The soul that took shape in the conference room was almost visible as Schofield Martin, but not quite. It was man-high, and had a head, arms, and shoulders, but the bottom half dribbled away in wisps of that darkness that meant no light at all. The voice was equally problematic; it was like getting messages from a cell phone with a failing battery.

"Mr. Martin?" Bree said.

". . . SET UP!" the voice said furiously.

Bree wasn't sure how long the manifestation was going to last, so she brushed aside any preliminaries. "Do you remember taking the chest containing the relic to the *Indies Queen*?"

". . . . . . ."

"Mr. Martin?"

". . . PUSHED . . . BOARD!"

"You were pushed overboard?"

"DROWNED!"

"I'm sorry," she said, in reflexive sympathy. "Who pushed you?"

". . . JILLIAN! MURDERED! ME!"

Martin's shade vanished, in less time than it would have taken her to snap her fingers.

"Jillian!" Bree said. She bent her head, and took a deep breath. Leah was innocent. Innocent. If Martin could be persuaded to tell her more . . . She patted the Cross a couple of times, afraid of damaging the filigree, but nothing rose into the air. She took a moment to compose herself before she said wryly, "Do you suppose that was a definitive response?"

"Hard to say," Ron admitted. "But it does appear as if Jillian Chambers is guilty of at least one murder."

Petru shrugged. Lavinia came into the room with a fresh pot of tea. Ron poured and handed out cups. Bree took a sip and felt her tiredness ebb. "Is it a conflict of interest?" she said. "Will I get kicked out of the Celestial Bar Association if I defend a client who's murdered another client?"

"Kicked out for finding out the truth? I don't think so," Ron said. He squeezed a lemon half into his tea.

"When Jillian passes on to her own Judgment Day, it would be, perhaps, wise to wait for the next advocate if she is inclined to appeal any sentence," Petru said. "But for now, the two jurisdictions are not connected. I do not think we can help you with this temporal defense."

"I'll have to depose Jillian about Schofield's knowledge of the Cross to address the charges of abuse of a sacred relic." Bree said. "If he didn't know what it was, his ignorance should be exculpatory. And maybe get an admission that she pushed him overboard, if that's what happened. Then I have to interview her again about her role in White's death? I'm not so sure the jurisdictions are that far apart. I think you guys can help on both of these cases."

"You are not obligated to inform the state of Georgia about a past criminal offence," Petru pointed out. "And if the poor woman's sanity is in question, there is always the usual not-guilty plea. The two cases are not related, Bree."

"I disagree," Bree said. "We need to get started. The state will be after her psychiatric records, and they are going to be essential to establish her competency the day the murder occurred. It'll be weeks before EB can get them, and Petru, you can have them for me by this afternoon." She clasped her hands behind her back and began to pace up and down the small room. "As for you, Ron, we've got two avenues for Jillian's defense. Right now, I think the best is to present an alternate theory of the crime. I'll need background checks on Charles Martin and Alicia Kennedy. I'll want to interview them myself as soon as I can. If you could set up appointments for each of them . . ."

She looked up.

Ron and Petru were gone. A handful of golden mist was the only occupant of Ron's chair.

"I guess EB can do that," Bree said to the air.

Lavinia chuckled. "You let Sasha take you on home now. It's late. You need a good night's sleep."

"How come you're still here?" Bree said, not rudely.

"I live here, remember? You sleep. You dream about what a good woman your mamma was." Lavinia didn't move, but Bree felt a feathery kiss on her cheek. "Good luck with the case, child."

She faded, in a wisp of violet light.

Bree pulled out her cell phone. Too late to call EB. But she could text her:

SET MTGS CHAZ MARTIN, A KENNEDY SOONEST. CU AT 9 A.M.

She looked at her dog. Sasha yawned, stretched fore and aft, and pattered to the tiny front foyer. Bree put on her coat against the chill weather outside and slung her bag over her shoulder. She paused at the front door, her hand on the switch to turn out the lights, and looked at the parade of angels marching up the wall to the second floor. The last angel in line wore scarlet robes embroidered with gold thread. The collar of the robe was a vivid blue. The angel's silver hair shone in a coronet of braids. The tiny painted figure looked up, its face turned toward the ribbons of sunshine curled above its head. The figure had held a cane in one hand, all through Bree's convalescence from her broken leg. The cane was gone. One small hand was raised, fingers curled into the palm, the thumb upright in the universal sign of approbation.

Twenty-one

"You're a little behind the time, Daughter," Royal said.

Bree stood up on tiptoe and kissed his cheek. There had been a message from her father on the answering machine at the town house when she came home the night before. She had agreed to an early breakfast meeting with McCallen at the Hyatt. "I overslept," she admitted. "Sorry."

"I'm glad you did. You're looking well."

It had been her first night without dreams for a long while. She and Sasha had gone back to the town house through the cool and humid night. Nothing had leaped out at her from the dark. No horned beings lurked in the depths of the mirror. She'd unbound her hair and fallen into the best sleep she'd had in weeks.

She had wakened with the conviction that Jillian was innocent.

"You ready to take on this case, Bree? I'm not at all sure it will be rewarding."

Bree looked at Royal with deep affection. Her father—Bree never thought of him as anything else but that—thought Jillian guilty. His circumspection was automatic; after so many years practicing law, he never passed judgment. Or almost never.

"If you've just asked me if this is a loser case—the answer is, I don't know. If it goes to trial, it's not going to be easy to get an acquittal." She lined the salt and pepper shakers up and stacked the sweetener packets in a little row beside them. "Something's off. I can feel it. I don't know what it is, yet. But, Daddy, I'm sure she didn't do it."

His eyebrows rose. "Intuition can lead you pretty far up the creek, Bree. I'd hoped I taught you better than that."

"You did. You did. And I'll be the first to admit I'm wrong. I've got a couple of avenues to explore."

"Not a lot of time before the hearing," he said.

"And I'll need a handle on the defense tactic. I know." She glanced at her watch. "I can't take too long here. I've got a lot of work in front of me this morning. And it's just EB and me now."

He raised his eyebrows. "You had someone else on staff?"

So the Angelus Street office was erased from her temporal family's memory. Bree wasn't sure how she felt about that. It made her secret life more secret, setting her further apart than she had been before. "No, no. Of course not."

"Use the Raleigh office if you get caught short. I like Mrs. Billingsley. She's smart and she's motivated. You can't ask for better. But she's new at it." He fell silent. "You'll take care of yourself on this one?"

"I surely will." She glanced at her watch again. "Cissy's late. And there's a lot to do." She glanced at her watch. "Allard Chambers is coming in for a meeting this morning."

"Good thing the Hyatt's close."

She nodded, looking out the window at the river rolling by below them. Royal had gotten a table overlooking the cobblestones of Front Street. They were a few steps away from the town house and a few blocks away from the Bay Street office.

Royal stood up. "Here they are."

"Bree, darlin'!" Cissy swept down on them in a flurry of perfume, cashmere scarves, and gold jewelry. She glanced at the other diners; then, with a mischievous look, she pulled her pants leg up to reveal a bare ankle. "Free!" she announced, and sat down with a happy sigh.

Lewis McCallen followed her at a more leisurely pace. "Morning." He shook hands with Royal, and saluted Bree with a warm grasp on her shoulder. "Happy resolution to the case, I think."

"I just can't thank y'all enough. Royal? You're stayin' for breakfast of course. Bree? You're looking wonderful this morning," Cissy bubbled. "Here, Lewis. Sit down by me. I'm just tickled pink this is all over!"

"It's not quite all over," Royal cautioned.

"Well, they hauled that lunatic woman off to the pokey, didn't they? I'd say it's all over but the shouting."

"You may be called to testify at the trial," Lewis said. "I'll be back to hold your hand for that, if I may."

Cissy shook her head so that her hair bounced flirtatiously. "I think I'd like that, Mr. McCallen."

Bree glanced at her father, who looked amused. You could knock Cissy down, but she wouldn't stay down for long.

"Anything I have to say to put that crazy woman behind bars for the rest of her life, you just tell me, Bree darlin'. And if she's gone and murdered Prosper, are the Chamberses still allowed to sue me?"

"Of course they can, Cissy, but . . ." Royal sighed, so lightly that Bree was the only one to know how exasperated he was.

"Outrageous. I'd like to see that over and done with."

Bree looked at McCallen. "You haven't told her?"

"Told me what?"

"Bree managed to get the suit dropped, Celia," McCallen said. "Isn't she something, your niece? Just like that."

"I told you she's the best lawyer in Savannah, just like you're the best lawyer in Atlanta, Lewis, and Royal, you're . . . Wait a minute. If they can still sue me, how come they're not? Suing me, I mean."

"I'm going to represent Jillian, Aunt Cissy. In exchange, the Chamberses agreed to drop the lawsuit over the *Photoplay* cover."

"What?"

"I'm going to defend her."

Cissy's voice rose several decibels, to the interest of the gray-haired couple one table over. "You're defending Prosper's murderer?! How can you?!"

Both men looked around uneasily. Nothing like a hollering woman to get Royal and Lewis upset.

"I don't think she did it."

Cissy was motionless, her face perfectly blank, her eyes terror-filled. Stricken, Bree leaned forward and touched her shoulder. "I know you didn't do it, either, and if you're thinking you're going to be rearrested, you are wrong, wrong, wrong. It's unbelievable how sophisticated forensic science is these days—and the more of it that comes back, the clearer it becomes. That you didn't do it, I mean. I never thought you *did*."

Cissy's eyes moved, first to Royal, then to Bree. "Well," she said finally. "As long as I don't have to go back to that horrible jail . . . I guess it's okay. You know what you're doing. I've always said so." She shook herself briskly. "So. If Jillian Chambers didn't do it, who did?"

Bree sent up a prayer of thanks for her aunt's family loyalty. It was good to have her mother's sister believe in her. It was even better that, for Cissy, blood was the strongest tie there was. "I don't know yet."

"She doesn't need to know who the murderer is, Celia," Lewis said. "She just needs to establish reasonable doubt of Mrs. Chambers's guilt in the minds of a jury."

"Let's roll this conversation back a bit," Royal said with a frown. "You said 'yet.' That you didn't know who did it *yet.* Are you planning on investigating the murder further, Bree? You know your aunt is right about the poor woman's sanity."

Bree looked around the room. The other diners were too far away to overhear normal conversation. "I have to admit, the evidence against my client is fairly strong."

Lewis snorted. "Strong? That's understating it. She had plenty of motive: White ruined them. As for opportunity, her proximity to the victim is on tape. As for the evidence? Her fingerprints are on the murder weapon. Sounds like a slam dunk to me. Your only hope is an insanity defense." He sipped his coffee, managing to keep an infuriating grin in place. "From the little I've heard, the woman's got a psychiatric history as long as your arm . . . Although that defense is a lot harder to prove these days than it used to be." He set his cup down with an "ah" of satisfaction. It was a personality quirk that annoyed Bree profoundly. People should shut up when they drank coffee. "It's an interesting case. High profile, too. Let me know if you need an expert hand."

"Be a good fellow and drop the needle, Lewis." Royal

folded his napkin into neat thirds. "Your mother and I were hoping that you wouldn't get wrapped up in a murder investigation this time, Bree."

"I'll be fine."

"You're more than capable of handling an insanity defense. It might be something to consider." He glanced at Cissy. "White was mixed up with some unscrupulous people. Charles Martin, for example. The man's been indicted twice under the RICO statutes. I can't say I see much good poking around in his background will do you."

"I know all about Charles Martin," she said untruthfully. She made a mental note to have EB follow that up. "The thing is—she's innocent."

Lewis chuckled. "Look at her, Royal. She's got a righteous fire in her eye." He took a raisin roll from the basket and buttered it lavishly. "Ah, to be young again. Or maybe not."

Cissy took the muffin away from him. "Now, Lewis, you have to be watching your cholesterol. Use some of this margarine here. Close your eyes and you won't know that it's not butter."

Bree didn't dare look at her father again. Cissy was nothing if not undaunted in her pursuit of men.

"Does 'non compos mentis' mean she's crazier than an outhouse rat?" Cissy asked chattily.

"The insanity defense requires that the perpetrator not know the difference between right and wrong," Lewis said. "And the current law requires pretty stringent proof that the defendant didn't know right from wrong *at the time the crime was committed*. The poor woman would have to have been in the middle of a psychotic episode. You've got videotape that shows she was capable of planning the demonstration, recruiting the demonstrators, not to mention equipping them with last week's vegetables to pitch at the victim . . . Pretty hard to prove incompetence. Especially for newbies. Like your niece."

"I don't plan an insanity defense, Lewis," Bree said pleasantly. "Such an unimaginative strategy, don't you think? I prefer a straight on assault on the Prosecution."

That got the grin off Lewis's face. Royal's eyes twinkled. Cissy set down the muffin and looked from Lewis to Bree. "You two fighting over something? You are? You don't want to get into a you-know-what-swinging contest with Lewis, Bree. For one thing, you don't have one. So cut it out. For another, he's a tough old bird, and wily, to boot. I hate to see my niece go all wily on me. Most unattractive. Besides, this is a celebration breakfast." She banged her fists down on the table . . . not hard . . . and yelled, "Jillian Chambers is in jail, and I'm not! Whoop! I'm free as a flippin' bird!" which drew the attention of a group of salesmen in the far corner, a couple with two children three tables away, and the entire waitstaff.

Bree wondered if there was going to be yet another restaurant in Savannah she'd have to avoid. She decided not to risk it. She stood up, waved at the waiter, mimed signing the tab, and then pointed to Lewis, who looked startled. "Thank you for breakfast, Lewis. And the advice. You'll excuse me. I'm late for an interview." She kissed her father and Cissy and then turned on her way out of the dining room and said loudly. "Just so you know, I am absolutely confident that I'm going to win this one."

The salesmen in the corner could chew over *that* for a while.

⤜∞⤛

Ten minutes later, in the Bay Street office, she wasn't so sure.

"I don't know how we're going to win this one, EB." She dropped her coat in the corner, marched around the desk to the screen, and folded it up flat in two energetic jerks. She propped it against the wall. "There. Now we can discuss this thing without having to holler through wicker."

EB picked up her steno pad and settled in with a practical air. "What should I do first?"

"I have to file a request to remand Jillian into medical custody. She was in pretty bad shape yesterday, but I couldn't convince the prosecutor's office to send her to the psych ward. They did agree to get her evaluated this morning. E-mail my father's office and ask for a sample document, fill it in, and then file it at the courthouse. I also have to file a motion to dismiss, but that can wait until later this week. Jillian will be arraigned and a decision made by the judge to turn her over for trial. The motion hasn't got a chance, I'm afraid. The evidence against her is too strong. But I have to try. The problem is, I can't file a motion without a rough idea of our defense tactics."

"You mean the plea?"

"Exactly. We have a couple of choices: innocent because she didn't do it; innocent because she did do it, but she was out of her mind and wasn't responsible for it; innocent because somebody else did it."

EB had been scribbling away. She dropped her pencil. "Did she kill Mr. White?"

"I don't know." Bree rubbed her forehead with both hands. "But if she did, it wasn't her fault. That much I do know."

"Maybe you should ask her?"

Bree shook her head. "Not yet. Maybe not ever. What time is Allard coming in?"

"Another ten minutes."

"Okay. I'm going to take him down to the Pirate's Cove so you can start making phone calls and generating documents. First: I'll need written permission from him to access Jillian's medical records, all of them. Second: I'll need background checks on Charles Martin and Alicia Kennedy. Call the same firm my father used to investigate White. Their work was impressive."

"They got an impressive price tag, too. Are you going to get a retainer check from Allard Chambers?"

"He doesn't have any money. We can apply to the state . . ." Bree stopped her pacing. She really missed Petru. But she had faith in EB. "There's not enough time. You're pretty good on the Internet, too. Do a global search on Martin and Kennedy and see what comes up. Narrow it down to any way that either one of them made the news in the last five years—Martin in Texas, and Kennedy in New York. We'll see where we want to take it from there. Don't spend a lot of time on it—I need you to do something else today, if you can."

She perched on the edge of the visitor's chair and frowned at the floor. "Cissy's housekeeper's been with her a long time. Her first name's Lindy. I need to know how that knife got out of Cissy's kitchen and into Prosper White."

EB's face glowed so brightly, it looked as if she'd been plugged in. "You want me to question her!"

"I do. Find out when she first missed it. If she did miss it. Find out if there's any connection between her and the Chamberses, Martin, or Alicia Kennedy. And see if anyone was in her kitchen in the past three weeks who shouldn't have been there."

"Got it."

Somebody knocked at the office door.

"That'll be Professor Chambers." EB turned to her computer. "Requests for records, first. You bring him back here after you two talk; I'll have everything ready for him to sign."

"Thank you, EB." She looked up as Allard Chambers walked in. He was wearing a tweed sports jacket, a tie, and chinos and carrying a plastic grocery bag. "You're dressed up this morning."

"I stopped by the Chatham County Jail to leave a few things off for Jillian. They wouldn't let me see her." He swung the bag. "They wouldn't let me drop this off, either. It's just some shampoo and a few energy bars."

"It was good of you to try," Bree said kindly. "Mrs. Billingsley is going to make up a few documents for you to sign. While she's doing that, can I take you to breakfast?"

He blinked. "Breakfast."

"Some food will do us both good. There's a café right around the corner."

He kept his replies to a minimum as she escorted him down the elevator and across the street to the Pirate's Cove Bar and All Night Restaurant. Yes, he'd slept all right, considering. As for her fee—he had five or six hundred dollars in an emergency fund; he'd stop by the bank and get her a check.

"We can wait on that for a moment."

He waited courteously while she seated herself in the booth, and then sat across from her. "It's good of you to take this on, Athena."

"We have to talk about our approach to the defense."

"Is there one?" he said unhappily. He covered his face with his hands. "If there was any justice, I'd be sitting in that holding pen, not my wife."

"Is this an admission of guilt?" Bree asked drily. There

wasn't time for this. She bit back the words "man up" and forced herself to be patient.

"What? No. No. Of course not. You should have seen her thirty-five years ago. She was beautiful. Smart. Witty. You young women don't know what it was like back then, for women like Jillian, especially in the male-dominated professions like archeology. It was unheard-of."

Bree thought about Margaret Mead, who had indeed had a tough row to hoe. And the only one who made a point of recalling Jillian was a PhD archeologist was her husband.

"Jillian always said she had to be twice as smart as a male to get exactly the same kind of consideration. You know what they say about academe anyway, right?"

"The politics are so vicious because the reward is so small?"

"I think that's what started it. Her mania. I didn't recognize that it was an illness at first. I blame myself for that. When she"—he cleared his throat—"started in on the male graduate students, I retaliated along much the same lines. If you know what I mean." He stared at his hands. The waitress set a carafe of coffee on the table and then slapped menus in front of them. He looked up at her. "You wouldn't happen to have an egg-salad sandwich."

"Sure thing."

"Fine for me, too," Bree said absently. She hadn't eaten any of the breakfast at the Hyatt. She regretted it.

"So I got help for her later than I should have. If I'd known, our marriage wouldn't have taken the hits that it did. But we managed. We looked for the Cross for twenty-five years after we lost it. She was with me on each and every dig."

The first discrepancy. Bree reached for her yellow pad,

then thought better of it. "You lost the Cross? The newspaper article said it went overboard with Martin Schofield."

He looked puzzled. "The news . . . Oh! You found a copy of the article about the accident. I'm impressed."

"It's an Internet age," Bree said.

"Well, that's what we thought, initially. But, ah, it turned up. It wasn't in the box of artifacts that went overboard after all."

The waitress set the sandwiches down. Chambers took a couple of bites.

"Where was it?"

"The Cross? Oh. Jillian was in charge of measurements, taking photos of it, the sketches," he waved his hand airily. "Documentation's critical when you're doing scientific research. Turns out she still had it. Didn't give it to poor Schofield at all."

"But then?"

"Well, we had a volunteer with us—I told you about her yesterday. Leah. Leah Villiers. A law student, in between semesters. Very good at her job. Unusual face. Not the kind of face you forget easily. Leah was the one who reminded Jillian the Cross was still in the lab. So we locked it up, didn't want to take a chance on losing it this time. But we did, of course."

The sandwich was tasteless in her mouth. Bree set it down. "You said that Leah left the dig when you all broke up to come back here. Did she take the Cross?"

"Leah?" He looked astonished. "Never. She wasn't . . . No. No, she didn't. If you'd known her, that question just wouldn't occur to you. It was a sneak thief, most likely. There was quite a black market for antiquities, you realize. Still is. Istanbul isn't a third world country by any means, but there's a great deal of poverty. So we kept an eye out, Jillian and I, every year we went back to the dig."

Bree put her hand in her pocket and touched the pine box. "How important is the Cross?"

"Vastly important." The weary man in front of her was transformed. For a moment, she caught a glimpse of the passion that had driven him to his profession. "All artifacts and relics of my period are important. The monetary value isn't huge—it wouldn't be like finding an intact Victory of Samothrace or a Nike—but it's significant. And it doesn't add a large amount to our understanding of the Justinian Empire—although," he added, with an attractive air of self-mockery, "you certainly couldn't prove it by the importance I placed on it in my publications. But it's a piece of history. Irreplaceable."

"You said something about it, the first time I met you in your shop. That Jillian thought it was cursed?"

"Ah, well. Poor Jillian. It was one of her obsessions. It may have driven her to . . ." He shoved his plate aside. "I'm not sure what this has to do with our current problems, Ms. Winston-Beaufort."

Bree decided to come at him from a different angle. "What was Schofield Martin like?"

His eyes slid away from hers. As if he knew where the questions were headed. "Pretty good scholar. If he'd had a little more discipline, he could have made some decent contributions to the field. But he and Jillian got into some wild speculation about the provenance of the Cross and its ritual purpose. I'd say he was easily distracted from rigorous scholarship."

"What sort of speculation?"

"That it had some religious significance. That it was . . . What did he call it? A key to the gate of the eighth circle of Hell, if you want to be precise. Never mind that Dante didn't codify the nine circles until seven hundred years later." He peered at her in exasperation. "What the heck does all that have to do with Jillian's defense?"

"Hey!" The waitress said. She came out from around the bar at a trot. "You can't let that dog in here."

Sasha wound his way to the booth. He turned around, so that his hindquarters pressed into her hip, and stared out the restaurant windows. It was a glowering day, with no sun and a lot of low-lying clouds.

Caldecott pressed his pale face against the glass.

Bree raised an eyebrow and waved her hand at him. There was another shapeless figure in back of him. He was tall, whoever he was.

Stay here.

Bree looked down at Sasha. "Me or you?"

Wait.

"Miss!" The waitress said. "The boss will have my guts for garters if you let the hound stay in here."

"Is your boss in?" Bree asked.

Sasha lifted his lip in a silent snarl. Caldecott backed away from the window. Not backed away, she thought. He'd been engulfed by something that made him disappear.

The huge shadow moved across the window, smearing the glass with fog.

The waitress snapped her gum. "Who, the boss? No. He don't come in until five."

Bree, one eye on the window, dug in her pocket and found the twenty-dollar bill she kept for emergencies. She pressed it into the waitress's hand. "My dog will be very good, I promise. And we won't be here too much longer."

The waitress, whose name tag read DONNA LEE, looked down at Sasha. He waved his tail and then thrust his nose under her hand. "Okay. But no peeing on my nice clean floor, buster." She ambled back behind the bar and settled onto a stool behind the counter.

Bree turned her attention back to Chambers. "According to the newspaper article I found, Schofield Martin drowned that summer, swept away in a storm."

"Drowned." Chambers's voice was hollow. "Yes."

"The body was never recovered? The police report from the Turkish government said it was an accidental death. Do you believe that?"

"Okay," Chamber said, with a kind of despairing cheer. "Okay. I don't know how you found out. We tried to keep it hushed up at the university, but the poor boy committed suicide. Jillian didn't mean anything by these little flings. They were a part of her illness. Schofield didn't understand that. He thought she loved him. He thought they'd go away, together, and when I told him, no, no, she's done this before, she's had these flings before . . . The poor boy just couldn't take it."

The second discrepancy. "Professor Chambers." Bree kept her voice low, but she put all the comfort and authority she could manage into it. "I don't believe Schofield jumped off the *Indies Queen* on his own. I think he was pushed. I think Jillian pushed him."

Chambers's eyes were haggard. "Are you asking me to turn in my own wife?"

"No." Bree sank back. She needed to breathe. "I'm asking you what would be best for her for the rest of her life. I'm asking you if we should consider a plea of not guilty by reason of mental incompetence. If she should be in a place where she can get some kind of treatment for her problems. Where other people, you, for example, can be safe from her."

Sasha nudged her.

We can go now.

The windows overlooking the street were clear. The fog had gone. No faces pressed in to peer at them. Bree's heart slowed; there had been something ominous about that tall figure behind Caldecott.

A second shadow darkened the glass doorway.

"Anything the matter, Athena?"

It was Hunter. He pulled the door halfway open, caught sight of her, and motioned her toward him.

"I'm fine, Allard. Look. I've got to go to another meeting. I'm pursuing what's called an alternate theory to the case. It may be that I'll turn up enough mitigating evidence to convince a jury that someone else killed Prosper White. In the meantime, I'd like you to think about your alternatives for the defense."

"And my options are?" He lifted his hands. "She didn't do it. She did it and didn't mean it. Somebody else did it."

"That's right, Professor Chambers. Those are the options in the state of Georgia." She got up, and put her hand on Sasha's collar. "Take a few minutes and go sign those documents Mrs. Billingsley has, will you? We'll be in touch later in the day."

"I've lost her," Chambers said. "Jillian. She's gone, isn't she? Whatever happens next, she's gone."

Twenty-two

Outside the Pirate's Cove, Hunter leaned against the wall, his arms crossed. The bearded face of a pirate on the restaurant poster leered over his shoulder. "You were meeting with Chambers in there?"

"Yes."

He touched her cheek. "You look sad."

"It *is* sad. They've been married for thirty-some years. His whole life's come down around his ears in the last eight months. And he's lying to me." She sighed. "Has Jillian been booked for a psych-eval?"

"Today and tomorrow. They put her in the Sampson Clinic. You're not thinking of using the insanity defense?"

She looked at the street. Savannah in February was blessedly free of tourists, and the sidewalks were open. "Let's walk a bit." She tucked her hand under his arm, and they started south, to the heart of the old city. Sasha wandered ahead of them, his head up, as if searching for something. Or watching. "What's the department think?"

"For God's sake, Bree. We arrested her. She stabbed Prosper White."

"Let me amend that. What do *you* think?"

"I interviewed her when they brought her in. But I can't—"

She nudged him. "Of course you can. You know I'll have access to the intake interview tapes if the case comes to trial. I'll tell you what's bothering me, shall I? I didn't meet her the day White was killed. You had her and Allard hauled off to the station first thing. But I did get a chance to see the surveillance tapes . . ."

"The surveillance tapes?" He stopped and faced her. "Those were entered in evidence yesterday. How did your office get hold of them so fast?"

"Copies from the museum," Bree said promptly.

"Copies?"

"Listen." She tugged him forward again. They had reached Oglethorpe Square. "You've seen them, too. It was she, not Allard, who appeared to be the organizer of the protest. And she seemed . . . what's the phrase . . . oriented times three; that's it. She knew who she was and what had happened when you questioned her?"

"She did."

"Have you stopped by the City of Light charity yet?"

"I sent McKenna."

"I'll bet you a lunch at Huey's that Jillian recruited the homeless people. She needed the crowd to get the TV people out there. Right? And again, Hunter, I don't need to remind you that I'll find this stuff out in discovery anyway."

"Okay, yes, you're right. The demonstration appeared to be Jillian's idea. The director of the center is a nice old guy named Foster. Not the brightest light in the chandelier but what you'd call a good soul. Jillian convinced him that there'd been a grave injustice done to her and her husband. She's done a lot of volunteer work with the charity, taking the patrons, clients, whatever they call them, out for picnics, to doctor's appointments, things like that. The morning of the murder, she handed out twenty-dollar bills left and right to the center residents. Before Foster knew what was happening, they were on the bus headed to the Frazier."

"Twenty-dollar bills?" That was interesting. Allard was broke.

Wasn't he?

The third discrepancy.

She put a firm hand on her speculations. First things first. Were the Chamberses lying to her? It wouldn't be the first time a client lied, nor the last. What she needed was evidence. And Petru was the best there was at gathering that.

Except Petru wasn't available. Maybe she could petition Goldstein to get her staff back. She paid her staff, didn't she? If she paid them, didn't she have some discretion about how her own employees spent their time?

"You with me here, Bree?"

"Sorry. Yes. Just thinking about the system."

"That'll drive you crazier than Jillian Chambers."

Bree stopped before the statue of James Ogelthorpe and sat down on the wrought iron bench in front of it. "When you arrested Jillian yesterday, you saw what I saw, didn't you. A badly disoriented woman. A distraught husband. A history of . . . What's her illness, again? You've gotten at least a verbal description of the diagnosis by phone from the university medical center, haven't you?"

"Bipolar disorder. They called it manic-depressive illness back when she was first diagnosed."

"Could she go from organized thinking to disorganized thinking overnight? Was she taking her medications?"

"I don't know the answer to either of those questions. I'm a cop, not a shrink."

"I'm a tax attorney, not a criminal defense lawyer." She traced a circle on the pavers with the toe of her shoe. Maybe she should give Lewis McCallen a call after all. The pompous jerk.

"What?"

"Sorry. I didn't realize I was muttering. Maybe I'm not the right lawyer for this case."

Hunter moved closer to her on the bench. She felt the warmth of his shoulder, the length of his arm, and his hip. The only good thing to come out of this arrest is that she could see him again. "You might think about pleading her out. Ask for mitigation due to diminished capacity. If you want me to tell you that she behaved in a rational way on the day of the murder, and an irrational way the day she was arrested, I will. It's true."

"She's innocent."

Hunter grunted. Then he sighed. Then he asked, "Why are you so sure?"

Bree put her head back and stared up at the sky. It was going to rain. A breeze whipped along the square, kicking up stray leaves, a couple of leaflets, and a little dust. "There's all these little pieces that don't fit."

"There always are."

"Did you know that the Chamberses are connected to all of the principals in this case?"

"Of course they are."

She ignored the slight exasperation in his voice. "Thirty years ago, Allard Chambers taught a graduate seminar in Roman antiquities. He and Jillian led an archeological expedition to Istanbul. You know who was on that dig? Schofield Martin, Charles Martin's younger brother. Terrance Kennedy, who later had a daughter named Alicia. Prosper White, who went on to a not-very-distinguished career as a curator. Chambers flunked White out of his course the semester following the dig. Did you know that? And there was a fourth person on the dig . . . who doesn't come into this case."

"Don't tell me you think there's a thirty-year-old conspiracy that's ended up in White's murder. You're smarter than that."

"Nope. I don't think that. But I'll tell you what I do think. Resentment, jealousies, hate—all that existed among these people for a long time. Chance brought Chambers and White together again. Chance didn't dictate what happened next. That was somebody who got pushed a little too far. Somebody willing to let the old resentments ride until there was one more event. A tipping point."

"What event? What are you talking about?"

"I don't know yet. But I'm going to find out. You interviewed Charles Martin, didn't you? And Alicia Kennedy?"

"Yes."

"I want to see Bullet Martin first. He's most likely to leave town. Where is he? Where's he staying? Come on, Hunter. He's a material witness in the case against my client, and I'm going to be allowed to cross-examine him later on. What does it matter if I see him now rather than later?" She resisted the urge to punch him in the arm.

"He's at the Hyatt. He wants to go back to Texas, and we're letting him go as soon as we retake his statement. He might have left already."

Bree was already on her feet and headed back toward the river, her cell phone in her hand. She called 411 for information and connected to the hotel as soon as she got the number.

She didn't like the look on Hunter's face.

She turned her back so she wouldn't have to look at him and completed the phone call. "He's in. He'll see me." She tucked the cell phone into her pocket. "What's the matter?"

"I'm working on it."

"Working on what?"

"On the fact that given your job and my job, this sort of thing is going to happen occasionally."

"So what are you going to do about it? You can see what I'm doing about it. I have to."

"You're right. We both have to."

"You're not going to come up with any rules? No 'don't go there'? No 'stop or it's off'?"

"Just one rule." He walked up to her and kissed her, to the amusement of a passing park worker. "If you get into a jam, call me."

Twenty-three

Charles Martin had a fifth-floor suite with a view of the Savannah River. When Bree walked in, the drapes over the sliding glass doors were open. The sun was making a determined effort to break through the cloud cover. The water was a color between ochre and steel.

The living room had the pleasant anonymity of its kind; dark wood desk, table and chairs, a sturdy, expensively covered couch that faced the balcony, frosted panes of glass that set the small kitchen apart. Martin was in shirtsleeves and tie, his suit coat tossed over the armchair. His briefcase was shut. A few papers stuck out from one end. Bree guessed he'd been working and hastily stuffed the papers away when she'd tapped at the outer door.

"Ms. Winston-Beaufort. You've been having quite a time of it, according to the newscasts." He gestured toward the couch. "Have a seat. Can I get you anything to drink? Coffee? Something a little stronger?"

"Not right now." She took a place at the small table and then took her iPad out of her tote. She took a moment to look at him. He met her gaze with a bland smile. "So you're representing the crazy Mrs. Chambers."

"Dr. Chambers, yes."

"And you want to talk to me about it? No problem. I'm going stir crazy here. Glad to see a friendly face. I'm checking in with some lawyer named Blackburn this afternoon, and then I can get my ass on back to Houston. Don't suppose she'll be too happy to know that I've agreed to talk to you. Seeing as how you're a member of the opposition and all."

The back of Bree's neck prickled. Sasha had gone back to the town house. The Hyatt had a rule against pets. She hadn't realized how much she depended on Sasha's sensitivities to threats from the true Opposition. She searched Martin's face. Nothing there but a pleased self-interest. No hint of anything darker.

"How's the poor woman doing, away? Your client."

Bree had considered several approaches on her way up to Martin's suite. She'd taken five minutes to call Royal and ask him about Martin's criminal record, and she wasn't sure at this point how it affected Jillian's case. He'd been accused, and cleared, of insider trading in the 2009 investment bank failures. He hadn't fared so well on the charges of embezzlement of client funds; he'd made restitution and then served eight months of a year's sentence in a minimum security prison in Connecticut.

He was probably tough, certainly greedy, and used to lying.

There had been one other whisper of criminal doings—and it was the most tentative of leads. Bullet Martin had an import business specializing in antiquities, and U.S. Customs had started an investigation into the legality of some of his cargo.

None of it pointed the way to the most urgent question.

She wanted to know if he was a killer.

"How old were you when your brother died in Istanbul, Mr. Martin?"

The question caught him off guard. His eyes widened. They were small and dark brown, a startling color with his white hair. After a brief pause, he grinned easily. "Schofield? Hell. That was more than thirty years ago." He sat down in the chair adjacent to the couch. "I was twenty-five. I'd just started with my first bank. Scooey was three years younger than me. Decided that dirt and pots were a better career than investment banking." He chuckled. "Given the crash of 2010, he might have been right. You probably know I import artifacts in a small way. It's a business that hasn't treated me too badly."

"Were you close?"

He shrugged. "He was my brother. Sure. Yeah. I guess so."

"When did you first meet Jillian Chambers?"

He smiled thinly. His drawl became more pronounced. "Lookin' for an alternate theory to the crime, Ms. Winston-Beaufort? You're barking up the wrong stump, honey."

"I don't know what I'm looking for, Mr. Martin." She did her best to look blonde, young, and helpless. The first two always worked, at least.

"Well, now, I sure didn't kill her thirty years later for messing up my baby brother."

"She did? Mess up your baby brother?"

"I caught a glimpse of her on the news last night. They reran her arrest. Looks bad. You should have seen her years ago. She cleaned up pretty nice, Jillian did. Scooey fell hard for her."

"How did you meet her, Mr. Martin?"

"Call me Bullet. Most folks do. How did I meet Jillian? She made a statement at the hearing. The family had to ask the court to declare my brother dead. Did you know that? Hell of a thing. Shook my folks up big time. Anyhow— Jillian was the last one to see Scooey alive before he got swept off the ship."

"The *Indies Queen*."

"Might have been. It was a long time ago. I don't really recall."

Bree's heart rate picked up. It was his first mistake. She hoped it wasn't his last.

"Your ship, Mr. Martin. Or partly yours."

He froze, like a rattlesnake staring down the headlights of a car.

"The *New York Times* did a series of articles about the failure of the investment banks in 2009 and 2010. You were featured in couple of them, and one of them listed some of your assets. You own some shares in the *Indies Queen*. Your brother died on that ship."

"An unfortunate coincidence, Ms. Winston-Beaufort." The tips of his ears were bright red. A flush stained his cheekbones.

"Maybe." She took the little pine box out of her pocket, opened the lid, and held the Cross up. It caught the weak sunlight pouring in from the balcony doors. The silver glowed like a small moon in her hand. "Do you recognize this?"

"No."

His second mistake. Bree's heart rate went up another notch.

"And you are an internationally known collector of such things? It's an artifact—or perhaps the replica of an artifact—from the late 700s. Found near Istanbul. I'll tell you what, Mr. Martin. I think you involved your brother in smuggling artifacts from Allard Chambers's dig."

His eyes flicked to the balcony doors and back again. His hands curled slightly. He shifted his feet under him and cocked his head to one side, as if assessing how much resistance she could offer. "My import business is completely legal, Ms. Winston-Beaufort."

"Is it, now," she said pleasantly. "The customs people have a lot of questions about that."

"I have partners. What can I say? I'm not responsible for their behavior. I can assure you, if you're looking to implicate *me* in anything illegal, you're not going to find a thing." He drew his lips back in a predatory smile. "It may interest you to know that I completed the sale of my shares in the *Indies Queen* just this morning. I'm completely out of the business."

"That's bound to impress customs," Bree said cordially.

Hostility rose off Martin like smoke from a banked fire.

"And in addition to Prosper White, your partners are . . . Pardon me, *were* . . ." She flipped through her yellow pad, as if searching for a note that would remind her.

"Terrance Kennedy and Allard Chambers. Terry bought shares in the business way back and hasn't paid a lot of attention to it since. Allard supplied the relics, or did until the university pulled his funding for the digs." He cocked his forefinger at her, as if pointing a gun. "Allard's the one you want to take a good hard look at if you think any of those goods were illegal. Last I heard, he's in a world of hurt for cash."

Twenty minutes later, Bree opened the door to Reclaimables and found Allard Chambers kneeling on the carpet, sorting through a dilapidated set of cardboard boxes. She grabbed him by the shoulder with one hand and hauled him to his feet. She pointed to his desk at the back of the store. "Back there." Then, "Sit down, please."

Allard sat, and fumbled for his pipe.

"I've just seen Bullet Martin."

Allard became very still.

"He said you supplied Prosper White with relics from your digs. For the past thirty years."

Allard nodded quietly.

"He didn't admit it—but the customs agents are likely to find out anyway: you've been smuggling illegally obtained relics out of the Near East for thirty years."

"Yes," he said quietly.

"When Prosper refused to authenticate the Cross—you lost your job, your funding, your whole life."

"Yes."

Bree was calmer now. She shoved a stack of old newspapers off the chair at the side of his desk and sat down. "Tell me. The truth."

"I told you it should be me sitting in that jail cell, and not Jillian. She loved . . . beautiful things. Not surprising. She was so beautiful herself. A modern Theodora. There wasn't any money, in the early days. Not enough to buy her what she wanted. And by the time I realized that her demand for jewelry, clothes—all of that—was part of the mania, it was too late.

"So when Bullet came up with the idea to start selling relics on the side, it was easy to slip him a piece or two. They weren't from the digs, you know. Or, at least, not many of them. When you're dealing with the kind of poverty that plagues the countries over there, you can always find a black market.

"At any rate. You're right. Scooey was onboard the *Indies Queen* with a load for Prosper White when she killed him. I don't know why she pushed him overboard—lovers' quarrel, caprice, the fact that Scooey, of all people, would have refused to be part of a smuggling operation . . . Who knows? When she was in the manic stage, all bets were off.

"I was trapped then. And for the next thirty years, I gave Martin what he wanted. And White what he wanted so they wouldn't expose her.

"It could have gone on like that until I retired from the university. I was so close. But the funding got pulled. So Jillian came up with the idea to fake the Cross and get the university interested again. White was an idiot about relics." Chambers paused and knocked the bowl of his pipe against the rim of the wastebasket. The ash flew upward in the currents of air. "I flunked him for good reason, you know. Not just because he was screwing my poor mad wife at the time. Anyhow. He wasn't an idiot about the Cross. So he called it a fraud. And it was over. We were pushed out. Jillian couldn't handle it. She saw White's actions as a personal betrayal. And she brooded about it and brooded about it. When the announcement about White's engagement to your aunt appeared in the paper, it triggered something. Her obsession about White grew to include Cissy, too." He darted a shamefaced look at Bree. "I'm sorry about that. I truly am. I should have known something was up when she insisted on the demonstration at the press conference at the steps of the Frazier."

Bree held her hand up. "Stop. I don't want to hear anymore."

Twenty-four

"So, you guys are back on duty," Bree said, after she had gone over Allard's revelations with her angels. "The case against Jillian Chambers is directly linked to Schofield Martin's appeal."

"I believe so," Petru said.

"Is there some kind of document I need to get? Shall I trot on over to Goldstein?"

"It's not complicated," Ron said. "We'll start investigating. If we're barred from the case, we'll know right away."

"How?"

"We won't get anywhere. Honestly, Bree, it's simple."

Lavinia ran the feather duster over the leather couch near the fireplace—her fallback tactic was office cleaning when she wanted to be in on a meeting and there was no real reason for her to be there. "So Professor Chambers was in cahoots with White all along."

"Yes." Bree drummed her knuckles impatiently on the

top of Ron's desk. "No proof, though, no proof, no proof. If I could talk to the customs guys about the investigation into the *Indies Queen* and her cargo, I'd be a lot further ahead."

"That Martin's skipped town?"

Bree grimaced. "Yes. I called Hunter on the way back here from Reclaimables and told him about the connection between White and Martin. But temporal law depends on process, and there isn't any. No evidence. Just supposition. There was no way to keep Martin in Savannah short of running him over with a truck, and Hunter said no when I asked him."

"You were joking, of course," Petru said.

"Maybe not." Bree bit at her thumbnail in annoyance. "Anyhow, Martin's halfway to Havana by now, or wherever crooks go when where there's no extradition. Damn. I had to push it, didn't I? He and White and Allard were in the illegal import business together. White travelled all over, buying stuff. That was his job as a curator. What if White had threatened him somehow—maybe asked him for a bigger cut? I may have let a murderer run free. So much for our track record."

Petru and Ron exchanged looks. "Uh, Bree," Ron said. "You're still convinced of Dr. Chambers's innocence."

"I am."

"But . . ."

Bree held up her hand in warning. "No. I'm not going there. Everything Allard told me is unsubstantiated. I've got to get corroborating evidence. If I can nail Bullet Martin along the way, so much the better. He had quite a motive to kill White, you know. It'd impress the heck out of a jury. After all those years, White wrecks the source of a very lucrative business?"

Ron was busy at his computer. "I've got something."

"Really?" Bree looked over his shoulder. "What's that?"

"You thought the one piece of hard evidence directly related to the killing was the knife from Cissy's kitchen. I'm checking Martin's airline and car travel for the last couple of months. This screen is his gas receipts for his credit card; this screen is his airline tickets. He was in Savannah three times in the past month, including this visit. Did EB interview Lindy, the housekeeper, today?"

"I don't know. Yes, I think so. I'll give her a call."

"Let me check and see if she's logged anything into your Bay Street files. Yep—she did. Just the date and time, though. No notes as yet. I'll bet she hasn't had time to breathe, what with all the stuff you asked her to do today."

"I did load her up, didn't I," Bree said guiltily. "Just goes to show how much I depend on you all. Which is *not good*. Shouldn't I be able to do most of this myself?"

"So Martin's still in the picture," Ron pushed himself away from his computer and stretched out. "What next, Bree?"

"Alicia Kennedy. She's got to know more than she's telling me or the police. And we've got a lot of catch-up to create this file. The psych records for Jillian—all of them. A list of all the shareholders of the *Indies Queen*, and her shipping history from thirty years ago, just for verification of what Allard dumped on me an hour ago. Let's see who else may have been in on this." She grinned, suddenly. "We'll need the murder book of course, from the Savannah PD and all the forensic reports . . . My goodness, it's great to be operating with all the lights on."

Petru wriggled his shoulders, as if adjusting his aura, which made Lavinia break into uncharacteristic giggles. "Like a dancing bear," she said. "Oh, my. It's good to see you happy again, child."

Bree glanced at her watch. "It's five thirty. With luck,

I'll find Alicia at the Frazier. After that, I've got a quick meeting with Cordy Blackburn."

"Her office has called twice, to confirm the appointment," Petru said. "Mrs. Billingsley has forwarded the phones. The young man also wishes to know what you will bring for dinner. He is somewhat callow, I find."

Bree shrugged impatiently. "Sandwiches, I guess. Gavin sure thinks a lot about his stomach." She headed for the foyer, noticing that the angel at the end of the frieze still gestured thumbs-up.

She hoped it was a good augur.

———∞∞∞———

"I don't have to talk to you," Alicia Kennedy said sullenly. She slouched huddled in White's office chair. When Bree walked into the office, she'd been weeping into a blue cashmere sweater. She suspected it was White's.

"No, you don't." Bree pulled a straight chair away from the conference table and sat next to Alicia, so they were on a level. "But you want his murderer caught, don't you?"

"You *know* who murdered him! They arrested that crazy woman."

Bree shook her head. "My client? My client's innocent." Even if Jillian had stabbed Prosper White to death thirty yards from where they sat—she wasn't culpable. A lot of other people were. She let the pause drag on; then she said, "Did you kill him?"

The shock tactics worked. Alicia stared at her, eyes narrowed. "You're out of your mind."

"Do you know what an 'alternate theory of the case' is?"

"I don't have a freakin' clue."

"The defense comes up with a solution to the crime that doesn't involve the accused."

"You mean you point the finger at somebody else?" Her cheeks flushed. "You're going to go after me?"

"That depends."

"On whether I answer your questions?"

"On whether you tell me the truth."

Alicia rubbed her face with both hands. Her cheeks were smeared with mascara. She'd chewed off most of her lipstick. Bree leaned over and opened drawers in White's desk until she found a box of tissues. She set the box on Alicia's lap. "Here. You'll want to tidy your face up a bit. Now. Listen to me. How long have you known Prosper White?"

"Forever. He and my dad were friends from way back. They went to school together."

"Were they in business together?"

"Business? No. My father's the president of a division of a copier company. Mr. White was an artist."

"Your father wasn't interested in Roman antiquities?"

"That? Sure. He studied archeology before he went on to his MBA. He says the best time of his life was when he was out on a dig in graduate school."

"And that's where your interest springs from?"

"I suppose."

"So your connection to White is circumstance," Bree said, more to herself than to the girl in front of her. "What about Charles Martin?"

"Bullet?" Alicia dabbed carefully at her face with the tissues. "I came to work for Mr. White right out of Columbia. That was three years ago. They'd known each other a while, I guess. Bullet's a collector, and he's very well funded—very. Very well known. Mr. White was a genius at finding pieces for him."

"Did Bullet have a large collection?"

"Not huge," Alicia said. "Sometimes he didn't keep things very long."

"You mean he resold them?"

"I suppose so." She bent from the waist and began to scrabble in her purse.

Bree picked the purse up and set it on the desk, which forced Alicia to look at her. "At a profit?"

"Of course at a profit. Art can't exist without money. Art . . ." She chewed at her lower lip. "You wouldn't understand."

"I'm getting a clearer picture by the minute. Let me see if I've got this straight. Prosper White was a genius at finding undiscovered Roman relics."

"Not just Roman. Greek, Ottoman, Arabic, Turkish."

"All from areas where Allard Chambers conducted his excavations."

Alicia folded her arms against her chest.

"Who supplied White with the relics?"

No answer.

"Was it Allard Chambers?"

No answer.

"Why did White repudiate the Cross of Justinian?"

Alicia's chin went out. Her eyes glowed. "It was a fake."

"So they had a falling out?"

"Mr. White," Alicia said proudly, "had his standards."

Bree regarded her thoughtfully. Alicia had just confirmed a good portion of Allard White's statement. As for the late blossoming of Prosper White's integrity? You just never knew about people. Cissy would feel vindicated.

She caught sight of the desk clock on White's expensive desk. Almost seven o'clock, and Cordy Blackburn was not a patient woman. She let Alicia go and headed out for the Municipal Building at a rate that would have displeased the traffic cops, if there'd been any around to catch her.

Twenty-five

Bree arrived at Cordy's office twenty minutes late for her seven o'clock appointment.

"Where's dinner?" Gavin said.

"I beg your pardon?" Bree's hair had loosened around her ears. She tucked it back.

"You said you were going to bring dinner. I told Cordy not to worry about dinner, because you were bringing it along. I checked with your office. Twice."

"Sorry, Gavin. I completely forgot. It's been a busy day."

"So I hear."

"But a successful one, thank goodness."

"I wouldn't call letting a notorious criminal escape justice a howling success, would you?"

"Excuse me?" Bree said stiffly. Formality between office staff and assistants had relaxed a lot since her father's day, but Gavin was pushing it.

"Charles 'Bullet' Martin? Smuggler?"

"That," Bree said, "is a matter of conjecture. But I expect to prove it soon."

"Right." Cordy's office door was closed. Gavin pointed at it with his pen. "She's waiting. And she's hungry."

"I'll order pizza."

"We hate pizza."

Bree knocked on the office door before she edged it open. Cordy sat at her desk with a legal pad. She looked up, unsmiling, and gestured at the chair that faced her desk.

If there were an Olympic competition for Most Intimidating Assistant DA When Annoyed, Cordelia Blackburn would take the gold, hands down. She was in her midforties, a well-dressed, comfortably sized African-American woman with a pleasing contralto voice. When she wasn't mowing down defense lawyers, she spent a lot of time with community-service groups. An array of framed photographs over her bookcase showed Cordy with the current president, two past presidents, the governor of Georgia, and a T-shirted, baggy-pantsed basketball team from the projects down on Magnolia Street.

"Sit," Cordy said.

Bree sat.

Cordy put her elbow on her desk and leaned forward, her chin in one hand. She held a heavy buff piece of stationary in the other. "You know what I have here in front of me?"

"I assume that's a rhetorical question? No? It looks like a letter."

"A copy of a letter to the Georgia State Bar Association Grievance Committee. It's about you. The allegation is improper behavior in regard to your clients Allard and Jillian Chambers. The complainant requests immediate action on the part of the committee. You understand the Grievance Committee's powers, do you not? They can issue a Letter of Censure. They can recommend that you be disbarred. They can, and will, ruin your life." She sat back in her chair, her gaze level.

"Barlow and Caldecott," Bree said.

Cordy didn't say anything.

She thought a minute. That buff stationary was familiar. She came to a conclusion that was improbable, but not impossible. "Not Marbury, Stubblefield?"

Cordy blinked.

Marbury, Stubblefield made more sense. They loved trouble—the more public, the better. She doubted that Caldecott wanted any kind of visibility in the local bar association. She frowned. "You're not on the Grievance Committee, Cordy. How did you get a copy of the letter?" Letters like this one were never revealed to sources outside the committee.

"It was in the afternoon mail." She held the envelope up. "It's addressed right—the mail room said it'd been 'misdirected.' Gavin didn't pay attention to the addressee—just opened it up. Part of his job is to read and file mail."

That went some way toward explaining Gavin's cheeky behavior. He thought she was scum.

"I should send the letter on to the committee, Bree. But somebody wanted me to see it before the donkey poop hit the fan. I'm making a couple of guesses as to why."

"You could have sent it on without talking to me, first. I'm glad you didn't."

"That's the point, isn't it? John Stubblefield's a sneaky son of a gun. My guess is he wants me to suggest you send Jillian Chambers to somebody else. What do you want to bet that if you drop her, Stubblefield's going to withdraw the letter?"

"He can send a boatload of letters," Bree said crossly.

"There's nothing improper about my representing Jillian Chambers."

"No conflict of interest?"

"If you're talking about the lawsuit against Prosper White's estate, Allard Chambers fired the lawyers handling it, then dropped the suit altogether."

"You've got a paper trail documenting that, of course."

"Not exactly. An e-mail from Caldecott acknowledging Chambers's request for the file. And Allard Chambers's verbal promise to drop the claim for damages against White's estate. That's about it."

Cordy didn't say anything. She didn't need to.

"I'm not dropping Jillian Chambers, Cordy."

"You're new at litigation, Bree. This is a high-profile case. You sure you have the chops to take it on?"

"Lewis McCallen's on the farm team, if I need him."

"Is that a fact." Cordy drummed her fingers on the desktop. "Maybe you ought to move him on to the majors. Like, right now."

"She's innocent of premeditated murder. I'm sure I can prove it."

"On what grounds?" Cordy said, with a lack of curiosity Bree didn't believe for a minute. "That she didn't do it and somebody else did? Maybe Charles Martin? That she did it, but there are mitigating circumstances? That she's nuttier than my grandma's Christmas fruitcake?"

Bree grinned at her. "Nice try. But I'll save my plea for the arraignment."

"The murder's been playing on the six o'clock news for two days straight. You know what I notice most about those film clips? That you're right in the middle of the action. You planning on calling yourself as a witness?"

"I assume that's another rhetorical question."

"I asked you here so I could go over your statement to the cops. I asked you here as a witness for the Prosecution." Cordy's full lips thinned. "I take it you're claiming privilege?"

"The suspect's my client. You know you can't compel me to testify."

"Fine. Go ahead. Jump off that cliff." Cordy picked up the letter to the Grievance Committee, tore it in half, and let it fall into the wastebasket. "Be interesting to see if Stubblefield calls wondering what happened to his misdirected letter. The man's got the balls of a buffalo." She frowned. "It's not going to keep him from sending it again and dropping it off at the right address this time. Expect a lot of sympathy from me when the papers start smearing your name from here to Topeka. You're going to need it. Now. We're coming to the third reason I'm sitting here with you when I should be home eating my dinner. Charles Martin."

"Dinner," Bree said guiltily. "Let me call out for something."

"I already did," Gavin said as he came into the room. He held a large paper sack in one hand and a large bottle of Coca-Cola in the other. "Not pizza. Shrimp po'boys from Savannah Seafood." He set the bag on the credenza, unwrapped the sandwiches, and set them on paper plates. "I got extra coleslaw and some of that cheesecake brownie that you like, Boss."

He set Cordy's plate down in front of her. He held the second plate out of Bree's reach. "That'll be forty-five dollars, please."

Bree took her emergency cash out of her suit-coat pocket and handed him fifty dollars.

"Do you need change?"

Cordy rapped her knuckles on the desk. "What are you doing, Gavin, training for the wait staff at 700? It's late. Go on home. I'll see you in the morning." She shook her head as the door closed behind her assistant. "How mad would you be if I made Mrs. Billingsley an offer she couldn't refuse?"

"Pretty mad."

"Guess I won't risk it, then." She took a large bite out of her sandwich. "How hard should I be trying to get Charles Martin back here? You think he had something to do with White's death?"

"Do you have the forensics back on the blood spatter pattern on his coat?"

"Heck, no. It'll be weeks." She glanced at Bree sidelong. "Your daddy paid to have a private lab do the tests on Ms. Carmichael's coat. They verified the fingerprints on the knife, too. Liberty and justice for all. The Winston-Beaufort motto. We poor folks who labor for the state have to wait while the underfunded state lab takes its own sweet time."

"Don't needle me, Cordy."

"Why not?"

"No special reason, I guess. Maybe because we mean well?"

Her expression softened. "Yes, you mean well. Tell me about Charles Martin."

"You know what I know to be fact; he owns shares in a ship that was the scene of a murder thirty-odd years ago in Istanbul. The victim was his younger brother, Schofield."

"No statute of limitations on murder. But what kind of treaties do we have with Turkey? Do I care? And even if I do, do I want to spend Gavin's valuable time chasing down a thirty-year-old murder case? Unless Martin killed his brother."

"No. He didn't."

"Do you know who did?"

Bree didn't say anything.

"So give me another reason to chase Martin."

"I may be able to prove that he's involved in the illegal shipment of antiquities."

"Not my jurisdiction."

"I'm almost certain he contributed to White's death."

"How?" Cordy demanded. "I need how, why, and when."

Bree rolled up the leftovers of her sandwich in her paper plate and tossed the remains on top of the letter to the Grievance Committee. "I'm doing my best to find out." She picked up her coat. "And when I do, you'll be among the first to know."

Twenty-six

It was late. She didn't realize how long the meeting with Cordy must have lasted until she walked outside the Municipal Building and headed toward her car. The sky overhead was pallid with veiled stars and a washed-out moon. The lights from the Municipal Building were dimmer than usual. She wondered briefly if the city was in the middle of one of its periodic cost-cutting measures.

She looked at her watch; it couldn't be six o'clock. The sun set at half-past six, and it was as dark as a tomb beyond the car. The second hand was fixed at twelve. She shook the watch. The hand didn't move.

She flipped her cell phone open. No bars in the little window. "Murphy's law, Sasha. Both batteries out," and of course Sasha wasn't there. He was at home, with Antonia, and she would be, too, very soon.

She'd parked under a streetlight at the foot of an alley

off Court Street. The streetlight was dimmed to a low, ugly orange. Her car was barely visible.

And there was something—someone—slouched against the hood.

Bree slowed down, and called warily, "Who's there?"

"Ms. Winston-Beaufort."

"Is that you, Caldecott?"

He stepped forward into the insufficient glow. "A word, if you please, Ms. Winston-Beaufort."

"I've got more than a few words to exchange with you, Mr. Caldecott." She opened the driver's door and tossed her tote inside. She was very aware of the pine box in her suit-coat pocket.

He smirked. "How was your meeting with Ms. Blackburn?"

"Very informative."

"Stealing clients, Ms. Winston-Beaufort, is an ugly practice."

"But not illegal," Bree said pleasantly.

He hissed, like a snake. "So you admit to stealing my cases."

"I admit nothing of the kind." She tapped his chest with her forefinger. He was spongy, like fungus. "Let's be direct about this, Caldecott. Allard Chambers fired you, hired me, and isn't interested in pursuing any action against the estate of Prosper White, which, I might add, is an estate no longer of interest to you, either, or it won't be as soon as we get you dismissed at coexecutor. You win some, you lose some, Mr. Caldecott. My advice to you is to man up."

He bared his pointed teeth, and for a moment, Bree was tempted to step back. His breath was fetid, and the texture of his skin repellant. Instead, she stepped forward, forcing him against the front bumper. He slid away and stood in the half darkness of the alley. Only his eyes were visible, the poisonous yellow with black, vertical pupils increasing his resemblance to a snake.

"Mr. Barlow is not happy."

"Too bad for Barlow."

Caldecott shot a nervous glance over his shoulder. Bree forced herself to stand, relaxed, one hip propped against her car.

"Mr. Barlow was not happy with my partner, either."

A brief vision of Beazley's gutted body flashed across her mind.

"Mr. Barlow is willing to let bygones be bygones. He is"—Caldecott slid a little nearer—"a merciful one, in his way." He held out his hand. "The Cross. Which does not belong to you. All he asks is the Cross."

"No dice."

Caldecott hunched over, as if he'd been kicked. "You will regret this, Ms. Winston-Beaufort."

"Perhaps, Mr. Caldecott." She reopened the car door, then stopped, halfway in. "I know you're not going to tell, me, but I have to ask. What kind of hold do you have over Stubblefield, anyway?"

"The Cross!" Caldecott howled. "You must give me the Cross!" He seemed, suddenly, to shrink. Or the space in the alley behind him had grown. Bree's breath caught in her chest, and she slid into the driver's seat, locked the door, and fired the engine.

She pulled away from the curb, and didn't look back.

She turned left onto Montgomery to make the short drive home, only half aware of the rising noise behind her.

It was big. Vast. A low, rumbling noise that swallowed

the sounds of her breathing and rose around her like a tide of water. It carried the dark. It was the dark. And it *breathed* with the slow, steady pulse of a muffled drum.

The dark light cupped the car, crawled over the hood, washed against the windshield, covered the side doors.

She braked.

She couldn't see where she was going.

She stopped.

The sudden silence was absolute.

Wherever she was, she wasn't on Montgomery.

Something tapped at the driver's window. Light taps. Polite, but inexorable.

Let me in.

Was that a hand pressed flat against the window?

Tap. Tap. Tap.

Let me in.

There was a shape behind the hand. So large that it blotted out what remained of the shattered moon. A smear of fiery orange red slashed across the head. The place where the eyes would be. The door rattled, as if battered by a huge wind. Bree grabbed the door handle and felt a force, immense, implacable, pulling from the other side.

She held on, her palms slick with fear, and felt the handle slip. She braced her feet against the floorboards and held on, with a grip so strong the metal bent, twisted, and began to rip away.

The door bulged out with a shriek of metal rending.

A crash of silver light split the darkness outside, and for a moment, the door steadied in her hands. Behind her, around her, in front of her, three columns of familiar color danced, spun and coalesced:

"I, Matriel."

"I, Rashiel."

"I, Dara."

Violet.

Green.

Blue.

The car door wrenched open, and they spilled out onto a plain of fire.

Petru and Ron stood at her right and left. Lavinia stood in front of her, blocking the terror that grappled with Gabriel. This wasn't her universe. This was a place she had never been before. The strikes of silver reminded her of lightning, but of a kind never seen by mortals. And the terror . . .

"The nephiliam," Ron said.

The terror had fire and worse at its command.

"He is lost," Petru said. "Our Gabriel."

"It will come for it," Ron said.

And to her, it seemed that this was an evil, terrible truth. The brilliant silver dimmed to metal gray. The tidal waves of burning burst mountain-high and began rolling toward them, swallowing the distance, eating it.

Lavinia turned and faced her. "The key, child. Give me the key."

"No," Ron said. "Not you. I'll go."

"Perhaps it will take all of us. If so . . ." Petru said. He touched Bree's shoulder, and laid his cheek briefly against hers.

"It's for me." Lavinia held out her fragile arm, her hand out, palm up. "Come, child. There isn't much time."

Bree fumbled the Cross from her pocket, her hands still slick with fear.

"Not that." The lightest of touches at her throat. "The key."

She slipped the scales of justice free and held them. It

was all she had of Leah, and for a moment, she hesitated, unwilling to let go.

The angels stood there, waiting.

Bree dropped the charm into Lavinia's hand. She brought it to her mouth and swallowed it.

For a long, aching moment, nothing happened.

Lavinia dissolved into a feather of brilliance like a peacock's wing.

Then, it shrieked. The fire roared into a hideous shape and thrashed against the heavens, half-man, half-demon, driven by a pair of sulphurous wings. It shrieked again. The sound was so high, so loud, so rage-filled that Bree clapped her hands over her ears in agony. The hate in the voice brought her to her knees. The stink of evil choked her.

The fire collapsed into itself. For a long, terror-filled moment, there was silence so crushing Bree couldn't breathe.

A ferocious wind of dark rushed at them, rushed through the silver light, scattering the shards into uncounted pieces, rushed over them and barreled into nothing.

Beneath her feet, a mighty gate clanged shut.

It was the last thing she heard for a long, dark time.

———

"Hey," Antonia said. "You awake? Bree?"

Bree swam out of sleep. She lay flat on her back, staring up at the bedroom ceiling.

"It's after ten," Antonia said. "I started to get worried. You've never gotten up this late in your life. And you fell asleep in your clothes."

Bree sat up. She wore the clothes she had worn the day before. Her silk T-shirt. Her light wool trousers. Her suit coat lay crumpled on the floor. Her hand flew to her neck. The scales of justice were gone.

"Did you get mugged or something? Come on, Sister. Say something."

"What time is it?"

"I just told you, it's after ten."

"What day is it?"

"What *day* is it? It's Friday." Antonia grabbed her hands and pulled her forward to the edge of the bed. "Now I'm starting to get seriously worried. I'm going to call Mamma."

"Don't do that." She stood up. "What time did I get home?"

"I don't know. I got home about one, and you were in bed already, if that's any help. What—did you go out and get drunk with Hunter or something?"

"No." She shoved Antonia's hand away. "Don't tug at me." She stumbled across the room and looked at herself in the bureau mirror. Her hair hung in tangles around her face. The flesh beneath her eyes looked bruised. The place beneath her heart felt hollow.

"Did . . . Did you and Hunter break up, or something? Bree! You look so sad."

"I've got to get to the office."

"EB will be glad to hear that. She's called twice, wanting to know where you were, but I didn't want to wake you up."

"I mean the Angelus office."

"Shall I make you some cereal or something?"

It was as if Antonia hadn't heard her.

"Where's Sasha?"

"In the living room. So, there isn't any yogurt left because I ate most of it. All of it, actually, but I can run out and get you some."

"No. No." Bree knelt and searched under her bed for her shoes. "I've got to get going."

"Not like that, Bree. You're a mess."

She worked her feet into her shoes on the fly, grabbing

her coat and her purse from the end of the bed where she *must* have put them when she got in last night, but she didn't remember. She went into the living room, where Sasha lay by the fireplace. He raised his head at her approach. Bree went on her knees beside him.

"Lavinia," she whispered. "Is Lavinia all right?"

He didn't answer, but he followed her out the door, and across Bay, and down Mulberry to Angelus Street, and was with her when she unlocked the door to the little house with painfully slow fingers.

The painted angel on the wall next to him held her hands cupped over her eyes. Crystal tears dropped between her fingers.

She was halfway up the stairs and on the landing to the second story before Professor Cianquino's voice called to her.

"Bree. Come down."

She went to the head of the short flight to the first floor and looked down. Armand was in his wheelchair, a blanket folded over his shriveled legs.

"She's gone," he said. "Come down and I will tell you how it happened. And why."

Armand pivoted the wheelchair with sudden, fluid grace and disappeared into the living room. Bree followed him with leaden steps.

Twenty-seven

"Lavinia became the key." Armand had steered the wheelchair to Lavinia's accustomed corner in the conference room. Ron sat at the table. Petru stood looking out the window at the graveyard beyond, his hands clasped behind his back. "Her light, her spirit, all of the energy that was Lavinia is now the key to the eighth gate. It was a sacrifice that the nephiliam couldn't, wouldn't make. Lavinia could, and did. She knew when she joined the Company that it could come to this. We all did."

"And the nephiliam?" Bree asked. She stood at the doorway, unwilling to come in.

"Barlow," Ron said. "That was the name of its presence here."

"What happened to it?"

"Gone back to where it came from, I hope." He and Petru looked at each other, and then glanced away. "Then again, maybe not."

"Wherever it is, the key is out of its grasp now," Petru turned his attention back to the cemetery outside the window. "Of that, at least, Lavinia made certain."

"What about Lavinia?" Bree's throat was tight. She bit her lip, hard. The tears came anyway.

"Alive in memory," Armand said. "She is part of the eternal now."

Petru spoke. "Come and see this."

Bree stepped into the room. Ron put his arm around her waist, and together they joined Petru and looked outside.

Lavinia's grave stood in the middle of the cemetery, a glory of spring in the middle of Savannah's winter. A marble column as tall as Bree served as the base for a statue of an angel. The figure was so like her friend that Bree half expected it to move. The angel stood with its face upturned to the sky, wings folded closely about its slender form.

A riot of flowers surrounded the base of the column. Creamy gardenias, white roses tipped with pink, and most evocative of all, a spread of lavender in full bloom.

"They will always bloom, these flowers," Armand said. "But they will need attention. It will help your grief, to be among the scents and colors of her garden. It is a reminder, too, that among the desolation of this place, where the bones of wicked men and women lie, there are forces that can prevail."

"I expected her to go," Bree said. "But not this way. Not this soon. I didn't get to say good-bye."

"We'll miss her," Ron tightened his arm around her. "We'll miss her terribly. But she was fading; we knew that. She was wearing out her mortal body, and she was moving on."

"It is a chance not given to many, to defeat a nephiliam," Petru said. "Gabriel himself was gravely depleted. If she had not come forward as she did, he would have been transformed forever, too. As it is, it will be some time before we see him again. And Lavinia? She had a sea of love in her." He looked down, to keep them from seeing his tears.

"An ocean," Ron murmured. "I'll tend the garden, Armand. We all will. We'll sit in the sunshine and think of her. We'll put up a bench."

Bree smiled at that, then drew the backs of her hands underneath her eyes, as if she could push the tears back. "Maybe we can have her tea out there. It's an oasis in the middle of all that other dreadful stuff."

"Hope in the middle of despair," Armand said. He rolled his wheelchair to the conference room door. "It's done. I will leave you now. There is work to do. You still have a case to appeal, Bree. Schofield Martin and Jillian Chambers both require that grief and your work can coexist. Lavinia knows that better than anyone. "

She started forward. "You're not staying?"

"I rarely leave Rosemont, as you know. It's time for me to get back."

"But I thought . . . I hoped . . . That is, the Company is one less now."

"Is it?"

Lavinia knows. Not "knew." So she did live on, just not in the form that they could see? Bree took a breath to ask the question.

Armand was gone.

"I have collected some interesting data on the *Indies Queen*," Petru said.

Bree turned around. Petru and Ron were in their accustomed seats at the table. Ron had his iPad out. A stack of files sat in front of Petru. She walked to the window and stared at Lavinia's tomb. The vivid colors of the flowers blazed in the dreariness of the cemetery. The lavender seemed brighter than before.

"I've got the autopsy results," Ron said. "The forensics team videotaped the crime scene, too. We should be able to get some good leads from that. As soon as you're ready, Bree."

"Give me a minute, will you?"

She didn't wait for them to respond, but walked out of the room and on through the little house to the foot of the stairs. She looked up, half-hoping that she would hear the familiar soft clatter in the rooms above, the sounds that meant Lavinia was taking care of her small charges.

There was no sound. But the scent of lavender was strong.

Bree turned to the brightly painted cavalcade of angels on the wall. The last angel, the one with the silver hair, was smiling, and she cupped a sheaf of Madonna lilies in her hands.

Bree touched the wall.

The angel was warm to her fingertips.

———∞———

Bree sat at the head of the table some time later. She pulled a yellow pad out of her tote. "So we're assuming that Schofield Martin's death is linked to White's?"

Petru adjusted his glasses. "The evidence seems to be accruing quickly."

"Because these cases revolve around the Cross? We still have the Cross." She took the pine box from her pocket and opened it. Such a small and insignificant thing to have caused so much trouble.

"Leah did not have the opportunity given to Lavinia—

the chance to return the key to the gate before she died," Petru said. "That is perhaps why she placed the energy of the key into the talisman she left to you, Bree. To hide it. The cross drew the attention of all who knew what it was— like Barlow—and those who suspected what it was, like Chambers."

"Which one is this?" Bree asked. "The real one or the fraud? Leah had the real one, and she put the energy from the Cross into the charm she left to me. So the original Cross did what? Disappear? Fall apart? End up in another museum somewhere? Or is this the original after all?"

"Jillian made a fake one, to get the funding back from the university," Ron said. "Or did she?"

"I do not know," Petru said. "There is a fifty-fifty chance the Cross you hold is either. Where did the true artifact go after Leah made the talisman key? It was not much of a question for Barlow and his ilk. Whether the Cross dated from the 5th century or from this one, it was a cross in the form of this one that they were after. For them, the Cross is now moot. There is an expression which covers this, I believe. Leah pulled a fast one on Barlow. The key has been returned to the gate."

"Okay," Bree said cautiously. "So we can forget about the nephiliam."

"For now," Ron said. "You can never forget about a nephiliam."

"It killed Beazley. Caldecott said as much."

"We're lucky it didn't kill you," Ron said bluntly.

Bree's eyelids felt sandy. Her head ached. She suddenly realized she needed a shower. "We need coffee. Tea. Something. Or at least I do."

"I'll get it." Ron bounced up and left the room.

She stared down at her yellow pad, which was frustratingly blank. "If the Cross is the key to both murders, Martin's of thirty years ago, and White's today, we have to figure out who had it, and when. First, Chambers uncovers it on the dig, thirty years ago." She wrote that down. "Then, Jillian Chambers takes it. Then Leah takes it. My mother sees it here in Savannah just before I'm born. So Leah has it thirty years ago. At some point, the energy in the Cross passes to the necklace Leah left me. And the Cross is . . ."

"Lost," Petru said gloomily. "The Cross that Chambers gave White for authentication was indeed a fake. But Leah would not have mistaken the real one. It is not a matter of importance now. I have some interesting facts that may be. I would prefer to concentrate on that."

Ron set the tea tray down in front of her. She poured for each of them and then took a cup for herself. It wasn't at all like Lavinia's. She pinched her knee, hard, to regain control, and said, "Okay. Let's have a look."

"Me first." Ron handed her a printout. "I looked into the whereabouts of all the suspects for the last three weeks. There's a timeline for Dr. Chambers, Professor Chambers, Bullet Martin, Alicia Kennedy, and Lloyd Dumphey." He wrinkled his nose fastidiously. "There's parts of Dumphey's time line that are truly revolting."

Petru picked up the stack of folders and began to lay them in a neat row down the table length. "There is much of interest here, too." He tugged a sheet of paper from a folder and laid it in front of Bree. "Professor Chambers's personal balance sheet."

"Good grief," Bree said after a moment. "He's loaded."

"*Was* loaded," Petru corrected. "He lost what you would call a bundle in the crash of 2009 and 2010."

"A lot of people did," Bree murmured.

"Now, this," Petru said, "is a copy of the partnership

agreement between the shareholders in the *Indies Queen*. May I draw your attention to the paragraph marked in yellow highlighter."

Bree read it.

"Well," she said, "this changes everything."

She jumped up. "I have to talk to Chambers again. I'll do it at the Bay Street office, of course. I'll see you all later, shall I?"

Sasha nudged at her knee. She looked down at him and fondled his ears.

Shower first?

<hr />

"You're late," EB said disapprovingly, nearly forty-five minutes later. "I thought you wanted to see Allard Chambers ASAP."

"I did. I do. I'm sorry."

"He'll be here in another twenty minutes." EB cocked her head. "You look like something happened."

"It has." She drew the visitor's chair up to EB's desk. "You saw Lindy yesterday? About who had access to Cissy's kitchen?"

"I did. Her last name's Hawthorne, by the way."

"I should have known that. I've known her for years."

"Uh-huh."

Thankfully, EB didn't make the point she should have; most people didn't inquire closely into the names of the servants. "I taped it, like you said I should. Then last night, I transcribed the tape."

Bree looked at her assistant more closely. There were dark rings under her eyes. "I'm sorry. You put in a long day yesterday."

"It's excitin' trackin' down a murderer." EB tapped the

printed sheets into a neat pile and handed them to Bree. "I did a summary. It's at the top."

> *Witness stated that boning knife is one of a set that's been in her kitchen since she started work there some twenty years ago. She send them out regular to be sharpened at Collard's Sharpening Services down by Liberty Street. She noticed boning knife was missing when she went to carve a turkey for a buffet party on February 10. It was a Valentine's Day theme to celebrate Miss Cissy's marrying that Prosper White. Guest list attached. Suspects at party included that Alicia Kennedy. The time before that she remembered using the boning knife was about three days before when Miss Cissy asked for chicken on account of she was dieting. So for the three days between the chicken and the turkey, Miss Cissy had lots of callers, including Mr. White, Ms. Kennedy, and Professor Chambers, who came to try and get money from Miss Cissy but didn't get any.*

"So we have a three-day window," Bree said. "Very helpful, EB. Now look at this." She pulled out Ron's account of Jillian's whereabouts for the past two weeks.

"She was on a church retreat with those City of Light folks when the knife went missin'."

"She sure was. And this is the shareholder agreement for ownership in the *Indies Queen*. The sale of the ship was completed this morning, according to Bullet Martin. Look who inherits if Prosper White is dead."

EB read it twice. She sat back, her eyes large, her lips pressed tight. "So. What are we going to do now?"

The doorknob rattled, and Allard Chambers stepped in.

"Ms. Winston-Beaufort. Mrs. Billingsley." He let the door close behind him and advanced tentatively into the room. "I'm grateful that we're talking this morning. I've come to a decision about Jillian." He indicated the visitor's chair. "May I sit down?"

"Suit yourself," EB said.

"Thank you." He sat. He smiled. "I believe you're right. About the insanity defense. You see I . . ." He took a deep breath, and then blurted, "She did it. She stabbed him. I know that spouses can't testify against one another, and that I won't be called upon to say it in court. But you need to know. I saw her. I tried to stop her. I forced the knife from her hand and threw it away. All I could think about was how to get her out of there. So yes. I've made up my mind. I want you to plead her guilty. The only hope we have is that the state of Georgia is merciful and will keep her safe from harming herself and others."

EB swung around in her chair and glared at him.

Bree folded her arms and leaned against EB's desk. "I know about your part ownership of the *Indies Queen*. And I know that the shares revert to the rest of the owners when a shareholder dies."

For a moment, the mask dropped from Chambers's face. The amiable expression was gone. His eyes narrowed to glittering blue slits. Then he smiled engagingly. "I can explain."

"Can you? I don't know that I need to know much more than I already do. For years, you've been using your trips abroad to sell illegal antiquities on the black market. You used the *Indies Queen* to transport them to Bullet Martin. Martin had them authenticated by Prosper White. White sold them back to you on the open market. You resold them to collectors. It's ingenious, really. An antiquities-laundering scheme, rather than a money-laundering scheme. You did this for your wife. Your poor, mad wife."

"Yes. Yes. You understand. I was a victim here."

"Sure. It could be exculpatory when it comes to motive. That's a defense I might use if I were defending you for White's murder, for example."

His shoulders relaxed a bit. "So, let's assume that you're right. And I'm not admitting a thing. After all, Jillian killed White."

"Jillian didn't do it."

"Both of us appreciate your passion as an advocate, Ms. Winston-Beaufort. But you were the first to point out how the hard evidence stacks up. She was at the scene. Her fingerprints were on the knife."

"How'd she get that knife?' EB interrupted. "We'd like to know."

Chambers pursed his lips. "I don't keep tabs on her every minute. She has a real vendetta against your aunt. You saw that for yourself. She's a clever woman. I suppose she saw the opportunity to slip in the back way to your aunt's kitchen and find a suitable weapon."

"You'll need to explain how the murder weapon went missing at a time when your wife was on a three-day retreat with the City of Light churchgoers, too." Bree leaned forward. "You'll need to explain how she knew the layout of the kitchen. She had no idea where Cissy lived."

"I'm sure she looked it up in the directory."

"Cissy's listed under 'Smallwood.'"

He frowned, puzzled. "Smallwood?"

"Her ex-husband's name."

"Then she must have asked somebody."

"Who?"

"Who knows?" He spread his arms in a conciliatory gesture. "Look. I hate to do this. I really do. But she killed him. I saw her do it. If you look at the footage on Channel 5, you can see that I didn't leave my wife's side for a minute. I was there when she slipped the knife into him. I was shocked, of course. I picked it up . . ."

"Your fingerprints weren't on it."

"I mean I kicked it away. I was scared senseless that she was going to get arrested right then and there. And if I'm asked in court if that's what I witnessed, I will have to tell the truth."

EB made a noise of disgust.

"You asked me to think about the best plea for my wife. I've thought about it. I came here this morning to tell you my decision. You wanted to know: What is best for Jillian?" His gaze was candid and open. His tone was earnest. Bree studied her yellow pad so she wouldn't have to look at him. "Guilty by reason of insanity. It's the only way to go."

"Maybe." Bree stood still and considered her options. Chambers crossed his legs and gazed at the wall over Bree's head with a sorrowful expression. EB took a couple of deep breaths, then clamped her teeth firmly on her lower lip.

Bree smiled at him. "I'll tell you what, Mr. Chambers. I'm going to have to turn you over to another firm."

"Jillian trusts you," he said. "She'll be sorry to hear that."

"Oh, no. Not Jillian. Just you. I'll be representing your wife. We'll be entering a plea of not guilty. I'll be presenting an alternate theory of the case. Would you like to know what it is?"

"Since I witnessed her kill Prosper White, I can't imagine what it is."

"I know you did it. And I'm going to prove to a jury that you did it."

He paled a little. He breathed a little faster. Otherwise he didn't move, just sat there in that same, confident pose.

"I have just the advocate for you, too. Mr. Barlow, downstairs. When we first met, you said you like lawyers who can stand a lot of heat? He's going to suit you just fine. I think if you call on him right now, he won't ask for much of a retainer." She pulled the pine box with the Cross in it out of her pocket.

Fifty-fifty, Petru had said.

"Just give him this."

He frowned. "That's a fake."

"Does Mr. Barlow know that?"

He grinned and winked at her. "Gotcha."

───※───

"I don't believe it," EB said, after Chambers slammed out the door. "I mean the man practically confessed he did it and you let him walk right out the door!"

"There's no hard evidence against him, EB."

"It'll be his word against hers. He's a big professor. She's a poor crazy woman. What kind of jury is going to believe her over him? We got ourselves a real loser of case, here."

"Exactly," Bree said. "You've hit the nail on the head."

Mr. Barlow isn't happy.

"I don't think he's going to have to worry about a trial, EB. Not in this lifetime, at any rate."

Twenty-eight

Bree called the Sampson Clinic to set up an interview with Jillian Chambers and her therapist. Then she spent the rest of the morning bringing EB up to speed on the matter of the People of the State of Georgia v. Jillian Knoles Chambers. She was grateful for two things: the offer from her father to support the process from his law firm in Raleigh and EB's brains.

"So we're not going to try the case at all?"

"I hope not. We're going to file a motion to have her declared non compos mentis. Roughly translated from the Latin, it means not in her right mind. I don't believe at this point that she's capable of understanding the charges against her. Then we're going to ask that I be appointed her guardian. That's the second motion. I do not want Chambers anywhere near the defense."

EB shook her head slowly, "How that man can think of testifyin' against his own wife, I do not know."

"He can't. She has spousal privilege. But there's nothing to stop him from poisoning the Prosecution. We've got to move fast, EB."

EB looked at the items she'd listed neatly on her steno pad. "Then we file a third motion—"

"To dismiss the charges altogether. And to do that, I have to prove the case against Chambers."

"So we don't go to trial."

"Not if we have a humane, compassionate, smart judge."

"Lot of those around, are there?"

"I hope so." Bree sighed. "I hope so."

EB looked at her watch. "'Bout time you got on down to the Sampson Clinic."

"And you're comfortable with calling my father's paralegal and getting him to e-mail all correct templates for the motions?"

"He was real helpful with the letters asking for all those documents." EB sighed happily. "I'll tell you something, girl. This beats scrubbing toilets for a living by a country mile."

⚬⚬⚬⚬

The Sampson Clinic for the Rehabilitation of Nervous Disorders was tucked on an unnamed side street off Washington Square. It was a square, three-story concrete-block building surrounded by an eight-foot wrought iron fence. The first floor was almost totally concealed from view by dense bushes. Bree showed her ABA card and her driver's license at the guard gate and parked her car in the half-filled lot around back. She gave her card to a second guard inside the glass double doors at the entrance and was left to wait in a small, thickly carpeted foyer with one barred window and a small love seat in the corner. Classical music drifted through speakers in the ceiling. It was Bach—something from *The Well-Tempered Clavier*. Its soft, clean intricacies were very soothing.

A door in the wall opposite the love seat opened partway. A pleasant-faced, middle-aged woman came in. She wore a white lab coat over a dark navy pantsuit. A cluster of keys was chained to her belt. The name tag around her neck read DR. SANDRA PHILLIPS.

"Ms. Winston-Beaufort?" She extended her hand. "I'm Sandy Phillips."

"And I'm Bree."

"You're here to see our patient?"

"Jillian Chambers, yes. How is she doing?"

"As well as can be expected."

Bree followed Phillips through the door down a long corridor floored with terrazzo tile. The walls were painted a thick, glossy beige. Indifferent artwork had been placed at intervals along the walls. The frames were nailed in place. The lighting was subdued and indirect. There were no windows. Bree hoped none of the patients suffered from claustrophobia.

"In here." Dr. Phillips stopped at a metal door with a small window inset at eye-level and selected a key from the bunch at her waist. She opened the door and stepped back. "I'll be with you throughout the interview. We don't take violent cases here. It's primarily the ones on suicide watch or prisoners in danger of self-mutilation."

"That's very sad."

Dr. Phillips looked surprised. "I suppose it is."

Bree looked inside the room. Jillian wore a pink hospital gown over a denim skirt. Her hair had been washed and rebraided. Her Doc Martens had been removed and replaced with paper slippers. She was shackled to a metal table. The chains ran between her ankles and up to her wrists. The chair she sat in was bolted to the floor. There was a chair on the opposite side of the table. That was bolted to the floor, too. Her thin fingers picked restlessly at her cheek.

"The chains," Bree said. "Are they really necessary?"

"Procedure," Phillips said briskly. "Now, we have forty-five minutes. Shall we get started?"

"I'd like to get a preliminary statement from her. And I'd prefer to be alone with her." Dr. Phillips opened her mouth to protest. "Not for evidentiary use. Just so I can get a handle on how to conduct her defense. What kind of medications is she on?"

"Are you familiar with psychotropic drugs?"

"Not really. But I intend to be."

"I'll keep to layman's terms, then. She's on medication for depression secondary to bipolar syndrome. It takes a while for that to kick in—as long as three to six weeks. She's on a tranquilizer, because of her anxiety. We haven't seen any evidence of full-blown psychosis yet, but the depression is so significant that she's not really oriented to time and place. And there's a mild dissociative state, which has resulted in moderate cognitive impairment."

"Layman's terms?" Bree said.

Dr. Phillips had a thin smile. "I'll give you some of the literature we hand out to families of prisoners."

"That would be a great help. And Dr. Phillips? I'd like to talk to her alone, if I may."

"I don't think . . ."

"I'm her attorney. You've got a preliminary diagnosis but not a definitive one. I want to be absolutely certain of attorney-client privilege. So if we could arrange that we talk privately, I'd appreciate it."

Phillips pulled her cell phone out. "I'll have a guard standing outside. He'll escort Mrs. Chambers back when you're ready." She stepped inside the room and pointed to a red button next to the lintel. "That's an emergency button. Use it if you need to."

"Thank you. And it's 'doctor.'"

"Pardon me?"

"Dr. Chambers. She's a PhD archeologist."

"Huh. Fancy that. Nobody said a word to me."

Bree waited until Phillips had locked the door behind her. She sat down. "Now, Jillian. We need to talk about Schofield Martin."

❧

The interview lasted forty-five minutes. Bree was at the Angelus Street office less than twenty minutes after that. She felt as if it'd been a week since she left Petru and Ron. She checked her watch twice to be sure. It was only three o'clock.

Bree tossed her wool coat onto the leather couch, sat down, and put her feet up on the oak chest they used as a coffee table. Ron looked up from his iPad and tsked. "You look beat."

"I missed lunch."

"Petru's sister made scones. There's a couple left. Shall I get you some?"

"Maybe later." She stared up at *The Rise of the Cormorant*. The skies over the ocean were less bloody than they had been before. The cormorant itself had circled upward, away from the waves created over the prow of the ship. The dark-haired woman reached over the side of the ship. She looked down at the drowning souls. Bree couldn't see her face. At that moment, sitting there, she would have given anything to see her face. "I think we're ready to ask the Celestial Courts to allow a review of Schofield Martin's sentencing."

"That's good news." Ron set the tea tray on the oak chest.

"Eat something, please." He sat across from her. Bree picked up a scone and set it down again. Petru stumped in from the kitchen, leaned on his cane, and watched her. His thick beard made it hard to see his expression.

Bree held up her small recorder. "I've got Jillian Chambers's statement. I'd like you to hear some of it." She tapped at the keyboard, then placed the recorder face up on the chest. Jillian's hoarse, exhausted voice was slurred.

Yes, I remember Scooey Martin.

"They had her on a number of medications," Bree said. "But she seemed oriented to me. I hope the Angel in Judgment will show some leniency and agree to have it entered as evidence. If not, I've got a backup plan."

He was a lovely boy, Scooey was. Under the thumb of his big brother, Bullet, of course. And trying to make his own mark in the world. It was my fault he got mixed up with Allard and that business about shipping the artifacts back to the States to White. He wanted me to run away with him. Just leave the dig, and my work, and Allard, too, and go live somewhere on a beach in California. Like I said, he was a lovely boy. I told him we couldn't do it without money, and that the best chance we had was to take a box of the things we'd gotten on this dig, and sell them ourselves. He didn't want to do it, but I told him Allard and Bullet and White were all in on it, and what did it matter who benefited from the stolen artifacts? Better the two of us than all of them.

He must have let something slip. Allard caught us as we were about to leave on the Indies Queen. *There was a*

*storm, a fight, and poor Scooey went overboard. Allard
fixed it with the police. I don't know how. I don't remember much about the period right after Scooey died.*

*Who pushed Scooey? Nobody pushed him. He
jumped, trying to get away from Allard. Jumped
over the side. Just didn't make it to shore.*

Bree tapped the recorder, and Jillian's voice stopped.

"I can argue that Chambers threatened Schofield and
drove him to his death. That Chambers is guilty of con-
tributory negligence at best, and of second-degree man-
slaughter at worst."

Petru frowned. "That statement of Jillian's? Uncorrobo-
rated? I am not so sure. As for Chambers—you will not get
him to admit to that while he is alive."

"I've got Martin's statement that his younger brother
wasn't a part of the smuggling scheme, too."

Ron went to his desk and sat at his laptop. "I'll recheck
that. As I recall, Bullet Martin said his younger brother
'didn't have any interest in the family business.'" The
screen came up with Bree's case notes. Petru leaned over
Ron's shoulder and stared at them. "Maybe. It is thin. But
it appears as though we have little else."

"I've got one more arrow in my quiver," Bree said.
"We'll see if I need it. Anyhow. I'm ready. If you've got the
box with my robes, Ron, I think I'd like to take care of this
as soon as the documents are prepared."

"It will, only take me a moment" Petru said.

Bree nodded. "All right. I'm going upstairs. I'll be back
in a bit."

She didn't wait for either angel to respond but went out to
the foyer. She paused at the foot of the stairs. Her painted
angel stood with hands folded, facing its gloriously robed

cohorts parading up the wall, as if considering whether to rejoin the procession. Bree took her time ascending to the second floor. As she rounded the stairs to the landing, she saw there was a sign on the door to Lavinia's living quarters.

FOR LEASE
INQUIRE, BEAUFORT & COMPANY

The door was slightly ajar. Bree pushed it open and walked into Lavinia's former home. The pine floors were dusty, with a shimmery violet dust that floated around her feet and glimmered in the sunshine coming through the windows overlooking the cemetery below. The air held the scent of flowers and spices of a kind Bree had only encountered in the company of her landlady.

The furniture was gone, except for a rocking chair near an old cast-iron stove in the far corner of the living room. As Bree watched, the scent of lavender grew stronger, and the chair creaked back and forth on the rockers, and then stilled.

Bree waited a long moment. Her heart ached. She wanted to say something. She wanted to embrace Lavinia, one last time. She opened her arms, as if the angel would rise from her chair and come to her.

The air stilled. The scent of lavender faded. Bree closed her eyes against a sudden rush of tears, and then turned and went downstairs.

Ron waited in the foyer, the parchment roll of pleadings under one arm, and her coat and tote in the other. He'd slung the strap of the wooden box carrying her robes over one shoulder.

Bree put on her winter coat and dug the car keys out of her tote. "Can we drive?"

"Sure."

"I mean, is my car in one piece or not?"

"It's fine," he said easily. "It's parked right outside in the usual spot."

Bree decided she didn't want to ask how she had gotten back to the town house the night before—or who had driven her car back to Angelus Street. But as she turned onto Montgomery, heading back to the Municipal Building, she couldn't help casting frequent glances out the side window, just to be certain the street wasn't taking her places she never wanted to see again. She avoided the parking spot on Market, too. And if Ron was amused, he didn't show it.

He did, however, say hello to Cordelia Blackburn as they exited the security check into the lobby.

"It's Ron Parchese, isn't it?" Cordy said. "Nice to see you again." Then, to Bree, "You're looking a little ragged around the edges, girl. Did you have a rough night?"

"I was up late, settling a dispute."

"Well, I hope you didn't lose any sleep over that matter we discussed in my office yesterday. I had a word with Stubblefield. He won't be sending out any inappropriate letters any time soon."

"Thank you, Cordy. I appreciate that."

"No problem. Nice to see you again, Ron. You ever decide to leave private casework for the state, you let me know."

Bree didn't say anything to Ron until they were in the elevator—which was, for once, empty of other people. "I suppose I should be flattered that that's twice in two days somebody's tried to swipe my staff."

Ron smiled. It was the kind of smile that never failed to lift her spirits.

"Why did you decide to be visible to Cordy today?"

"I like Cordy. And I'm a little jazzed. Always am before a courtroom appearance."

The elevator went past the sixth floor and stopped. The doors hissed open. Bree stared at the bronze medallion on the wall. The winged scales of justice seemed to glow more brightly than usual. "Lavinia was spending herself out. If I'd known from the outset that each time she appeared in temporal form it took energy away from her, I would have . . ."

"What? Asked her to slow it down?" Ron set the box on the floor, then shook out the red velvet robes and held them out, ready to drape them around her shoulders. "Not a decision for you to make, Bree. Not for her, not for Petru, and not for me." He twitched the stiff collar up, so that it framed her face. "There. Shake out the lapels a little bit. Lavinia finished the border, by the way. Take a look."

Bree lifted the hem. An exquisitely stitched figure embroidered in gold thread filled the last empty space on the edge of the robe. It looked a little like the painted angel on the foyer wall. It looked more like Bree herself.

"Ready?"

She tucked the parchment roll more firmly under her arm. "Ready."

Ron led the way down the hall to the door marked CELESTIAL COURT COURT OF APPEALS. ANGEL JUSTICE AZREAL PRESIDING.

The door opened into a vast, cavernous room that always reminded Bree of an airport terminal. An escalator took them down three flights to the courtroom below. The painted murals on the walls showed scenes from Schofield Martin's life. Bree wanted to pause at the scene that showed Martin on the deck of the *Indies Queen*, but the mural faded to his family at his graveside before she could catch more than a glimpse of the shadowy display.

She stepped off the escalator at the bottom. The marble

aisle led up to a huge dais, empty of the judge's presence at the moment. The defense's and the plaintiff's areas were on opposite sides of the aisle, and were identical. Each had a long oak table with carved wooden chairs that faced the dais. Bree went to the right-hand side, sat down, and unrolled the parchment containing the motion to review Schofield Martin's sentence. Ron busied himself with the pitcher of water that was the only other item on the table, and poured them each a glass. A few moments later, Lloyd Dumphey and Caldecott took their places on the left.

Somewhere in the reaches of the courtroom, a brass gong sounded. A soft voice announced that the Celestial Court was now in session. A gold replica of the scales of justice appeared on the dais. Behind it, a soft glow grew to twice the height of a man.

"All rise for the Honorable Angel Azreal," the disembodied voice said.

The four of them got to their feet.

"Be seated." Then, "Miss Winston-Beaufort, the Honorable Justice wishes you to present your case."

"We are representing the soul of Schofield Martin, Your Honor, and requesting a review of his current sentence, an eternity in the seventh circle of Hell. The plaintiff will be offering facts not in evidence when the case was first adjudicated. These consist of statements made by witnesses privy to parts of Schofield Martin's activities not made available to the defense at the time of this trial.

"But these statements are unsupported. In order to verify them, I ask that the Court call an independent witness to these events, and that her testimony be entered into evidence.

"I ask that the court call Leah Villiers Winston-Beaufort to the stand."

Epilogue

Bree stood in front of Lavinia's grave. The stone angel's gaze was turned to the heavens. Her wings were folded around her slight, fragile figure. Bree felt, for a fleeting moment, as though the feathery lightness was wrapped around her, too. A breeze stirred the flowers clustered at the base of the stone pedestal. The welcome scent of out-of-season roses filled the air. The smell of lavender was intense. Outside the circle of green hope and sorrowful joy, the graves surrounding the Angelus office lay as dank and grim as ever. Safely inside the circle, Bree was at peace.

"I couldn't speak to Leah, of course. Not personally. Not mother to daughter." Her cheeks were wet with tears, but it wasn't grief that drove them. "The important thing was that I saw her. I heard her voice. In her death, she was as real to me as if she were alive and here in the world of mortal men.

"Leah is beautiful, Lavinia, at least to me. It's not a soft face. It's a very wise one. High cheekbones. Her eyes are a very pale blue, like the water at the edge of a clear, calm beach. Her hair is very dark. No reddish lights in it at all— more blue, like a blackbird or a raven.

"Ron thinks that we sound alike. So I have her voice. And at the very last, before she stepped down from the stand and went back to whatever part of the Sphere that her soul resides in, she looked at me. Really looked at me."

Tears collected at the corner of her mouth, and she swiped her sleeve across her face to dry them. "You know how Goldstein always spouts off about 'what is time to an angel?' I got what he meant. Finally. That look we shared was a lifetime. All that I missed of her growing up—it was there, as if there had never been a hole to fill at all.

"I know everything now. There's nothing missing. That she liked the Beatles. That she wanted to be an archeologist because her adoptive father loved old things. That she had a little sister, like Antonia, who drove her crazy, just like Antonia makes me crazy. And that her mother, my grandmother, loved a man who was killed in Vietnam, and never loved another."

Bree scrubbed the tears away from her face. "There's one last thing, which you knew, I think, before you left me, too. That I will have a daughter. All of us have daughters. The advocates."

The thought of Hunter filled her with a fierce, momentary flare of pure joy.

"At any rate. I wanted you to know." She reached out and touched the cold stone. It seemed to warm to life under the palm of her hand. She stood there, under the gray sky of a Savannah winter. She was never more at peace.

"Bree?" Ron stood at the cemetery gate. His fair hair was ruffled so that it stood up in tufts around his face. His smile made her feel even better. "I got hold of Goldstein. We've got a ruling."

She left the protected circle of flowers and scented air around Lavinia's grave and stepped into the mire of the cemetery itself. "How'd we do?"

"There was the little matter of adultery with Mrs. Chambers . . ."

"Dr. Chambers," Bree said, momentarily diverted. "I'm thinking that this particular secular case is going to bear down on how much the poor woman was marginalized, both in her marriage and her profession."

"It sounds like a tactic EB will greet with joy," Ron said. "She's left a couple of messages on your cell phone. She's tracked down a colleague from the Chamberses' former university who's more than willing to talk about how Allard's behavior hindered Jillian's recovery. That's going to help a lot with your petition to be appointed guardian."

"Good. I'm feeling more optimistic about this case by the minute. And you said you called Goldstein about the disposition of Schofield's plea?"

"The Court's agreed to a thousand years in Purgatory for the adultery. Piece of cake, considering."

"Good," Bree said. "That's one for the good guys."

"There's more news. Hunter found another body. Same place as poor Beazley, the parking lot behind the Bay Street building."

"Caldecott?"

"You'd better hurry. Hunter wants to talk to you. And no, it's not Caldecott."

She stepped back, to allow Ron to open the gate so they

could leave, and caught sight of a new grave, next to the headstones for the murderers she had brought to justice before.

ALLARD CHAMBERS
1947–2011
I AM JUSTLY KILL'D WITH MINE OWN TREACHERY.

The Hierarchy of
the Crystal Sphere

PERFECT LIGHT

The First Sphere—The Guardians of the Light
Seraphim, Cherubim, Thrones

The Second Sphere—The Governors of the Spheres
Dominions, Powers, Virtues

The Third Sphere—Messengers in the Temporal World
Angels, Archangels, Principles

The Fourth Sphere—Temptors in the Temporal World
Fallen Angels, Fallen Archangels, Principles

The Fifth Sphere—Governors of Hell
Dominions, Powers, Sins

The Sixth Sphere—The Warriors of the Dark
Nephiliam, Fallen Seraphim, Fallen Cherubim

ENDLESS DARK

5343

ALSO FROM
MARY STANTON

ANGEL'S
Advocate

Money's been tight ever since Brianna Winston-Beaufort inherited Savannah's haunted law firm Beaufort & Company—along with its less-than-angelic staff. But she's finally going to tackle a case that pays the bills, representing a spoiled girl who robbed a Girl Scout. But soon enough Bree finds that her client's departed millionaire father needs help, too. Can she help an unsavory father/daughter duo and make a living off of the living?

M557T0809

Mary Stanton is the author of eighteen novels, including five in the Beaufort & Company Mysteries, and the senior editor of three short story anthologies. Writing as Claudia Bishop, she is the author of more than twenty novels, including the bestselling Hemlock Falls Mysteries. A dedicated horsewoman, Mary divides her time between a working farm in upstate New York and a small home in West Palm Beach, Florida. Mary loves to hear from readers, and she can be reached at her websites: www.marystanton.com and www.claudiabishop.com.